Vice

A Novel

GW00499481

Terry Stewart

For the original four, for all the adventures.

Venatrix

Chapters

"In order to know virtue, we must first acquaint ourselves with Vice."

— **Marquis de Sade**

The Hall

"Life is a Party, dress like it."

Audrey Hepburn

Hunter stared into the extravagant array of latex, leather and lace that made up the majority of her wardrobe and wondered what to pack for the dinner party. Usually, the answer was simple – a half-decent bottle of wine and some supermarket-bought flowers were all that were generally required for such occasions – but tonight was different. Tonight, the dinner party was to be held at 'The Hall,' and this would require something a good deal more glamorous and a great deal more risqué, not to mention at least two costume changes, one of them latex.

She had already dismissed the coal-black cobra-skin Louboutin heels she was wearing, as far too painful to last the night. These were shoes for sitting drinking cocktails, or as part of a lingerie ensemble where she knew she wouldn't be on her feet for long. That said, the skin-tight, negroni-red latex dress she was wearing above her excruciating fuck-me heels would *definitely* work for after dinner. If only she could find the right shoes.

Peering deeper into her wardrobe, Hunter shivered slightly. Latex was beautiful and completely lust-inducing, but also incredibly chilly when first put on. *Funny that they never show that bit at fetish fairs,* she thought, with a wry smile.

Standing five foot and eight inches, even without her signature heels, Hunter was taller than most women, and when she wore her preferred 4-inch stilettoes, she was eye-to-eye with most men. She loved to comment that her height would have made her eligible to be an authentic Las Vegas Showgirl in the 1950s. She had been called 'statuesque' and 'curvy' for her entire adult life. Her figure was certainly more boudoir than catwalk, but she remained lithe and toned, which complimented her enviable cleavage and shapely legs.

It also helped that she had been given such an androgynous and unusual name. 'Hunter' had vaguely masculine connotations, which was a delicious counterpoint to her incredibly obvious and deliberately hyper-sexualised femininity.

She often precipitated delighted surprise in those she was meeting for the first time; people who, upon seeing the name 'Hunter Blair', had assumed a gung-ho Scottish country gentleman type, and whose expectations were quickly recalibrated when she arrived, stiletto-heeled, corseted, with eyes flashing an amused challenge at their misconception. Hunter was the millennial Marilyn Monroe with a master's degree and BDSM fetish.

She picked up the invitation which lay coquettishly against her mirrored dressing table, seeming to mock her wardrobe indecision, and ran her perfectly manicured fingernail over the elegant script.

Richard and Tiffany invite you to The Hall on Friday October 12ᵗʰ
Join us for dinner, drinks, debauchery, and debasement
Dress code: cleavage and heels (ladies) waistcoats (gentlemen)
Following this a shoot shall take place in the grounds on the Saturday, for
this -
'Dress to kill'

The pun in the invitation was classic Richard, Hunter thought, as she imagined him chuckling to himself as he penned it. Cleavage and heels were easy enough; if you threw a champagne cork into her wardrobe, it would be hard not to hit something that would work. But the shoot was another matter entirely. There was absolutely nothing in Hunter's own wardrobe that was sturdy or plain enough to suffice. Fortunately, she knew that – if the worst came to the worst – she could borrow from Tiffany's ample supply of country casual.

Tiffany Hadleigh was one of Hunter's dearest friends, a confidante, a kindred spirit, and a consummate dinner party hostess. Hunter knew the drill. Inevitably Tiffany would have orchestrated some sort of temporary liaison for her for the event, though Hunter was never completely convinced whether the benefit of such fixups was intended for her, or for the sex-starved colleague of Richard's that was usually on offer. Still, she didn't mind, even though Tiffany got it completely and somehow charmingly wrong most of the time. The liaisons were generally entertaining enough to last the evening or, occasionally, an entire weekend.

Hunter frequented dinners at The Hall because they were gorgeous, glamorous, and pretty much the only excuse that she had to show off the best of her wardrobe with her other similarly inclined female friends. Unfortunately, the likes of corsets, stockings, suspenders, and latex were usually frowned upon in 'polite' company. Not at The Hall though, at The Hall nothing was off limits. Especially when the party progressed into The Stables. Whatever Tiffany and Richard had planned for the evening, it never disappointed. Where else would colour-coordinated and silver-plated butt-plugs be given out as post-prandial party-favours?

Hunter plucked a plunging, blood-red, long-sleeved shift dress from her wardrobe and, with a quick nod of approval, slid it into her overnight bag. That, coupled with some matching red stilettoes, would do for dinner. She then peeled off the latex she was wearing and put that in too alongside some matching PVC heels. Tacky but cute. She smirked. She probably wouldn't be in them that long anyway.

Finally, she looked in her lingerie drawer for something even more revealing, just in case it was called for later in the evening. *You never could tell at The Hall*, she thought, then, *who was she kidding? You could always tell at The Hall.* She grinned and carefully manoeuvred her gold nipple-tasselled chain-link playsuit from its opulent protective box and added that to her bag. It was her very favourite outfit. She never failed to feel like a goddess whenever she wore it. She would slip the chains over her head and feel the cold weight caress her skin and be completely empowered.

'Done,' she said aloud, examining the contents of her bag. As she leaned down to close it, she felt a flutter of excitement in her stomach.

*

At the same time as Hunter was selecting the perfect wardrobe for her weekend adventure, Tiffany was trying not to lose her almost infinite supply of patience and stab her housekeeper Marissa with the corkscrew she was currently holding, somewhat too tightly, in her curled fist.

'Yes, I understand what you're *saying,* Marissa,' she hissed through gritted teeth. 'But what I *don't* understand, is why, with six people arriving for dinner in two hours, you've chosen *this* moment to start polishing the silver!'

'It's the decanters,' Marissa said, clearly harassed and not a little cowed. 'Richard told us he wanted them for the dinner. The stags-head ones specifically.'

Tiffany took a deep breath. She loved her husband dearly, but sometimes she wanted to bash his head in with one of those decanters. She'd married a man twice her age – Richard was well into his fifties – but he had the same energetic capacity as a speed-addled Spaniel. There was always some scheme or activity, some plot or business idea that he was immersed in. This unstoppable attitude extended to every part of his life, including his parties. But while the parties were endlessly exciting and had brought her in touch with many fascinating guests from all over the world, it was Tiffany that had to deal with the endless planning and inevitable post-bacchanal clean up. Now her dinner party was running late because Marissa was busy polishing those bloody decanters, when she should have been setting everything up in the dining room. Tiffany knew that there was no need for these particular decanters at dinner; no one would be even remotely aware of their absence. But just because they were going stalking tomorrow Richard had insisted. Once that man had an idea he was like a bloody bullterrier, and he wouldn't let go until he'd seen it through to fruition. Or just as often, to destruction.

It wasn't just the decanters. At Richard's instruction, Tiffany had also been wearing the nipple-clamps for over an hour now, and she was starting to let them get to her. She adored the sex-games between herself and her husband, but the overlap with real life could be both figuratively and literally unbearable.

Breathe, Tiffany, just let it go. She repeated this mantra over and over in her head.

'Thank you, Marissa,' she said, flashing a sweet but brittle smile. 'I know it's not your fault. But please, if Richard has any other requests, just tell him to sod off will you.'

Tiffany was still relatively new to life in Scotland, having arrived from Indiana eight years earlier, and there could be no doubting her American heritage. Tiffany was American, with a capital A. She'd been a cheerleader and a sorority sister and had been on track to marry her high-school sweetheart until cruel fate had forced her to leave her beloved country behind.

The one thing that rankled with her friends was how dissatisfied Tiffany was with life in Scotland. Early on in their friendship and having listened to Tiffany complain for an entire hour about life 'North of the Wall,' Hunter had asked Tiffany why she'd come to study at Glasgow when she so obviously preferred England. It was at this point that, Tiffany had, somewhat sheepishly, explained that she'd thought Scotland was just another part of England. Wow. Hunter had been stunned but had since learned that world geography was not necessarily high up on the curriculum in all of Indiana's schools. According to Tiffany, most of the people she grew up with got their information about the UK through television shows like *Downton Abbey*, or even more worryingly, *Game of Thrones*. Lord save us.

Tiffany was now married to Richard, or as he was referred to in less subtle, but arguably more honest, society, 'Dick Hard', in reference to his several wives and countless mistresses. Tiffany looked like she should be called Candy, or Brandy, but there was so much more to her than that. For one thing, she actually loved Richard. This incorrigible and infuriating man-child, with his air of... what? Not sadness – he was far too in love with life to be sad. And it wasn't melancholy either, or even something as specific as dissatisfaction. No, it was none of those things, but that made it even more poignant as there was nothing you could specifically put your finger on. It was undeniably there though, there was something in this billionaire ringmaster's past that left an indelible stain of loss, like the elegant watermark on his opulent office stationery, so imperceptible as to underline its own significance by its very subtlety. That may be why Tiffany complimented him so well, as she was in no way melancholy or subtle; she was completely blonde, brassy, bombshell, burlesque, and bordello.

Hunter had been as sceptical as the rest of their friends when Tiffany had told her about the man she was seeing. It was so much of a cliché as to have almost ceased to even be a cliché anymore. Hot young girl hooks-up with rich older man. Predictable. Finite. Depressing. Tiffany had spent a summer at university working on his ranch in Texas. By then, Richard was already tiring of wife number three, and had been on the lookout for a younger and brassier model for some time. He and Tiffany had begun an affair and when the summer ended, he flew her over to numerous European cities where he lavished her with gifts, attention and hotel-room destroying sex. Within six months he was divorcing, a year later they were engaged and now they'd been married a respectable (and some would say frankly astonishing) three years.

Tiffany had first introduced Hunter to Richard in the Balmoral hotel in Edinburgh, an evening which had precipitated one of the worst hangovers of Hunter's life. The night had ended with the three returning to Hunter and Tiffany's Glasgow apartment, where Hunter immediately began to perform a drunken striptease that only ended when her head hit the pillow an hour later. Richard had deliberately left her clothes in a mural of shame on the floor for her to find the next day. Whatever you might say about Richard and Tiffany, evenings spent with them were certainly never dull, and dull was what Hunter hated more than anything in the world.

That night had been three years ago, right before their opulent Scottish country-house wedding, and they were still going strong, issues with nipple-clamps and decanters notwithstanding. Tiffany frequently talked about transferring down South to what she considered the 'real' UK, but Hunter never missed an opportunity to regale her friend with the historic and contemporary superiority of Scotland, from the friendliness of the people to the strength of the drinks. In doing so, she was hopeful Scotland would eventually become her friend's real home.

*

Hunter loved travelling up to The Hall. Technically it was possible to get there by train, but the journey was so convoluted that driving was always preferable. The road wound through the hillsides of the central highlands and it didn't matter how many times Hunter completed the journey, she always found it breath-taking. The Hall was a good three hours from the centre of Edinburgh, but it was worth the effort.

As Hunter had left Edinburgh, she'd felt a rush of exhilaration at leaving the city behind and heading out into the wilds of Scotland. The weather was closing in, but she didn't mind; it added an ominous and vaguely dangerous atmosphere to her journey. It was threatening atmospheres like this upon which Hunter thrived. She was aware of a darkness inside her, and she was always comforted by the rugged harshness of the Scottish wilderness. She watched the sky bruising as she skirted a shadowy loch, the wind sending ripples dancing across its surface.

Suddenly, there was a flash on the road ahead of her. Instinctively, Hunter swerved into the right lane of the narrow highway before slamming her foot onto the brakes. The car screamed to a halt and Hunter looked over her shoulder, her heart hammering in her chest. There, in the centre of the road, a majestic stag stood and stared directly at Hunter, his breath steaming against the freezing air. It was shock that kept him standing there, it must have been. Hunter knew how he felt; she looked down towards her lap, and to her hands, which were shaking like leaves in the wind. She took a few breaths, desperate to collect herself, before looking once more in the rear-view mirror. The animal was gone. It was as if it had never been there at all.

By the time Hunter reached The Hall she was much calmer. She pulled off the main road at a slight depression in the dense fir trees that lined her way, a depression you would only notice if you already knew it was there. An entrance into the forbidden forest indeed. She made her way to a set of wrought-iron gates, which opened onto an ornate driveway that quickly disappeared into the trees. Hunter remembered Tiffany telling her about it when she was first invited here. Tiffany had told her with a smile, 'Honey, the drive from the gates to the house is super long, so if you've been driving for about twenty minutes seemingly into the middle of nowhere, don't worry; you're on exactly the right track.' Richard certainly seemed to like his privacy, that was for sure.

After the requisite twenty-minute drive, The Hall finally appeared as if conjured by Hunter's thoughts from the foliage and the dampness. In the dark and the rain, the façade of The Hall looked like a medieval masterpiece; not quite a castle, perhaps, but imposing, nonetheless. The near miss with the stag had unnerved Hunter, and once she had pulled up outside, she sat in her car for a few minutes, listening to the rain fall rhythmically against her windscreen before she steeled herself to rush inside.

The wind tore at her hair as she grabbed her things from the boot and ran, high heels sinking through the stones of the driveway, towards the pillared archway that framed the front door. Although a guest, Hunter was expected to let herself in and find her bedroom without help; she had, after all, been at The Hall at least a dozen times over the years. She considered it a privilege to be so trusted, and at moments like this she appreciated that she didn't have to confront anyone with her rain-lashed face and wind-tousled hair. She shivered, gathered up her overnight case and opened the door into The Hall, and whatever lay ahead.

*

Hunter had quickly navigated her way through The Hall's labyrinthine corridors towards Tiffany and Richard's room, which had been filled with the raucous laughter of her three best friends. She had arrived later than any of the others, but it had taken no time at all to catch up with the day's news. Now, Darcey Bell, the third member of the kinky quartet, and Hunter's oldest and dearest friend, was looking with curiosity and a little trepidation at a small pink plastic egg that nestled in her palm. 'You want us to do *what* with them?' she asked, unable to keep the nerves from her voice.

Astrid rolled her eyes with mock-impatience. 'Okay. For the last time. When we serve the champagne there will be four remotes on the tray, each of which will correspond to one of these little beauties. Each guy will take a remote at random and, well…' Grinning, Astrid stopped for a breath. She'd almost been tripping over her words in her excitement to get them out. 'If you manage *not* to have a breathy orgasm at the dinner table, you win! But if you give in and anyone notices you come, then you're both out of the game. The kicker of course, is that none of us is going to know who's in control of our love-egg! See? Totally freaking awesome!'

'Well,' Hunter began with a slow smile, 'if it's a test of discretion, we know who's got the upper hand already.' Immediately, the women turned to look at Darcey, who gave a slightly nervous acknowledging wink. Darcey hid her 'alternative lifestyle' under hospital scrubs and a military uniform, whereas Hunter wore hers openly, even brazenly, practically daring the world to express an opinion.

Now this *is my sort of game*, thought Hunter. Knowing Richard, the prize would be champagne, and a different kind of sex toy presented to whichever pair managed to keep a lid on their dinnertime pleasure. Hunter had amassed quite the collection of exotic sex-toy prizes from dinner parties at The Hall.

Astrid was no doubt the architect of this little debauchery. She was, without a doubt, the most sexually adventurous person Hunter had ever met, completely uninhibited, fun, and feisty. There were adjectives not yet conceptualised that would one day describe the pixie-haired powerhouse that was Astrid Stephens.

Yet, for all her experience, Astrid was also scarily naïve, and on more than one occasion had got herself into a potentially catastrophic situation. Condoms were often anathema to her, which could lead to its own specific form of nightmare, a nightmare that all the women knew Astrid was desperate to avoid. She'd gone as far as making an appointment to have her tubes tied. However, the anachronistic and misogynistic doctor had refused, insisting that she may, 'want children someday.' Prick.

Astrid had also famously fucked every one of Tiffany's three brothers at Tiffany's own wedding. But as Tiffany had put it at the time, 'at what point does that stop being a gang bang and just become an outward manifestation of a complete lack of self-respect?' As sex positive as all four women were, that sentiment still nagged at Hunter sometimes, like chipped nail varnish on an otherwise perfect manicure that you just couldn't ignore.

Maybe it was the stripper thing? Astrid was the quintessential ex-stripper with seven personalities, zero self-awareness and an MBA. She was, in a way, the tacky success story of a hundred bad movies. At 27, she had earned her MBA before taking a job at the marketing company owned by one of her clients. She had made the career move because, as she said, 'If you don't have an exit strategy in place by the time you're 30, then you're fucked. Your tits start to go south, you can't compete with these 21-year-old new girls. You. Are. Fucked.'

Hunter and Darcey had actually been friends since childhood. But they had met Astrid and Tiffany when they were all at Glasgow university studying various very different degrees. Hunter was doing her master's in ancient history, whereas Astrid was doing her MBA. Darcey, naturally, was outdoing them all in academics, training to qualify as a surgeon. Meanwhile Tiffany was studying 'Equine Science,' which Hunter was convinced was her way of actually studying how to become an English Princess.

Because they were all postgraduate students, they got to patronize the post-graduate club, and this was where they had all met one drunken and surprisingly debauched evening. A week later, they had all attended Club Noir together, Glasgow's slightly more 'socially acceptable and mainstream' fetish club. Their lives had remained inexorably intertwined ever since.

*

Jesus Christ, this is a nightmare, Darcey thought, as the love eggs were handed around by Astrid. She tried to be as enthusiastic as the other women, and she knew Hunter was being supportive when she had pointed out her talent for discretion. It was so incredibly frustrating because she *did* love the sound of the game. At the same time, she knew that her husband would not be able to handle it if someone else got her remote. He was possessively jealous, which was a turn-on in the bedroom, but *nowhere* else. She began frantically trying to work out how she was going to manage this little scenario. The disappointing story of her life right now.

Darcey did like coming here – it certainly felt like an escape from her quotidian suburban existence – but nowadays she was undoubtedly the most conservative of the four women.

14

Darcey's nickname had been Double D for as long as any of the women could remember. Those inclined to casual cruelty might suppose it was intended as a slight in reference to her diminutive breasts. They would be wrong. Rather, it referred to her dominant character. Darcey was always in control, in the military, in theatre, in life and in the bedroom.

Darcey was also smart, like scary smart. She was currently a military surgeon and had previously spent a few years as a research scientist. She had both an B.Sc. in biochemistry and a degree in medicine, and yet she couldn't help but feel she was living someone else's life. She loved surgery, she loved the military, she was a ridiculous over-achiever, but she was always looking for the next thing, never in the moment, never truly happy.

This could have something to do with the fact she had married the wrong man and couldn't bring herself to divorce him. In her family that just wasn't done. She also couldn't have that failure on the Curriculum Vitae of her life, 'divorced before thirty.' No. That was not going to happen. Ever. She would just suck it up, like she had for the past few years, and learn to deal with it. For tonight, she'd just have to work out a way to let her husband know which remote was hers, or fake reactions at the table every time he moved his finger. Lose the game but spare the drama of a scene later. She'd figure it out. She always did.

Once the eggs were in place and the finishing touches to outfits and make-up had been tended to, Tiffany led the women down the elegantly curved staircase and through the concealed wood-panelled drawing room door. You could enter from the perfectly obvious door at the other side of the hallway, but between Richard's flair for showing off and Tiffany's desire to make an entrance, the concealed door was far preferable.

The women looked delicious, and they knew it. Astrid the exotic bird of paradise in a kaleidoscope of colours, Tiffany a shimmering mermaid on dry land, Darcey elegance and class personified, and Hunter, provocative, red heels and lips, a woman on the hunt indeed. They entered the drawing room with perfect poise – no easy thing considering their astronomically high-heels – to audible appreciation from the men.

Richard was standing by the marble mantel piece, in which a roaring fire was not only giving off significant heat but was also turning the lighting in the room into a cosy orange. The drawing room was large and lined with books on all four walls, peppered with comfortable antique couches and elegantly appointed drinks tables. Dressed in his trademark turquoise waistcoat, his ruddy features lit up the moment he saw Tiffany, whose aquamarine Hervé Léger bandage dress was the perfect complement to his own outfit. Hunter was happy to see that, even after three years of marriage and a fair few lovers' tiffs, they remained as besotted with each other as when they'd met. They shared a long, deep kiss, before Richard turned to his guests with a magician's flourish.

'Welcome to The Hall!' he boomed. 'Thank you so much for braving the hideous Scottish weather to come all the way into the central highlands. It is, as ever, appreciated. Even more so though, is the effort everyone has made with their attire. Gentlemen, thank you for donning the traditional waistcoats, of course. I know a few of you find my necessity for waistcoats at dinners peculiar, but when I was growing up it was the mark of a true gentleman. And I'm sure you'll all join me in congratulating the ladies who, as ever, have put us to shame! Astrid, never fails to amaze, sexy and bloody ridiculous as ever.'

Astrid laughed; she was used to Richard's good-natured ridicule. He never quite understood her chaotic style, it being so at odds with what he was used to seeing in his conservative English circles. She had once come to a black-tie dinner at The Hall in an outfit that was described by one guest as something you would see on a Las Vegas rodeo-matador-cowboy, which was quite an achievement in just one dress. Tonight, she was more conservatively dressed in an outlandish neon orange shoulder-padded mini-dress, with a V-shaped slit to her navel. Absolutely no-one else Hunter knew could pull that off, but somehow with Astrid's shock of spiked black hair and wide Bambi face, it just worked. With her signature kohl-rimmed eyes and diamond stud in her nose, she looked every inch the naughty pixie.

With Richard's greeting complete, it was Tiffany's turn to take centre stage. 'Just before we get started with the aperitifs. some information for the gentlemen. Please, when Marissa brings you a glass of champagne can you also take a remote control from the tray. Each of our lovely ladies, has for our mutual enjoyment, added a little extra adornment to their already delicious outfits this evening, and you, gentlemen, are in control of them. The extra excitement being that you have no idea whose pleasure it is that you are in control of. We are at your mercy gentlemen.

Be kind.' Tiffany finished, with a bad-girl grin lighting-up
her already flirtatious features.

*

Tiffany had no sooner finished welcoming her guests when
Marissa arrived with the promised aperitifs. As Hunter took
a glass from the tray, she found herself entranced by the
beautiful choker that Marissa was wearing. At first glance,
it seemed to be nothing more than a thick strap of black
velvet, which encased at Marissa's delicate throat a violet
porcelain cameo of what looked to be a Victorian lady. It
was astonishingly simple and yet Hunter couldn't take her
eyes off it. It reminded her of one she had seen on display
at The Hermitage Museum in St. Petersburg, which had
been gifted from Josephine to Alexander for his assistance
and chivalry. She felt there was more of a connection there,
or some vague significance that her brain was missing,
some reason Marissa would have chosen tonight to wear
such an impressive necklace. Unfortunately, at that precise
moment, she was far too distracted by her anticipation of
the evening's events to properly think about it.

Glancing around the room, two things troubled Hunter. The
first was that they appeared to be one guest short. Hunter
knew that Richard always had even pairs at an event like
this. He didn't care whatever gender the pairs were, same-
sex, opposite sex, or indeed everything in between. But the
numbers were always even, and by Hunter's count they
were missing someone.

The second thing that troubled Hunter was the sight of
Richard's oldest friend, Trigger, standing by the antique
drinks cabinet. Trigger had tried it on with Hunter (to her

initial dismay and current despair) every single time their paths had crossed at one of these things. He just would not accept that she was not, had not, nor ever would be, remotely interested in him.

Trigger, unfortunately, was a frequent fixture at these events, as he was an obsessive hunter. Ostensibly that was what this dinner party was all about, a precursor to a weekend of shooting in the beautiful Scottish Highlands. Hunter, however, knew better, as what it actually was, was a two-day-long glorified orgy with canapés.

Plus, the only one of the women that gave a damn about the shoot itself was Darcey. She was a crack-shot and had been trained since birth to be the perfect Scottish gentlewoman, meaning that she actually enjoyed the pursuit. Hunter, Tiffany, and Astrid meanwhile, were far more interested in the après-shoot activities.

Though she had planned to strategically avoid Trigger for the entire evening, he had disappointingly appeared by her elbow before she had even finished her first glass of champagne.

'Darling!' He'd slurred into her ear whilst clinking his glass against hers and trying to kiss her. Thankfully though, this was not Hunter's first rodeo when it came to avoiding unwanted male attention, and she deftly sidestepped so that he barely grazed her cheek. Which was still significantly too much contact for Hunter.

'Good evening, Trigger.'
'God, you look good enough to eat.'

Ick. Hunter rolled her eyes and turned slightly away. 'How are you?'

'All the better for seeing you here tonight. You look just wonderful.' His eyes pointed directly at her cleavage.

'Yes. You said. Thank you.' She sighed.

'And I bet you have something even kinkier for later don't you, you naughty thing.'

Jesus Christ.

'Have you spoken to Astrid yet this evening? Surely, she's more your speed if it's 'kinky' you're after?' Hunter gave him an icy smile whilst motioning towards Astrid with her glass. Hunter sent a silent prayer to any god that happened to be listening that this would in fact turn out to be the case.

Her deflection onto Astrid wasn't completely un-altruistic, as Astrid was known for her complete lack of discernment about the men that she bedded. More than once – much more than once – she had woken in the morning in full knowledge of having slept with someone, but completely oblivious as to who they were. She'd slept with married men, single men, several men simultaneously, men who said they were gay, she really did not seem to mind. Come to think it, she'd slept with women and everything in between as well. If sexuality was a spectrum of colours, then Astrid was determined to paint herself a rainbow. Hunter really hoped that, for tonight at least, she would extend her generosity as far as Trigger. Anything to get the lecherous old git the hell away from her.

'Oh please!' he replied, slurring. 'She's a woolly jumper, a… an object of necessity, but you, you're a silk kimono, something decadent and elegant.' As he said this, he ran a finger down Hunter's arm. Inside she retched.

She was half laughing, half dying. What was it with men and touching women they didn't know? Clearly, she couldn't be less interested in him, but he still felt he had the right to paw at her. She consoled herself that this 'old-guard' of misogynists, as she liked to think of them, would be dead soon. In her darker moments she seriously wondered at helping some of this 'old-guard' shuffle off. Although these were thoughts, and nothing more, if someone had slipped a cyanide pill into her pocket at that precise moment, it would have taken some serious willpower not to discretely palm it into his glass and drift innocently away.

'I've always loved the feeling of a silk robe on a woman, come to think of it, undoing that tie and putting my hand inside...' He trailed off, trying, Hunter assumed, to look alluring, but succeeding only in looking especially creepy. The man was so crass that words failed her. A self-styled Benny Hill without even the attempt at horrendously cringe-worthy slap-stick humour, this man (if he was even worthy of being called that) had no redeeming features whatsoever. He was a raging misogynist. If Hunter was given a choice between sucking Donald Trump's cock or shaking this man's hand, you better bring a folding chair, a book, and a glass of wine, because the deliberations could last a while. *Please, somebody, anybody, save her.*

And then, in a silent answer to her silent prayers, the most perfect example of masculinity that she could ever have imagined walked into the room. He did so as if nothing of import could have possibly happened before his arrival. He was a walking growl. Pure predator, the perfect dominant. Tall, rugged, a slash of stubble complimenting the broad shoulders and almost superhero stance. *Who was this man?*

The answer was not long in coming. As soon as Richard spotted him, he stamped across the room and shook his visitor's hand so enthusiastically that his guest couldn't help but smile. *Well, they're clearly old friends.* Hunter thought. But *I wonder why I haven't met him before?*

Hunter felt almost woozy as she watched Him take a silver champagne flute from the housekeeper Marissa's tray. She had never had such an immediate physical desire for a man in her life.

He had an easy smile and the effortless movement of someone with perfect control over their body. He was everything that made for an ideal lover. A searing flash of jealousy at Astrid coursed through Hunter as she watched the two exchange pleasantries that were achingly out of earshot. She would give her favourite leather corset for this man to take possession of her remote tonight. Whereas if it were the man opposite her, she'd have to bathe in disinfectant for days afterwards.

Hunter gulped some champagne down to distract herself. She'd deftly thinned out the bubbles with her silver champagne swizzle-stick, a girl's best friend and a godsend at a party like this, where the champagne would undoubtedly flow all night.

Astrid was still busy flirting with Him, much to Hunter's displeasure. She could also see Darcey whispering urgently into her husband Peter's ear, as she searched wildly for an escape from The Letch. *I wonder what that's all about*, she thought, noting the obvious tension on Darcey's face.

Hunter was desperate to go and introduce herself to Him and find out His name. Although knowing The Hall it wouldn't necessarily be His real one. A particularly odd proclivity of Richard's was to re-christen his guests with names he found more indicative of their personalities. Take Trigger, the hunter, for example, though Perve might have been better.

Although Hunter had been teased mercilessly for her own name at school, where 'safer' names like Morag, Laura and Caitlin were the norm, she had learned to love it in later years. Something that Hunter certainly was not, was 'normal'. She'd die before she'd let that happen, so perhaps her name was appropriate after all.

Trigger had noted her interest in the new arrival with obvious displeasure. He immediately and loudly started extolling his own virtues with even more energy than he had Hunter's. Although he did concede that the object of Hunter's interest was a 'bloody good shot actually'. His one redeeming feature according to Trigger, and the explanation for His presence at their little soirée.

Finally, she'd had enough, she excused herself and took a determined step towards Him. He, who at that precise moment was decorously refilling Astrid's glass and laughing at something she'd said. Naturally, at that moment, her progress across the room was halted abruptly with a word from their hostess. Hunter cursed her terrible timing.

'Ok everyone,' Tiffany said, beaming. 'It's time to head into the dining room. There's no need to bring your glasses, but gentlemen, don't forget your remotes. The game begins at dinner!'

'Damn!' Hunter exclaimed, as everyone put down their glasses and headed towards the dining room. *Oh well, maybe I'll get to play with Him later.*

Little did she know, it would very much be Him who would be playing with her…

The Dinner

"In this instant of danger, they realized they were each other's reason for living, and into this instant they threw their whole being."

Anaïs Nin

Hunter often dreamed of spending time surrounded by the elegance and beauty of the eighteenth-century salons. Whenever she stepped into the dining room of The Hall, these dreams came absolutely no closer to being met. The whole setting reminded Hunter of something that her mother used to say growing up, 'all fur coat and no knickers'. All glamour but no substance. Somehow, that seemed to Hunter to sum up her experience of The Hall perfectly. Always fun, but somehow, not quite real. Like the entire place was trying just a bit too hard to be decadent and debauched.

Hunter put the various design flaws down to a mix of Richard's over eagerness to 'out sex' everyone and Tiffany's ongoing struggle to define her own sense of style. Tiffany would have sorely loved to make all the cosmetic decisions herself, but she found it difficult to assert herself in her Scottish surroundings, and frequently found herself deferring to Richard's tastes. This would have been fine twenty years ago, but unfortunately Richard's tastes were now tragically out of date.

Hunter would have loved to make her mark on The Hall, but at the same time, the mishmash of cheerleader chic and aristocrat élan somehow suited the couple. She also knew, that if it was perfectly tailored and manicured into the den of iniquity it inspired to be, then it would undoubtedly lose some of its charm. Hunter knew she could be overly critical at times, her standards were often too exacting, and her friends never shied away from telling her as much. They knew she fantasised about living in a high-class eighteenth-century brothel and had to keep reminding her that this was never going to happen. Unfortunately, she'd been born too late for the opulence she so desired.

Regardless of the dining room's many flaws, the table itself was undoubtedly gorgeous. Tiffany had outdone herself here, and in view of their planned highland shoot tomorrow, the silver stag head decanters were a nice touch. Matching solid silver antique candle sticks offered the room's only lighting, bathing everyone in a warm, ethereal glow, reminiscent of historic dinners at royal courts. Hunter closed her eyes for a moment, immersing herself in the almost edible atmosphere of pheromone-laced anticipation.

The rules precluded the use of the remotes until the ladies were all seated, so everyone was impatient to find their appropriate place. It was at this point it became clear that Hunter's silent prayers had indeed been answered. The Letch was, alas, seated on her right, but on her left, was Him. And there, to the left of the Letch, sat Astrid. Hunter could have kissed Tiffany! The Letch *was* for Astrid, and He, He was *all* hers.

Tiffany and Richard were at opposite heads of the table. Hunter was closer to Tiffany's end, with Darcey and Peter facing each other across the table next to Richard. Tiffany's practice was always to have people sitting next to someone of the opposite sex, and couples were never allowed to sit next to one another.

Immediately the atmosphere was saturated with the tinkle of champagne flutes and the sound of expensive cutlery on even more expensive plates. It reminded Hunter of a scene from High Society, and she could well remember Celeste Holm's famous words; 'You know, one of the prettiest sights in this pretty world is the sight of the privileged class enjoying its privileges.' Watching that film as a child, Hunter never thought that she would be included amongst that class, even if it were only as a guest. Weekends at The Hall were the epitome of this ideal.

Richard absolutely refused to ever hide from or apologise for his wealth. This was fair enough, as far as Hunter was concerned. She had much the same attitude to life herself. Perhaps that was why, despite a lack of natural simpatico, they both got on so well. If you have it, flaunt it, because life really, really, was too short. She knew that from bitter experience. Her eyes rested once more on the beautiful stag head decanters. She wasn't sure if it was the aspect of the silver antlers or the thought of the hunt tomorrow, but she was suddenly overwhelmed by a vision of her stag, standing proud by her car on the road, its powerful breath misting the air. Then, just as quickly, it was replaced with the image of a rivulet of blood running through tawny fur. She was shocked at this invasion into her imagination, as if a fragment of a dream she'd had. But she was sure she had never had such a dream before. One thing she was certain of though, was that she was now absolutely dreading the hunt tomorrow. She frowned.

Although, as He was going to be there tomorrow, she would at least have something to distract her. She watched Him discretely from the corner of her eye as she unfolded her napkin. She could see the muscles moving in His forearm and the tightness of the fabric of His trousers across His thighs. Her mouth opened as she imagined being pinned beneath His obviously powerful body, His stubble grazing her skin, His hands pinning her wrists and forcing her to obey. Her eyes strayed lower.

'Do you trust me?' He asked suddenly, this god-like man next to her, as He poured some wine into her crystal glass.

She stared open mouthed for a second unable to formulate a coherent response at this sudden direct address. She could feel the heat rising in her whole body as she fought to control herself. The man hadn't even introduced himself yet and she was already a sticky mess of desire. He was definitely *not* the usual business associate of Richard's…

'Um,' she faltered, 'well, I think on an occasion such as tonight, and considering you're an invited guest of some of my best friends, I'm going to take a risk, and say… yes.' She smiled as she regained her confidence and poise with the words.

He laughed, turning in His chair, and looking directly at her, as if about to elaborate. Suddenly, an overwhelming pleasure shot through her, giving her such a shock that she involuntarily started and thumped her crossed legs off the underside of the table.

'You shouldn't,' He said, nodding to the remote that rested in His hand.

'Bastard,' she gasped laughing, enjoying herself beyond decency. She was thrilled that He had her remote. The fact that He had it heightened her arousal immediately, which was impressive as it was already at fever pitch.

'Oh, you have no idea,' He said, the hint of something unspoken behind His eyes. 'And I am going to be having a lot of fun with you over dinner.'

Yes, yes yes yes yes yes! Hunter's body sang.
'Oh, I think you'll be surprised by just how much I can take. I won't let you win that easily.'

He smiled. 'Considering you're so sure of yourself, how about we raise the stakes?'

Dear god, she thought, *this is escalating quickly, we haven't even had starters yet and He's determined to torture me. How utterly fabulous. Still,* she considered, *the things He has in mind can't be that bad. I already have love eggs inside me – how much more risqué can it get?* The phrase 'Famous Last Words' flitted unhelpfully around her head. She ignored it, and carelessly threw sexual caution to the wind. Not for the first, nor the last time.

'Absolutely,' she said. 'Do your worst. Or best, depending on how you define something like this.' Grinning playfully, she took a sip of her Montrachet. She was just beginning to guess when He might press the remote once more when, to her surprise, He pulled an evil-looking knife from His inside jacket pocket. She was so shocked by its sudden appearance that she somewhat inelegantly aspirated her wine.

Being Scottish, she was no stranger to men wearing blades. Even at high school dances, boys of sixteen would wear the traditional Scottish Sgian Dubh in their kilt socks with pride. What He was holding, though, was definitely not the traditional Scottish 'black knife', and certainly not something you'd give to a boy, regardless of tradition. This was something far more sinister sharp and its blade was almost black.

'Jesus, Hunter you're really not going to last if you're choking already!' exclaimed Astrid delightedly, as The Letch began enthusiastically rubbing Hunter's back.

Hunter looked up to find the entire room looking at her with amusement and a smug self-assuredness that, although they may not actually win the game, at least at this rate they'd outlast *her*. She batted The Letch's roaming hand impatiently from her back and forced a smile. 'I'm fine,' she said, shooting daggers at her knife-wielding tormentor. 'I just inhaled my wine. Which is delicious, by the way, Richard.' She cast an appreciative tilt of her glass in her host's direction in a semi-successful attempt to divert attention away from herself and onto Richard's perfect choice of wine. Hunter worked in wine sales, so she knew a good bottle when she drank it.

Everyone went back to their own private conversations, although Hunter could hear Astrid's squeals as she was already failing to hide her excitement. Astrid would never win a game like this, but she would enjoy herself immensely regardless.

Hunter was struggling not to stare at the knife that He continued to hold in His hand. Noticing this, He chuckled. 'Don't worry,' He said. 'You have nothing to fear from me. For now, at least. I will ask you again, though. Do you trust me?' His eyes were insistent, probing, engaging, almost daring her *not* to acquiesce, daring her to run away frightened and keep the night's festivities at the darker shade of vanilla that they were currently at. Well, two could play at that game. It was simply not in Hunter's nature to shy away from anything. Besides, she was already imagining having that knife at her throat as He held her down and did unspeakable things to her.

'Yes.' She stated simply, looking him straight in the eye. One word spoken without fear or hesitation. Damn Him if she was going to look like a scared little girl. If He had any idea what she could do to Him, He would be a damn sight less cocky, she was sure. And yet…

*

'Richard you are terrible!' Tiffany said. She was only barely managing to eat her starter due to the continuous throb between her legs and pull on her nipples. My god, she loved her dirty, insatiable husband. She'd already come once right as Marissa put the starter of home smoked pheasant and bramble salad down in front of her. No one had been any the wiser.

'Oh really, and in what way this time?' Richard asked mock innocently.

'You set it up completely with the remotes didn't you. There's no randomness here at all. You've got mine, obviously, as it hasn't been switched off for even a second. Clearly the couples all have each other's, and you gave poor Astrid to Trigger, didn't you? Which leaves Hunter with –'

'Ok, yes, you're right. I couldn't mix them up anyway after Peter threatened to, and I'm quoting here, 'batter' anyone who got Darcey's. I mean, what the hell am I supposed to do with that? Anyway, I thought you'd be pleased with the pairings. Things will still heat up after dinner, I'm sure. Plus, I got the impression that Hunter can't stand Trigger, so I thought I'd throw the poor girl a bone. She's done well servicing all the men we put in front of her but even she deserves a holiday.'

Tiffany looked towards Hunter, and the man who was so clearly enamoured by her. 'She certainly seems happier than usual tonight. And he certainly makes a nice change from your usual colleagues. They're all just so old and boring.'

'They're only old and boring compared to me, my dear.' He grinned as Tiffany gripped the table in an effort to disguise *another* orgasm. 'Getting to be too much is it?' he enquired politely.

'Yes!' she squeaked. 'You win!'

Richard smiled. 'Always, darling.' With expert precision, he pulled the clamps from her nipples. She exhaled in relief, desperately in need of respite.

*

32

It wasn't so much pleasure that pulsed through Darcey with each flick of her husband's wrist as it was pure and unadulterated relief. Thank god Richard had given her remote to Peter. She couldn't have cared less whether it was by accident or design. She was just relieved that she could relax and try to enjoy each sensation now.

There was no question of her giving the game away. A public orgasm would have been impossible for Darcey, as inappropriate as it would be embarrassing, even in this setting. She knew they would win; they always did.

Darcey looked at Peter, his Captain America image accentuated by the spitfires on his waistcoat and clean-shaven visage. She was already preparing to bury that clean-shaven face in the pillows of their opulent antique four-poster bed later.

She couldn't help feeling it was all just so terribly unfair. Peter presented this hyper-masculine, clean-cut image, and yet, when it came to his sexuality, all he wanted was to be dominated and humiliated. There was no doubt that Darcey preferred to be the dominant one in her relationship – that had always been the case. It's just that Peter's tastes were very different from her own, and not ones that she'd ever been keen to try.

She had a sudden flashback to the night she met Peter. God, that felt like a lifetime ago. Another life, a life where she and Hunter were just two girls at university, living their best life, with nothing to worry about and everything still to play for. She still couldn't believe how quickly everything had changed. She truly hadn't seen it coming.

A vibration in her already sticky underwear brought her crashing back down to earth. She looked over at Peter and smiled, stifling a slightly disappointed sigh, and trying ever so hard to enjoy herself. After all, it wasn't his fault she was unhappy. Not really.

*

Astrid, who had zero interest in competition, only in pleasure, had already come loudly and wildly twice. She wasn't even disappointed that her remote was in the hands of Trigger. She knew how repellent Hunter found him, but she didn't care. He was funny, wealthy, and dirty as hell. He was also part-owner of a London-based arms manufacturer, which gave him a tangible air of danger and immorality. Which Astrid had to admit that she found that immensely appealing. Though if she was completely honest, she knew she'd find him appealing no matter what.

She knew that she wasn't the same as other women. She genuinely found something attractive or intriguing in every guy she met. Whether it was due to a laugh, a scar, an attitude, or even an expression, she was unable to escape even the most grotesque man's charms. Having said that, not one of them ever managed to hold her attention for long. Men were like ice cream, and she was determined to eat them before they melted.

Despite her current fascination with Trigger, she was, at that precise moment, completely focussed on Hunter and the fun she was having. Trigger might think his prowess with pushing buttons on a remote was the *only* reason a small puddle was forming in her lingerie, but the sexual chemistry between Hunter and the new guy was even more of a turn-on.

Hunter's moan of complete and utter pleasure momentarily distracted the other members of the party, their eyes rising from their plates in such perfect unison it looked like they'd rehearsed the move. In fact, the spectacle was so erotic that no one could tear their eyes away, including Marissa, who had stopped short in the doorway as she was about to serve the main course.

Unbeknownst to the rest of the guests, the knife that had so startled Hunter a mere half hour before had since been put to good use. He had used it to cut lengths of cable tie, and then proceeded to tightly secure Hunter's wrists and ankles to the arms and legs of the Hepplewhite chair she was sitting in. Now, to the delight of the remaining guests, He slowly removed His tie, sliding the silk between His fingers, and tied it around her eyes as a makeshift blindfold.

Hunter was unable to move a muscle; there was barely a ribbon's width of space between skin and chair. But while this kept her completely immobile, it also stopped short of pain or serious discomfort. She was kept waiting for some time before she was given any clue about how this meal was to continue. Then He began to feed her delicate mouthfuls of wine between bites of the delicious starter, describing in detail each morsel before placing it in her mouth, His fingertips intentionally brushing her lips with the lightest of caresses each time He did so. Hunter was only vaguely aware of what she was eating, so focused was she on the sensations He was creating within her. She wasn't even hungry anymore; her appetite was only for Him. Even without the cable-ties, the eroticism of Him feeding her blindfolded would have nailed her to the chair.

She thought that she was going to die of desire. Every sense and nerve were stretched as taught as piano-wire. She could feel the restraints nipping gently at her skin like a lover's bites. She also knew that He had her remote next to His plate. He'd made a show of putting it there before blindfolding her.

She was so aware of the object inside of her precisely because it *wasn't* vibrating, that she knew she'd come as soon as He switched the damn thing on. She could barely take the tension that He was creating inside of her. His decision to keep her on the precipice of such extreme pleasure was almost painful. What made this even more unbearable was that she knew that *He* knew this. Every move and gesture He made were meticulously calculated to draw the most exquisite pleasure from her. *This is not a man*, she thought, through the fog of desire and pleasure. *This is a God. My God.*

Once more, He dipped a finger into her wine, and ran it tantalizingly along her lips. When the tip of His finger slid into her mouth, she moaned before she could stop herself. She ran her tongue down the inside of His finger before gently sucking and biting the tip. Then, just as she suspected she was about to lose the game, the Letch knocked his glass over and sent a cascade of chilled Montrachet down the inside of her right leg.

Although, outwardly, Hunter barely seemed to react, inwardly she was screaming every profanity under the sun at this bumbling moron, desperate to tear at her restraints and punch him square in the face. Sensing this, her other, more welcome tormentor chuckled.

Then, with infinite care, He removed the blindfold from her eyes, before kneeling on the floor at her feet. He slowly removed her stiletto heel and began gently, achingly, to lick the wine from her ankle right up to the top of her knee. He never took His eyes from hers the entire time.

Hunter wasn't sure how much more of this she could bear. His tongue felt like hot whiplash on her skin and sent every one of her nerves straining for more of His touch. Without thinking, she leaned forward and kissed Him, her lips open and wanting. The bite of the restraints at her wrists and ankles only increasing her pleasure. Smiling, he pulled away and retook His seat next to her. Once more, everything she desired was just a chair's length away, and she was completely powerless to do anything about it.

'God you two are hot!' Astrid exclaimed. 'Wow, like wow!'
There wasn't a word of dissent from around the table, as everyone seemed suddenly eager to be done with dinner and onto the rest of the evening's more exciting activities.

The Stables

"Imperfection is beauty, madness is genius and it's better to be absolutely ridiculous than absolutely boring. "
Marilyn Monroe

On her way out to The Stables, Hunter was carefully negotiating the paving stones in her four-inch heels, and slowly massaging some feeling back into her cable-marbled wrists. She was still dizzy with desire, having watched Him wield His knife for the second time that evening and cut her loose from her bindings. To her relief, the ladies had divested themselves of the eggs soon after dessert, and it had been decided by unanimous vote that Darcey was the mistress of poise and discretion, winning the game without the barest hint of arousal on her face.

Hunter didn't mind losing, particularly considering the pleasure she had experienced over dinner. The thought of Him made her pulse quicken and muscles tighten. She quickly negotiated the rest of the pathway and slipped through The Stables' heavy oak doorway, which had been left open.

Already, Hunter could hear a cacophony of giggles and exclamations, which signified that the post-dinner wardrobe change was in full swing. She was about to make her way through the stone archway that led to various side-rooms, when she was suddenly confronted by the largest mounted stag's head that she had ever seen.

Now, Hunter had grown up in the Scottish countryside and was in no way squeamish. She came from outdoorsy country people who regularly hunted, shot, and fished. Hunter herself had gut mackerel as a child (her grandmother, a fishing champion, had insisted she learned how to prepare the fish if she wanted the pleasure of eating it) and she'd even fetched the odd pheasant or two from the pantry. But even she baulked at this macabre trophy. She was surprised Tiffany allowed it. Much as she knew that her friend enjoyed the occasional shoot, surely this was going too far?

Hunter's attention was still on the stag's head when Astrid broke her from her melancholy. 'Hey!' she yelled. 'Get in here and get the latex on, and for the love of god stop worrying about the hunting trophy!'

Hunter smiled wryly. 'You know me too well,' she said, sashaying into the room, unzipping her dress, and letting it fall to the floor. 'Still, you have to admit it's a bit over the top, surely?'

Tiffany was the first to assent. 'I hate that bloody thing! It's new, someone bagged it on the last big hunting day. I forget who, but Richard couldn't let the thing leave the grounds he was so impressed. Frankly I think it's overkill, if you'll excuse the pun.'

Darcey grinned mischievously. 'Nice use of the word "bloody," Tiffany. We'll make a Scot of you yet!' Tiffany flushed, horrified that she'd used one of the Scottish inflections that, as a devoted Anglophile, she'd been working so hard to avoid.

'I'm kidding!' Darcey assured Tiffany, smiling. 'You've got more plums in your mouth than the rest of us put together! Honestly, not one of us speaks 'the Queen's English' quite like you do when you try Tiffany.'

'Seriously?' said Astrid, 'No one is going to make a 'plums in your mouth' joke?' She laughed. 'Ok, Hunter, hurry up. You're the only one not dressed.'

Hunter grabbed her overnight bag and made her way to the side of Tiffany, who was putting the finishing touches on her make-up while examining her lithe form in the powder blue latex mini dress. She looked like she'd walked out of a vintage advert for Pan Am, or – less charitably perhaps – a high street advert for Ann Summer's vocational section.

Astrid, meanwhile, looked delectable if somewhat outlandish in an acid-yellow fishnet bodysuit that was more holes than net. The outfit made zero attempt to conceal her pierced nipples. She also had her 'stripper' shoes on, enormously heeled and equally tacky PVC numbers that were covered in lime-green horns, disconcertingly reminiscent of a triceratops at a rave, or possibly an orgy. If a small pink lizard tongue snaked out of one of the shoes Hunter would officially lose it.

Astrid's outfit, Hunter knew, was due to her impending performance on the pole. Although she was no longer a professional pole dancer, she maintained it was the best way to stay in shape. Judging by her incredibly taught arms and thighs, not to mention an ass you could serve drinks off, the women were all inclined to believe her.

Astrid may have been small, at only five foot two, but her muscles gave her the hint of curves in all the right places. Her Indian heritage and coffee-coloured skin also gave her a deliciously exotic, almost forbidden, look. It had made her incredibly popular in the clubs she had worked in. There was a huge Indian diaspora in Glasgow, but as far as Astrid knew, she was the only pole dancer, and she loved that she was considered so unique among her clientele.

Hunter had divested herself of everything except her shoes and was unselfconsciously fastening golden nipple jewels onto her naked body. They were evocative of carved fleur-de-lys and hooked around her erect nipples with tiny, disguised ties which Darcey diligently tightened, ensuring that they wouldn't slip during the evening's festivities.

The scene in the 'dressing room' was being hungrily observed by Him, and although he made no effort to hide his presence, he hadn't openly announced it either. He couldn't help but feel that he was being given a stolen glimpse into a modern version of some ancient myth or legend; nymphs, perhaps, tempting unsuspecting male virgins into debauchery, or sirens punishing unsuspecting sailors with an insatiable death, or even the inimitable Bacchae.

He was entranced. He had always loved women; he'd devour them all if he could. His dealings were usually over after a day, a weekend, a week or two at the outside, and yet… And yet, he couldn't deny that the one called Hunter who had reacted so exquisitely to his ministrations over dinner undoubtedly intrigued him. She was so unselfconscious in her body, in her sexuality. He sensed a hunger in her that could possibly match his own. He was only cautiously optimistic however, having been so used to disappointment in the past. Women could never keep up with his appetites for long. Their desires always became so depressingly quotidian and predictable. The danger and lust disappeared, leaving half-hearted obligation and boredom in its lipstick-stained wake. Those were things he worked hard to avoid at all costs.

His mouth parted involuntarily as he watched Darcey slip the ornate golden chains delicately over Hunter's head. They fell like folds of the most extravagant silk over Hunter's high and proud breasts, the cold of the metal causing her nipples to tighten. The chains fastened around her back and fell delicately around each buttock before looping around her waist to drape elegantly over her thighs. She was, for all intents and purposes, naked, draped in nothing but golden chains, and yet at that moment she was the most sexually sophisticated woman he had ever seen.

He was so engrossed in Hunter's costume that he didn't even notice as Tiffany and Astrid walked directly past him and out of the room, sharing an amused and knowing look between them.

'Damn,' breathed Astrid grinning. 'It looks like someone's fallen for Hunter's ample charms! Which means...I'm stuck with what's-his-name from earlier.'

Tiffany grinned. 'You don't have to sleep with him just because he's here, you know.'

Astrid tilted her head towards her friend. 'I'm sorry, sweetheart, but have we met?' The girls broke into laughter as they split up to perform their allotted tasks for the evening's enjoyment.

One immovable tradition at The Hall was the serving of espresso martinis after dinner. This was always done, without exception, in The Stables, and if Astrid was staying, to the accompaniment of an impressive pole dance. A further mainstay of this tradition was that the drinks were served from the body of one of the naked guests. In this instance, it was Tiffany. Tiffany, as hostess, had changed the rules slightly for tonight though, wanting something faster and more powerful to kick things off. She had supplemented the drinks menu with shots of tequila. Quick, popular, and much easier to either grip between your thighs, or balance in your cleavage.

Hunter glanced around the room. It was quite the scene, akin to a Jack Vettriano painting, if Jack Vettriano did fetish wear anyway. Astrid was methodically rubbing down the stripper pole, which was a professional affair, bolted into both the ceiling and the small, raised stage – called the 'bar' – at the back of the main room. This room was the largest in the old stone building. It contained the usual array of Harris Tweed and tartan upholstery, old-boy leather chairs in front of a roaring fireplace and a few rather insipid hunting watercolours along the walls.

The Stables itself was actually run as a going concern, a profitable shoot that people would pay to come to partake and stay at. Ostensibly a cross between a stone crofters' cottage and an elegant Scottish hunting lodge. Anyone in the know however, could spot the small notes of discord

in the otherwise classic Scottish country scene. The
patently obvious stripper-pole and stage notwithstanding.

Some patrons may wonder why, what had been an actual
functional horses' stables, had since been remodelled into
accommodation for the aforementioned shoots, had been
arranged in such an unusual layout. The bar room for
instance was the largest in the old stone building, and
there were little give-aways all over the scene. The fact
that the bar itself, which ran the entire length of the wall
as you entered the room to your left, as well as having the
traditional but unnecessary brass rail, had hooks at 24-inch
intervals. Seemingly innocuous to the unobservant or
uninitiated, but clear indications of some pretty serious
bondage to those in the know.

The books inside the ornate oak cases were all slightly
suspect as well, works by the likes of: Sade, Petronius,
Montesquieu, and Aretino, then Defoe and Cleland to say
nothing of the hostess's favourite, Réage.

Then there were the bathrooms, or more pertinently, there
weren't. There was only one, and it was enormous on a
grand scale. Every fixture seemed to be made of the same
dark marble, but what was really impressive was the
bathtub. It was giant, yes, but more so it was divine. A
claw-footed masterpiece of wrought iron feet and the same
dark marble design. Into which, you could comfortably fit
six, with several more lounging along its wide tiled edges.
Hunter knew this for a fact, having done so herself after a
rather satisfying Hogmanay party.

The room was also filled with candle sconces, not in itself
indicative of any nefarious goings-on, but couple this with

all the cabinets featuring a selection of condoms, lubricants, oils and stimulants among the more regular cotton-buds and nail varnish remover, and the signs were all there, *if* you knew where to look. It never ceased to amaze the guests 'in the know' that people actually stayed here with no inkling of what went on when Richard had his more *private* parties. It was amazing that which people did not want to see. Or perhaps it spoke more to the characters of the currently assembled guests, that where regular people would see decanter stoppers, picture hooks and pastry-cutters, others would see butt-plugs, bondage hooks and pinwheels.

Hunter sighed happily. It was nights like this that had led the four women to become firm friends. By then, they had all come to realise that their sexual proclivities were a lot more adventurous than the average woman, and that these proclivities tended to make their more traditionally minded girlfriends decidedly uncomfortable. Astrid couldn't even remember the first time she had received a disapproving look from a peer when mentioning a particular kink or asking a particular question; it happened almost continuously. Unlike her three friends, however, she genuinely didn't give 'a single solitary fuck' about the opinions of others.

Tiffany's first experience of disapproval had come indecently early, according to her high school friends, whose views were far more in keeping with those of their Bible-bashing parents. She had excitedly explained how she'd lost her virginity to two older boys simultaneously, and how she'd since become an avid practitioner of spanking. The girls in question had looked horrified and refused ever to speak to her again. Very quickly, vicious rumours began to spread that she was a freak and a pervert, and she was dropped as the captain of the school cheerleading squad. Distraught, Tiffany had vowed that in future she would only reveal her secrets to people who were as interesting and exciting as she was.

The ultra-conservative views of her Bible-belt contemporaries had been one of the main reasons Tiffany had chosen to do her postgraduate study in the UK. She had always considered the UK quaintly camp and far more liberal than her home country. She remembered listening to Elton John and Freddie Mercury as a teenager and had always suspected that she would be more accepted across the pond. It turned out that when she moved here, she had been proved right. As if called into existence by her thirst for friends like her, she met Hunter, Astrid, and Darcey almost immediately. In many ways this meeting had saved her.

For Darcey, an intensely private person who was slow to confide in others and ruthlessly self-controlled in public, it had taken slightly longer to be called out as being somewhat unusual. Her husband had hosted a poker night for some of the other Royal Air Force officers on base, and after a few drinks and a few losing rounds, one of the other players had suggested it might be time to throw their car keys onto the table. Darcey, who by then was a little worse for drink, had immediately risen from her seat and stared with confusion at the men around her. 'But... I'm the only woman here!' she had slurred, half indignant, half laughing. 'How the hell can we hold a fishbowl party with only one woman?'

Her husband had stared daggers at her, clearly enraged at his wife's blunder. 'No darling,' he said, through gritted teeth. 'He meant to use his car as collateral for the bet.'

Darcey had been devasted at her mistake, and retired to bed shortly afterwards, mumbling something about a migraine. She had felt the sting of the injustice, though, as her husband was well aware she had a kinky side and frequently made use of it when the two were alone. She wasn't sure that she'd ever be able to reconcile herself with his uncompromising possession of her sexuality.

In short, the four friends had never had sex lives that *most* people would consider 'normal,' but once they had found each other at university, life had become a lot more fun.

Before Tiffany had first introduced them to The Hall, the friends had all met down in London for a girls' weekend. Tiffany was already there, doing some property thing with Richard, and Darcey was attending a surgical conference at the RCS, so Hunter and Astrid had decided to hop on a plane and join them. The highlight had been a trip to Coco De Mer, individually beloved by each of them, and as Hunter often put it, her personal 'chez away from chez'. They had each bought tiny matching vibrators, elegantly reminiscent of vintage 1950s necklaces, when pencils would be worn on chains around the necks of office secretaries for convenience.

These charming devices were to make pleasure accessible anywhere, and the fact that they were hidden in plain sight appealed to them all. They decided that, from then on, they would wear them whenever they got together, like some sort of R-rated friendship bracelet. They also had a challenge going as to who could wear theirs in the most daring scenario without getting caught. So far Darcey was winning, having worn hers during a surgery that she was performing. A close second was Hunter who had worn hers *over* her form-fitting shift dress on the way home from the London trip, whilst she went through airport security. Unsurprisingly, Astrid was the most daring, but also almost always caught or questioned by some innocent as to her 'unusual jewellery.' The game was ongoing, with the winner democratically decided upon, and the leader board continuously updated.

Regardless of whatever men they were entertaining at the time, these women were undoubtedly meant for each other. They would defend their relationship to the last, and no mere man would ever come between them. Men would inevitably come and go, but the women's friendship was forever.

*

Astrid's performance on the pole was, as always, impressive, in equal parts erotic and athletic. Watching her perform, eight feet from the stage and leaning back in a perfect backwards swan dive, it was impossible not to be impressed. Gyrating and twisting in time to 'Pussy Liqueur,' a song steeped in sex, she had the whole room in raptures, and no one could tear their eyes away. Trigger practically salivated throughout the entire performance. When Astrid finished, sliding down the pole into a perfect full split at the bottom, Hunter thought that Trigger was going to have an actual honest-to-goodness heart attack, either that or spontaneously ejaculate into his boxers right there.

Astrid had a talent that others could only aspire to in vain. She was a beautiful pole-dancer, even though she was not necessarily considered classically beautiful. Darcey in particular had often commented that her garish make-up and over the top outfits made her look like a 1980s sweet, full of chemicals not entirely good for you, and yet somehow nostalgically wholesome. Her performance on the pole, however, would bring anyone to their knees, either with lust or in simple slack-jawed admiration. Astrid was also the most crazily comforting and loyal person you could meet.

The women helped their ecstatic and gently perspiring friend from her podium and made their way over to the stable bar. Astrid basked in the all-out adoration from everyone present as she sashayed her way across the room. She really came alive under the spotlight, and despite the obvious, Hunter always wondered what on earth had possessed her friend to give up the limelight (albeit the slightly seedy version) for life as an office corporate whore. She'd be much happier if she was still on the pole. Protestations about aging aside, Hunter could see Astrid kicking ass up there well into her fifties.

Tiffany, meanwhile, ever the consummate host, had shimmied out of her latex and hopped up onto the long, immaculately polished bar.

With Tiffany now lying brazenly naked, spread-eagled and expectant, along the bar, Darcey suddenly realised what everyone was waiting for. 'Bugger,' she said. 'I left the tequila next door. Hunter, can you do the honours while I fetch it?'

'Of course,' Hunter said, and began to balance the shot glasses on Tiffany's prostrate form. She placed four at varying intervals in between her thighs, the higher of which would invariably allow the drinker a taste of Tiffany as well as tequila. She balanced one more on each clavicle, and yet another in her cleavage. She was about to place a final glass in Tiffany's mouth when He appeared behind her as if by some deviant magic. 'Can I be of service?' He asked.

Hunter looked calmly towards Him. 'I think I can handle this, thank you.'

Just then, Darcey appeared with the bottle and Hunter began pouring a generous measure into each of the glasses.

'Shit,' Hunter laughed, 'I can't add! I've done eight and there are only seven of us drinking - obviously you don't count Tiff!' She frowned. 'Oh well, someone will just have to do two.'

'Or balance the other one on someone else?' He suggested lasciviously.

'But Sir,' Hunter purred at Him, 'wherever could I put it?'

'I can think of a few places I would certainly enjoy. May I?'

'No,' she smiled, knocking back the extra shot.

He laughed and leaned into her. 'You missed a spot.' He licked a drop of tequila from her lip, tracing the chains around her waist with His fingers as He did so. Hunter closed her eyes and pressed herself into Him, willing His clothes to evaporate from His body.

'For the love of God just fuck him will you!' hissed Tiffany lying unmoving on the bar and somehow managing to transfer all her pent-up energy into her words. She poked Hunter in the side, careful not to upset her glasses, 'He clearly wants you and I know you want to know what he can do with that knife.' She winked. Louder she added, 'Also get bloody on with it and fill the rest of the glasses with tequila will you! I want a drink and I want off this bloody bar!'

Hunter snapped out of the myriad sexual fantasies flicking though her mind's eye, stepped back and placed the final shot glass in Tiffany's mouth, filling it up. All the while He watched her ravenously.

A moment later, Richard took his cue like the ringmaster he was. 'Thank you, Astrid, for your delightful little precursor. Now, we have more drinks, dancing, and any other debauchery you wish to indulge in. But remember; guns at seven am sharp, and we will not wait for latecomers. I'm looking at you Trigger, I don't care how fucking hungover you are, you drag your pickled carcass out of bed and get in the damned Landy!'

Trigger laughed heartily, assuring Richard he'd be there, whilst casting lecherous eyes over Astrid.

'So,' Richard continued, 'please, enjoy the evening, and remember...' Richard allowed himself a small chuckle in anticipation of his oft-used pun. '...The drinks are on us!' Grinning, he looked to each of his guests and then, with a theatrical wave of the hands, shouted, 'To the shoot!'

With that, the guests bent their heads towards Tiffany and enjoyed a tequila body shot. Richard took the glass from between the apex of his wife's thighs, allowing his tongue to linger a little longer, eliciting a sweet moan from Tiffany.

The shots were downed, and the inevitably spilt tequila was licked from Tiffany's willing body, Tiffany herself greatly enjoying the process. There was something vaguely vampiric about it, Hunter thought, delighted. She looked up towards Him and, to her surprise, He delicately licked a drop from the top of Tiffany's clavicle. It was as if He had read Hunter's thoughts, and suddenly all she could think of was Him and what He might be able to do to her with that knife.

Once the tequila was drunk and Tiffany had shimmied off the bar, the espresso martinis made their traditional appearance, as if by some sort of dipsomaniac deity. From then on, the night quickly descended into the expected drunken bacchanal. Astrid and Trigger had barely swallowed the first shot when Trigger, roaring in triumph, hoisted her bodily over his shoulder and practically ran from the building back to The Hall. Astrid's raucous laughter had been audible even over the thumping base of the music that had been playing since her amazing pole performance. *Well*, Hunter thought, *that's the last we'll see of them until the morning.*

It was at that moment that Hunter decided that nothing was going to happen with Him tonight. She was already too drunk to enjoy Him fully, and she knew that she would want to have every sense heightened when she did. She also wanted the seduction to last as long as possible. Thus liberated, she decided to fully enjoy the party instead. She grabbed Darcey's hand and pulled her into the middle of the room. They both started dancing to one of both of their favourite songs, Billie Eilish's 'Bad Guy.' *How appropriate*, thought Hunter as she lost herself in the music, feeling completely content to be dancing the night away with her favourite people in the whole world, and the prospect of the most exciting sexual adventure of her life tantalisingly within reach.

Vice

The Hunt

"Either kill me, or take me as I am."
Marquis de Sade

Hunter awoke with the expected pounding headache. She reached for the pre-emptively placed Alka-Seltzer (drunk Hunter was a helpful Hunter). It didn't matter how drunk she got the night before, she always, *always* placed an Alka-Seltzer and a full glass of water on her bedside table. It had saved her life on more than one occasion. Hunter lived to enjoy life. Her father had once said of his eldest daughter, not quite joking, 'you'd go to the opening of a door if champagne was provided.' She hadn't been offended; he was right. Hunter could make an occasion out of a wet Tuesday in February. Hence her hangover avoidance ritual.

If she was relatively compos mentis then she would even do a quick 1-minute facial, moisturise, and take a vitamin before bed, but alas, none of that particular ritual had been accomplished last night, thanks to Darcey and some lethal cocktails. She tore the packet with a worryingly well practiced motion and quickly tipped the contents into the glass next to her. Even the gentle fizzing sound was comforting. After drinking it down, she noticed the time and gasped. *Only half an hour to guns.* She threw off her blankets and, with a shudder, tiptoed quickly towards her wardrobe.

With moments to spare, and bedecked in Tiffany's borrowed tweed, Hunter stumbled downstairs towards the main entrance of The Hall. She noticed, with almost tearful gratitude, that Marissa had left a platter of bacon rolls and ready-poured coffees on the hallway table. It was at times like this that Hunter could see the appeal of being rich. That, and every time she got on a plane.

Suddenly, a voice boomed behind her, causing her to jump and tip coffee all over her shoes. Luckily no Louboutins today. Nope, a sturdy pair of Hunter wellies to complement the tweedy country-chic ensemble she'd thrown together from Tiffany's capacious wardrobe. The voice was suggestive of the Peerage, of someone dressed in tartan and then liberally dipped in whisky. Hunter grinned and turned around.

'Steward!' She exclaimed, delighted. 'I didn't know you were coming this weekend.'

'Neither did I, sweetheart. It was all a bit last minute. I was supposed to be shooting elsewhere but it all fell through. So, I gave Dickie a ring and he said he could stand me a gun for the day.' Steward stepped forward and gave Hunter a kiss on both cheeks. He was older, titled and absolutely fabulous. He was also the only person on the face of the earth who Hunter knew could get away with calling Richard 'Dickie'. She loved Steward like an avuncular best-friend. He was the not-so-bitchy queen that everyone wanted to know. But Hunter and Steward had always had a particular rapport.

'Now come on gorgeous, I was sent in to fetch you and that demonic sex kitten Astrid, you're both the last.'

'Oh god, sorry! Hunter laughed. 'Though, I'm surprised Darcey made it down already. The two of us were up until three am. We ended up back in the drawing room... I think... making martinis out of whatever was in the drinks cabinet.'

'Jesus, darling, you're lucky you're still alive! The contents of that cabinet would have felled a lesser mortal. Especially drinking the dreaded martini, or as my dear departed grandmother used to say –

> *Beware the dreaded martini,*
> *Only have one at the most,*
> *With two you're under the table,*
> *But with three you're under the host!'*

And my dear it looks like you've been under more than the one host!'

Hunter laughed, wincing slightly as she raised her coffee mug in mock salute.

'Now off with you,' Steward commanded. 'I've the starting line-up to do and I will not be late.'

Hunter took a last swig of coffee before trotting outside, bacon roll still in hand. She spotted the party immediately, hovering in various states of hangover by several army-green Land Rovers. *It looks like we're invading the highlands, not enjoying them,* she thought as she hugged Darcey and Tiffany good morning. Darcey looked like she'd just stepped out of a Boden catalogue, of course, and Tiffany... Tiffany looked like the American perception of what country-chic would be, draped in tartan from head to toe.

'How are *you* looking so fresh?' Hunter asked Darcey, taking a last bite of her bacon roll as a panacea against the pain.

'Practice,' Darcey said, 'You work on-call in a hospital for a while and a late night followed by an early start doesn't even register.'

'Oh look!' Tiffany cried. 'Here's Steward coming to get this party started!' Then, when Astrid came into view behind the loping Steward; 'What the hell is *she* wearing?'

'I think a Barber coat, wellies and absolutely nothing else,' Hunter said, laughing.

'That's my girl!' Richard shouted. 'Perfectly bonkers as usual! Right, now that we're all here, it's a quick bang and then off we go!'

'Bang?' asked Astrid, blinking through last night's make-up.

'Brace your hangover,' Hunter told her. A moment later, Steward hefted his shotgun onto his shoulder, and fired two enormous blasts into the sky. Each one made little firework lights dance behind Hunter's eyelids.

'Right!' Steward roared. 'I declare this shoot officially open!'

And with that, they were off.

Vice

*

By the time everyone reached the destination point and began to organise themselves into hunting pairs, Hunter's heart had gone out of the hunt completely. The unease she had felt since her near miss with the stag hadn't left her, and that coupled with her hangover, made her an unsafe bet with a hunting rifle.

'Hey guys, I'm not going to join the hunting, I'm just going to walk the hills.'

There were protestations of, 'are you sure?' and 'is everything ok?' But the women knew that Hunter wasn't big on the actual shooting part of these events. Astrid was only going along as she had been paired with Trigger and thought they could probably manage an illicit shag along the way.
'Don't worry Dickie,' Steward said, 'I'll pair with Hunter's man.' The man in question waved a salute at Steward as He readied His weapon, all the while stealing glances at Hunter.

'Thanks, old boy. No problem darling, enjoy the landscape. If you head up that ridge over there, you're out of the way of the hunt, and the view is rather impressive.'

'Perfect. Thanks Richard.' She smiled in his direction and put her gun down in the back of the Land Rover. 'I'll be fine.' She assured them as she began walking into the hillside, giving Darcey a small wave and a reassuring smile. Darcey waved back. She knew Hunter could look after herself.

Hunter thought that she could feel His eyes on her back as she walked away.

God the Highlands are beautiful this time of year, she thought, as she began walking the track that led to the summit. Hunter loved Autumn in Scotland. She could feel the cold prickling even through her many layers, but she was soon warmed by her exertions. Her breath misted in the air, and she had to shield her eyes as the sun rose. It glinted off the berries on the bushes she passed, making them look like pinpricks of fresh blood. The noise of the group receded to nothing as she continued her walk. She was glad of her sturdy wellies as she pushed through the thick heather that carpeted the ground in front of her. It smelled vaguely of coconut, which Hunter always found incongruous. The incline was gentle, and the landscape was breath-taking. Rolling hills in every direction, and in the distance, she could see snow-capped peaks, mountains reaching to the sky like jagged teeth.

She had been walking for about thirty minutes when she suddenly became acutely aware of her isolation. She also realised that she'd become quite hopelessly lost. Where was she? Had she placed herself in danger? She thought she'd stayed well outside of the hunting range, but maybe not… She was, she had to admit, a bit fuzzier than usual this morning. The summit had never materialised, and she'd found herself following a track along the side of the hill as opposed to going up it.

Wherever she was, she knew she wasn't ready to be rescued. The morning mist curled lazily around the barren branches that enclosed her, leaving delicate pearls of dew in their wake. The air felt almost liquid with its silky, clammy caress. The ground was soft underfoot, blanketed in fallen leaves, the hills crowded around her like old friends, occasionally a break in the skyline would offer a glimpse down to the still dark loch below her path.

As she navigated the cool morning landscape, enjoying the dew that sparkled on the heather, Hunter's thoughts returned to the night before. Tiffany had noticed Hunter's obvious interest in Richard's friend, whom Richard had christened Lord Byron, and decided to tell Hunter everything she knew about Him.

Tiffany had described Him as dangerous, which had conjured up in Hunter's mind some tortured, James Bond-esque soul, or the villain in a bodice-ripping Mills & Boon romance. But no. This man was dangerous in ways she couldn't even begin to fully contemplate or understand. He voluntarily hovered between life and death, apparently enjoying the view, in no rush to pick a side. Bears were just one of the many animals He hunted, and when He was done killing the animal, He made sure to eat it. He drove his Aston Martin DB9 at a minimum of forty miles over the speed limit at all times, not in a desire to show off or be overtly ostentatious, but because of a perpetual feeling that time was running out. This feeling crackled around Him like a static aura. His personal clock was ticking, and this wild ride, whatever it might be, might be His last. This was a man who, if He hang-glided over hell, would complain that the view wasn't interesting enough.

Snap! The crack of a twig breaking scythed through the cool morning air and brought her hurtling out of her reverie, and back to the chilly Scottish hillside and her hangover.

She froze, straining her ears. It was Him, come to find her. She knew it. It was Him. Out of sight, perhaps, but she could sense He was close. She wanted Him closer; she wanted Him inside her.

The irony that she was now involved in a hunt of her own making was not lost on Hunter. But the question remained: was she the hunted, or the huntress?

She picked her way through the trees, her long hair catching and pulling in every twig and snarl. And yet, she was happy. She loved the smell of a damp Scottish morning, especially in the autumn and winter. Mulch, mould, and the musky hints of wet heather were forever reminiscent of growing up on her parents' farm and offered an inescapable sense of comfort and contentment. The overlying smell of wood smoke was the only thing that was absent from the olfactory trip down memory lane.

As she walked, the thundering tumult of a waterfall grew closer and closer. The scent of the churned water was riding on the air. *Where is He?* she thought, '*and come to that, where the hell am I?* She knew He had to be close. She looked this way and that, frantically searching for any sign of Him, all the while half expecting, half wishing a hand to grab her by the throat. Her heart pounded and her throat dried, the comforting Scottish atmosphere quickly disappearing over the lightening horizon.

Then, through the trees, she saw him, enormous and proud in the ethereal morning air. All the collective tension poured out of her in one huge breath. She could hardly believe her luck. For there, a mere twenty feet from where she stood, was the stag. She watched him, keeping her breath steady so as not to startle him away. Glorious antlers reached skyward, and giant hooves tore chucks from the forest floor as he looked around, emerging from the fog-laced foliage, seemingly unaware of her presence.

It was ironic, really, that she'd failed to load or even bring a gun, and yet here she was with the perfect shot. Trigger would have given his right arm to be in this position right now. She wondered if he would even believe her when she told him how close she had come to the very creature he was now searching for. And then it occurred to her; she had her phone, and from this vantage point she would be able to take a picture that would rival Landseer's 'Monarch of the Glen.'

The sun was beginning to chase away the mist and the animal was suddenly lit with warm streaks of gold. It really *is* the perfect shot, she thought, as she reached for her phone and steadied herself to take the picture. She slowed her breathing and made sure her movements were fluid and precise. She felt everything slow and crystallise around her as she focused completely on the magnificent animal. And then there was an explosion that forced an involuntary scream from her lips and knocked her onto her knees.
What the fuck just happened? she thought, her head swimming from the shock and a ringing persisting in her ears. *Am I hit? I can't feel anything. Have I been shot or am I numb?*

Slowly, she began to raise her head from the cold wet earth, and what she saw made her almost wish that the bullet had been meant for her after all. For there, on the grass, lay the stag, its final breaths escaping in wisps from its velvet muzzle, a trickle of blood running down its tawny coat.

Rising unsteadily to her feet, she stumbled towards the still body of the beast, shaking with fury and adrenalin. By the time she had reached its side, it was already dead. She felt dizzy. How could anybody do such a hideous thing to such a beautiful creature?

Too late she heard Him coming through the trees. She turned quickly, and there He was, all six foot five of him; broad shoulders and dark hair, eyes like granite taking aim with His rifle right at her. Her breath caught in her throat. In that moment her entire world became the look in His eyes and the barrel of that gun. She dropped to her knees in surrender and raised her hands instinctively.

Was it possible she had found her Master, or was He actually going to shoot her? This man, who simultaneously attracted and repelled her. Excited her beyond measure but offended so much of who she was. These thoughts were a maelstrom inside her head as she kneeled in front of Him, breathing heavily and defiantly holding His gaze, almost daring Him to fire. He sighted along his gun and maintained her gaze.

Slowly a wolverine grin stole onto his mouth. He lowered the gun and strode forwards until He was right there in front of her. He could see she hovered between submissive and defiant, and He was loving the challenge in her. Her eyes blazed fury in response. She hated herself for wanting Him so much and hated Him for his contradictions.

'Careful,' He said calmly, lifting her to her feet, 'If the beast twitches, those antlers could get you. I'd hate for anything but me to penetrate that beautiful skin.' He cocked His gun into the crook of his elbow and expelled the spent shell. 'First time you've seen a kill up close, I take it?'

She squared her shoulders defiantly. 'Actually, I *have* been involved in hunts in the past.'

'But never been this close to the prey,' He said, his eyes roving all over her. 'Well, do you like it now that it's more visceral? Now that you know how bloody and raw the experience is?'

'It's not bloody and raw, it's sad and unnecessary. Take a sodding picture for god's sake or get close enough to feel like a man by looking through your sight at it. Why kill something so magnificent?'

She expected a stock response, something about man vs. nature, the natural order of things, the usual dull platitudes trotted out by people with a limited grasp of ecology and too much time and testosterone. He surprised her by saying nothing. He just continued challenging her with His eyes. Then in one fluid, almost sensual movement He reached down into the wound on the stag's chest and bloodied His fingers.

As their eyes locked once more, the mist crystalized in the air between them, and the sun finally won its battle with the Scottish climate, streaking the landscape with liquid light. With His un-bloodied hand, He held her to Him, gripping her tightly around the waist. The air crackled with tension between them. Suddenly, He pushed her, roughly, against a nearby tree. She leant against it with all her weight, unable to control her limbs or even shout out in protest. Her lips parted and she breathed in, inhaling the smell of blood and Him. If you could bottle masculinity, then this is how it would smell. Wood, fire, power, earth. He pressed His taut body against hers, and then, holding her there, traced His bloodied hand across her mouth, his fingers slipping inside for the briefest moment.

The metallic salt of the beast's hot blood penetrated her lips, and it was all she could do not to retch. Then, without warning, He grabbed her hair and forced her head back, kissing her hungrily, His tongue forcing more of the blood into her mouth. She responded hungrily, lapping the blood from His tongue, and almost biting at His lips. She was beginning to think she might faint with pleasure when, suddenly, He pushed her roughly away. He looked deep into her eyes, panting, almost growling, and licked His lips.

She would have leapt on Him in that moment, but just then the rest of the party arrived jollily at the clearing. Breathing heavily, He discreetly bloodied her cheek with the remaining red stain on His fingers and then turned to greet them. For the second time that day, Hunter found herself deliberately breathing slowly and trying to steady herself. Inside she was almost snarling with want, their attraction was so visceral it could have ripped her apart.

'Oh my god!' Tiffany cried, the words tumbling from her mouth in a stampede. 'You got a kill? You didn't even take a gun!?'

'No,' Hunter replied, still breathless. 'It was His kill. I just… got in the way?'

'Ha!' exclaimed Astrid. 'Sure, you did. You're lucky all you got was bloodied. Want me to lick it off?'

Hunter smiled. 'No, I'm good. Anyone got a tissue?'

'Here.' He said, handing her a silk handkerchief. 'Bear in mind, though, they say it's bad luck to remove the blood before midnight.' He flashed her a roguish smile.

She looked at the handkerchief, secretly delighted. *Seriously?* she thought. *Monogrammed handkerchiefs? What century is this? And what the hell did He mean, was she seriously supposed to leave this on her face for the entire day?* Turning her eyes back to Him, she touched the silk to her cheek and removed the smear of blood. But she made sure to leave the merest hint of it there. She wasn't superstitious, but she gave more credence to obscure Scottish traditions than most. She also knew she'd be breathing into that handkerchief as she pleasured herself later that evening.

The men had already reached the stag and were congratulating Him excitedly on His stunning kill. Rolling their eyes, the women turned as one to join their male counterparts in the post-mortem party. It was Steward who stood holding court, rifle cocked jauntily in one elbow as he poured generously from a pewter flask. He embodied the adventurous spirit of Livingstone or Kipling, and images of overly romanticised colonial conquests flitted through her head as she accepted her drink. It was only slightly unfortunate that it looked like sparkling blood, as she was convinced that she could still smell the iron taint on her skin. But it turned out to be delicious, sloe-gin mixed with champagne, a drink Tiffany had christened the *Sloegasm*. Delicious but deadly.

*

Hunter could no longer trust herself around Him, that much was clear, she was too involved now, whether she wanted to be or not. He had a power over her, and she knew she'd give Him more, give Him everything, if He demanded it. He was enigmatic and powerful, a predator, and despite her repugnance at His obsession with His recent kill, she would now gladly make herself His prey. His slave. She couldn't help it, but could she handle it? She was still unable to reconcile His obvious unpredictability and contradictions with what she wanted from Him. In order to be a willing slave to a true master, you had to give yourself completely and entirely, and that required the purest form of trust. She worried that He was too unpredictable. Would He keep her safe, or would He abuse his power? In truth, she had no idea.

Part of Hunter's character, that the other girls teased her mercilessly about, was how seriously she took her family history and Scottish heritage. She lived to uphold her clan's name and maintain its traditions. Hunter Blair. The Blairs had been integral to Scottish history and culture for centuries. Her family were supporters of both Wallace and later Bruce. Hunter took things like this seriously. Including her clan's motto 'Amo Probos' – 'Love the virtuous.' Hunter always tried to surround herself with people she considered noble and moral. She was not convinced He was either of these things, and this had already awakened a conflict in her.

Fortunately, there was still time for her to decide what to do. Lucky, really, as committing to being someone's slave was not a flippant decision to make, and she would need to carefully consider it.

The Chase

"The only way to get rid of a temptation is to yield to it. Resist it, and your soul grows sick with longing for the things it has forbidden to itself."

Oscar Wilde

The water of the Scandinavian hot tub was deliciously warm and restorative as it kissed and swirled around their naked skin. The vista of the highlands that surrounded them was like something out of a scene in Braveheart, and you could almost imagine that hundreds of battle-crazed Scots were about to come cresting over the hilltop screaming bloody murder. Mist slithered amongst the heather, teasing out every available nook and cranny, whilst the hills glared down imperiously over the thickening drizzle, as if in disapproval of the weather spoiling such a stunning view.

'There are certainly worse ways to spend an afternoon,' Tiffany sighed, as she handed a glass of champagne to each of her friends. Although the giant hot tub was easily large enough for their entire party, they had all ended up sitting in gender segregated groups, the girls and Steward (who was one of the girls to them anyway) on one side and the men on the other. While the gentlemen swirled whisky in Edinburgh crystal glasses and deconstructed their days' shooting, the girls and Steward were far more interested in the beautiful surroundings, the crisp champagne and catching up on mutual friends' current situations.

When He had stepped out of the lodge completely naked, Hunter had thought her heart had stopped, her entire body had quivered so violently that Astrid thought there was something wrong with her. Despite her friends' joking she had just stared at Him, taking in every inch of Him with her eyes, as she knew she would soon with her whole body. He was magnificent. The most powerful man she had ever seen, muscles glistening slick with sweat that clung to Him like she desperately wanted to. His chest had a smattering of dark hair and with each stride the muscles of his thighs betrayed their strength. He knew she was salivating for Him, and He simply stared back at her, chest rising and falling, as she fought to keep her eyes on His and not where they wanted to go. She would not give Him the satisfaction. She wouldn't. Although she was practically vibrating with the effort of *not* looking.

They were close to finishing their second bottle of champagne when The Letch leaned towards Astrid. 'So,' he said, with a smirk that made Hunter shudder, 'how did you lovely ladies meet?'

Tiffany turned to Astrid. 'You mean you didn't cover this post-coitally last night?' she asked, sotto voice.

Astrid laughed, completely unabashed. 'You know after a night with me they can't even breathe, never mind hold a coherent conversation.' Then, looking at the Letch, she launched with tangible relish into their history together as university acquaintances and then best friends.

Hunter barely listened to the stories that followed. Her eyes were locked on His, and the six feet that separated them suddenly seemed insurmountable. She could imagine His powerful erection beneath the surface of the water. Her lips parted in reflex, but despite her desire she remained rooted to the spot she had taken between Astrid and Tiffany, sipping her champagne, and floating pleasantly in and out of the tales Astrid was telling of their early days together. It was tempting to use the texture of the water to disguise arousing herself further. She knew that if she did, He would know, and it would drive Him wild. But she also knew if she started now, they'd be fucking there and then in the hot tub, and one thing that Hunter did not want for this, was an audience. It was about the only thing staying her hand.

'Anyway,' Astrid was saying, as Hunter tried not to think about Him fucking her hard against the side of the hot tub. 'We all looked amazing in our various Halloween outfits, and we were in our element. Halloween is pretty much the only night of the year that perverts like us get to wear full bondage gear, and no one gives a shit. Plus, the amount of eye candy in the room was unbelievable. Hardly surprising, of course; it was a Royal Air Force party after all. Those pilot men were fucking beautiful!'

The Letch blinked, trying to hide his jealousy of the handsome men Astrid was describing. 'How the hell did you end up at a Royal Air Force party?' he asked.

'Oh, we were celebrating a… "Wing Procession," or something. Wait, what was it again, Darcey?'

'A Passing Out Parade' Darcey said. 'For some of the guys I knew from training. It was where I met Peter and you met Andrew.'

Vice

Astrid almost squealed in delight. 'Oh my god, Andrew! I'd forgotten about him.'
'Well, we hadn't,' said Tiffany. 'Or his bow-tie.'
'God he was fun. Such stamina!' Astrid grinned.

'He was also thick as mince!' Darcey said.

'True, but so cute. I forgot how much I love the military!'

Tiffany had only the haziest recollection of the night that Astrid was talking about. She did, however, remember having a delicious time at the party with a particularly stunning Navy pilot who was *very* into bondage. She had been incredibly willing, and also incredibly flexible. Tiffany had kept her beautiful Navy girl's thong as a souvenir, in fact now that she thought about it, she remembered having dressed up for Richard on a different Halloween in that very same thong, only this time she was in a rented Navy uniform. He had got a kick out of fucking her in the outfit that the Navy woman had worn when Tiffany had fucked her. This was the kind of kink that they both enjoyed, and why they were so suited as a married couple.

As the others laughed at Astrid's almost preternatural promiscuity, Hunter suddenly felt a wave of something hit her. She felt too hot, as if her skin was too tight for her. The damp-cedar smell of the forest immediately became sticky and cloying, as if turning the blood to sap in her veins. She knew it was just the champagne and the adrenaline, but still… Breathing as deeply as she could, she leaned over the edge of the hot tub, desperate to cool her skin in the gently falling drizzle. She was, if anything, feeling even closer to collapse when a voice appeared at her ear. 'Swim with me,' it said.

She turned dizzily to find Him standing by her side. 'What?' Even in her current wobbly state she kept her eyes riveted above waist height.

'Swim with me,' He said again. 'You're too hot. I can see it on your skin. Trust me, come with me.'

Suddenly His hand was around her throat, and He dragged his tongue down her face, savouring the final taste of the sin that he had left on her, that mixed with the salt of the sweat that was prickling her skin. Then, without another word He took her hand and pulled her up. She fell against him, unable to resist, woozy from the champagne. She cursed herself for finding herself like this, for allowing Him to caress her like a compliant ragdoll against His powerful body. She was caught somewhere between desire and despair when He suddenly heaved her into His arms and stepped down from the deck and across the wooden jetty that stretched far out into the loch. *God He was strong.*

'What are you two up to?' asked Darcey, ever watchful of her friends' situations.

'It's alright,' He replied, from over his shoulder. 'She's overheated, that's all. She'll feel better soon.'

'And she was never seen again...' Astrid said with a cackle, and they all laughed.

He was right; Hunter already felt slightly better as the cool air enveloped her in its soothing embrace. Her relief, however, was short-lived; when they reached the end of the jetty, she felt His muscles bunch beneath her, and in a moment, she found herself sailing through the air and into the soul-choking cold of Loch Tay. She knew what was coming, but it didn't stop the cold sucking the air from her lungs and stabbing her skin with what felt like a thousand ice-pointed needles.

Hunter was still catching her breath when there was another splash. A second later, He came roaring to the surface. 'Oh, come on,' He laughed, seeing her shocked expression. 'You've never done this in Scandinavia?'

'I'm not fucking Swedish. And actually no, I haven't. I prefer Southern Europe or Asia when I travel. Anywhere that's hot, sweaty, and exotic.'

'Well, I prefer the North,' He said. 'It's wild, and uncompromising, and if you take your eyes off it for even a second, you die.'

With a few practised strokes, He swam to where she was treading water, kicking her limbs despite the cold that was invading her body. She was almost annoyed to realise the cold water had made her feel completely okay again.

He must have noticed her expression because He began to chuckle softly. 'Feeling better?' He asked.

She nodded, reluctantly. 'I suppose I should thank you.'

'Never let it be said that I'll let a damsel languish in distress.'

She was already aware of how effortlessly His well-muscled body cut though the water. The sudden heat of her body contrasted with the chill in the air and the water. She felt the searing pull between her legs towards Him. She kept herself afloat with slow easy movements, feeling better by the second, and consequently even more aware of her arousal. He turned and swam back to her, panting in exhilaration.

'I love the water here, so clean and cold. It tastes pure.' He said. He looked so innocently delighted in His surroundings that she couldn't help but smile. The cold water swirled around her, insistent, commanding, mirroring the desire she felt for Him.

'I do too,' she said. 'I grew up swimming at North Berwick beach, so essentially the North Sea, which was bloody freezing as I am sure you can imagine. Even colder than this actually.' She laughed. 'There's something much more pleasant – something almost medieval – about swimming in a Loch, surrounded on all sides by the Scottish hills. It feels like a connection to the past, to the old clans who used to live here.' She trailed off, lost in history. Suddenly she felt His hands around her waist. She nearly choked.

'So, your Scottish lineage is important to you then,' He asked seriously, His eyes boring into her, as He held her fast.

'Well yes, it's an anchor. I can trace my family back centuries.'
'That explains your self-assurance then.'

'My what?' She was finding it hard to follow the conversation with His body so close to hers in the water.

'You're innate. You know exactly who you are and where you're supposed to be. You have an inner confidence I've never encountered in someone your age.'

She laughed again, flattered, but still not convinced as to what He was getting at. 'I've never felt the need to apologise for what or who I am if that's what you mean.'

'I just mean that you're completely comfortable. In any situation. With yourself, with your place in it. You play in obscenely wealthy and accomplished company as if it were nothing.'

She looked at Him, more serious now. 'You know as well as I do. It *is* nothing.'

He smiled. He knew she was right. He was also pretty sure she meant what she said. She wasn't interested in money. She saw through the shallow lives of the rich just as much as He did. Gazing into her eyes, He pulled her towards Him, His hands around her waist now and their legs intertwining as they sought to touch as much of each other as possible. She wanted to rake her nails down His back, but as she leaned in to kiss Him the water exploded around them as they were joined by the rest of the party, who had been watching amused from the hot tub. Whoops and shrieks pierced the still evening air as the six newcomers came to terms with the icy water.

'Come on, you two,' shouted Richard. 'This is a party, not a couple's retreat!' He lifted a naked and dripping Tiffany onto his shoulders and told Trigger and Astrid to do the same. 'Let's have some fun!'

With everyone splashing and play-fighting around them, He took her by the wrist and pulled her aside.

'Meet me inside in the sauna,' He commanded.

The response 'Yes, Master' sprang unbidden to her lips, but she bit it back just in time, simply inclining her head in assent.

Not yet. She thought cautioning herself. *Not my Master yet.*

*

Leaning blissfully against the smooth wall of the sauna, she enjoyed the contrast of temperatures, the heat of the air, the cold of the stone. She saw Him approaching her though the steam, barrel-chested and beautiful. He had the body of a fighter, male honour made flesh. She was surprised at how much He reminded her of the stag He had dispatched earlier. Perhaps He saw himself in the animal too? Was there a hint of self-loathing, of wanting to erase a part of himself He didn't like? She let these thoughts swirl idly around her head as she relaxed into her desire. He was here, He was hers. They were alone, in the most sexually charged setting she could imagine. They were literally in heat. He would have her, and finally sate this compelling longing.

'You were made for me,' He said. A simple statement of fact. A complete truth. She knew that He was right. Even the reservations she held about Him wouldn't stop her from succumbing. He was a match for her. She would just have to wait and see whether her mate had been gifted to her by a benevolent or a malevolent god.

'Yes.' She said.

He was standing by her side now, completely unselfconsciously naked and – she couldn't help but notice – impressively erect. When He noticed where she was looking, He grinned like a predatory version of the Cheshire cat. His movements were fluid and powerful, He was in complete control of himself, of His surroundings, and now, of her. She slid from the stone bench and kneeled in front of Him, face turned upwards, ready to acquiesce to His every command. He looked down towards her.

'Meet me at Ardanaiseig next weekend,' He instructed.

'Meet you where?' She asked.

Her eyes locked on His as her mouth hovered painfully close to His deliciously erect cock. She wanted to reach out with the tip of her tongue. But her desire kept her rooted to the spot beneath Him. Obedient. Still. Dominated.

'It's in a remote part of Argyll and Bute, it's a beautiful old country hotel. We can spend the weekend together completely alone. I need you all to myself. I need to take my time with you. You will be mine completely. I need you for me alone. Someone who chooses this life because they desire it, *not* because they want to be with me. Something about you makes me think that this is something you want. A different way to live. If it is, then we will be together, completely. And I will take you in a thousand ways that you have never imagined.'

She regarded Him slowly. He looked sincere, open, perhaps even a little vulnerable at having stated His desire so clearly. She knew what He was asking, it was everything she had ever wanted. A man worthy of her. A man she could gladly call Master. One whom she could trust with body and soul, who truly understood the mix of responsibility and desire, of pleasure and pain. She wanted to believe He could be that. He certainly seemed to have the personality and the temperament. 'I have wished for this for so long,' she said. 'Are you sure you're up to this?'

He laughed, a low, guttural growl. 'Am I up to this? I'll have you begging for mercy in the first twenty-four hours.'

She smiled back at Him. 'Try me.'

The Seduction

"He whom one awaits is, because he is expected, already present, already master."

Pauline Réage

'Divine. Absolutely divine. I'll need the last two cases.' Hunter snapped out of her fantasy and blinked at the rather dapper gentleman beaming back at her.

'Gosh, I'm so sorry, I was somewhere else.' She laughed. 'So, two cases of the Chateaux Laffite Pauillac Rothschild 1983. Excellent choice.'
'Well, it was your recommendation.' He winked at her and took another sip from his tasting glass.

Hunter smiled at him. A charming older gentleman, he looked like he had walked straight out of a Dickensian novel. He had come into the Wine Cellar where she worked earlier that day. He was there to choose wine for an upcoming dinner event. Ordinarily Hunter would have enjoyed the chance to discuss the different courses and wine pairings with another oenophile who was as enthusiastic as she was, but her mind had been elsewhere all week. She'd spent so long watching the seconds tick by on the clock in her office she was almost surprised the hands hadn't melted under the sheer force of her impatient gaze.

She organised the order and shared the last of the bottle he had been tasting, smiling and laughing. And although she made the appropriate small talk and he was clearly loving the attention, Hunter was entirely on autopilot. Her thoughts were consumed by Him, always Him. She woke with Him and slept with Him. She had grown bored and frustrated with every single one of her vibrators and toys within days of meeting Him. Using and discarding each one in turn, as she invariably wore out the batteries. Endless orgasms left her more frustrated than when she started. The handkerchief He had given her no longer carried His scent. Nothing sated her, she needed Him.

Her previously enjoyable, albeit mundane day-to-day life, had become unbearable since her weekend at The Hall. Now that she was so close to what she needed, to what she had always wanted, it was *all* she could think about. A Master to tame and care for her, a life lived less ordinary. She was in the thrall of a man finally worthy of her lust, worthy of her body, worthy of her soul. She had been in, what she was now calling the *'wine dungeon'*, all week, barely aware of who came and went, or of what wine they bought. The fact that she'd sold the last remaining cases of 1983 Pauillac in the word, at £1,000 a bottle, should have made her ecstatic. Instead, it left her cold. If she wasn't tied to His bed with Him licking the wine from her nipples, then she just didn't care.

The week since their hunting trip at The Hall had been the longest week of her life. She had been waiting for this for what felt like an eternity. Thank god, it was finally here. Finally, she was going to her Master.

Vice

*

She strode confidently down the beautifully appointed corridor to the hotel room door and knocked, the desire and demand reverberating through the elegant oak door. It opened. He stood there, glorious in his masculinity. James Bond on his day off. The object of all her desire. She was so ready for this man that she could almost smell her own arousal.

'Room service,' she purred. His laughter followed her into the room as He closed, and securely locked, the door behind her. Apparently, they'd need more than a 'Do not Disturb' sign tonight.

The hotel room was bigger than her first flat, and breathtakingly beautiful. Deep, dark claret DeVore wallpaper draped the walls. The bed was a proper four poster, solid carved wooden legs canopied in a similarly elegant style. She noted the chilled champagne on the bedside table with approval. That was a definite prerequisite. Cocktails were all very well, but it was champagne that was required on a night like this.

The sexual tension vibrated between them as they stood staring at each other. They both knew what was to come, what this meant, and yet neither was sure how to begin the negotiations. With a dominant/submissive relationship, consent and agreement were sacrosanct. Perhaps it was ironic that to a particular type of sexuality, hers included, only within distinct limits could she truly abandon herself. Could she be completely free.

The Seduction

He could barely control his ardour. His cock had been rock-hard and leaking in anticipation for the hour he'd waited for her in the hotel room. He didn't just want to fuck this woman; he wanted to possess and consume her. He remained controlled and calmly walked over to the table and carefully poured two glasses deftly handing one to her. Only His eyes betrayed his animal desire.

'To adventures,' He said.

'To adventures,' she answered. The uncertainty, the *shyness*, she was feeling was anathema to her. She was used to having men panting on their knees by this point. She always marvelled at the naiveté of men, thinking they had any say in when or how a woman gave herself to them. Insignificant boys all. Yes, they might think they were in control, but always, always, she had decided exactly what she wanted from them before anything had even begun. This was the power in the submissive.

But now everything had changed. She had literally no idea where to begin. She was relieved, then, when He stepped forward and plucked the champagne glass from her hand. They cleaved together, hands, tongues, limbs immediately intertwined. The force of it took her breath away. But He breathed more into her. They tore at each other's clothes, sending shirt buttons flying and tearing stockings without heed. She undid His belt and tugged at His trousers.

She had surprised Him with the force of her desire. 'On your knees,' He commanded, remembering the role in which He was cast, through the fog of pheromones and heat. He would make her submit.

She dropped immediately, obediently. It was a practiced response and one she had been looking forward to for so long. She didn't do yoga for the earnest conversations and chai tea. She did it so she had a body completely under her command, a tool of pleasure. Arching her back and looking up from her parted knees she delicately and deliberately slowly, licked the tip of His cock, and He roared.

What she was doing was nothing different to what He'd done with a hundred other women, and yet everything felt amplified, like she was teasing His soul from His body. Every movement, lick and touch made Him want to rip her apart in a sexual frenzy or crush the life out of her all together.

Her tongue flicked over the opening of His cock, and she dug her nails into His hips, pulling Him into her mouth. She would leave bloody welts on his body before the night was done. It was all she could do not to swallow every inch of Him now. She wanted Him so badly, but she did not want this to be over. Ever. She had to have this man in every way she could.

He had had enough of her torture. He grabbed her round the throat and dragged her up from her knees. She had ceased to exist, she was desire and feeling, skin and nerve endings, lust and want. She had never wanted a man so much. Holding her firmly by the neck, restricting her breathing just enough. He eased himself inside her, the culmination of her ultimate masculine desire, she felt every delicious inch of Him inside her, she felt the pulse of her muscles around Him, and groaned. There was nothing but Him. She was consumed and desperate. Licking, biting clawing, raking His back trying to pull more of Him into her. He, in turn, thrust with a power she had never felt before. Before she knew it, she was climaxing around Him. In that moment of instant abandon, He had her, completely. She was His. She hadn't meant to be so quick, hadn't known such a thing was *possible*. It had happened despite herself. She fell against Him, completely sated, completely owned, feeling nothing but pure joy as she panted into His neck. She was barely aware of Him lowering her forcefully onto the bed, until she felt Him grow even bigger inside of her.

*

Hunter had lost all concept of time. It could have been two o'clock in the morning or the middle of the following afternoon. She didn't care. She never wanted to leave this place, this palace of decadence and debauchery. She felt like she had fallen into a Victorian erotic novel, another place, another century.

They were reclining in either end of a claw foot bath, completely exhausted, spent and sated. When they had finally thundered to a stop, a sweaty tangle of limbs beneath a table on the floor, she had fallen asleep almost immediately, her body drained of lust but also artifice, naked in every sense of the word, sore, broken and yet completely at peace. She had only awoken when He lifted her bodily and slid her gently into the hot and fragrant water that now surrounded them.

'Here,' He said, passing her a generously filled glass of brandy. 'This will add to the afterglow.'

Vice

Hunter accepted the proffered glass and studied the gilded liquid, velvet smooth and warm. 'Another of my favourite tipples,' she said. 'A lucky guess?'

He looked towards her, that same enigmatic half-smile half-threat playing across His features. 'You're easier to read than you think.'

She laughed, delightedly, far too content to be offended. She took a deep draft of the liquid as the warm scented water licked her skin. She was being warmed both inside and out. She could see the scratches that adorned His skin, her want written into His body. He really was a master, of the senses if nothing else. She looked at Him, smiling. 'You know when you smell something it can make you remember a memory so vividly? But sometimes there's no memory, only a feeling?' She asked dreamily. Feeling everything so strongly because of the cocktail of hormones coursing through her.
'Yes.' He said.
'Well, I don't know why, but I love the *feeling* of brandy. Whenever I drink it, my whole person remembers the feeling of something, but I can't remember what it is, or was.' She said wistfully. *This really is heaven*, she thought, as she lay against the bath and closed her eyes, feeling each delightful wound He had inflicted upon her soothed by the heat, delicious bruises blossoming on her skin.

*

He watched from the bed as she dressed, grinning with delight when she noticed her shredded stockings. 'I'll be in Malaysia next week,' He said.

86

'Malaysia?' Hunter said, with genuine surprise. 'And here was me thinking it was the frozen Northern tundra of Siberia or nothing.'

He grinned. 'Not a lot of work up there, unfortunately. Although I do love the bear hunting.'

Hunter gave an involuntary shudder. 'Ick. Animal.'

'I'll take you sometime. I'll take you everywhere. You better practice having a stronger stomach for these things.'

'I think not,' she replied. She was fully aware that He was goading her and loving the ire He invoked in her.

'In any case, I will need you when I return,' He said, handing her the address of a different hotel with a room key. 'Meet me at this address on Friday evening.'

Hunter wondered how it was that He had a room key to a hotel almost a week in advance but filed it almost immediately under 'not her concern.' One of the many things she adored about being a submissive was that the liaison organization was always at the behest of the dominant. She knew there were those who treated their submissives as day-to-day slaves, and many submissives who enjoyed it, but she made sure that in her dalliances she just had to turn up and be the glamorous and willing participant.

No sooner had Hunter placed the key in her bag, He was by her side again, grabbing her by the throat and pulling her to

Him, forcing His tongue into her mouth. She moaned, loving every hungry taste of Him.

'Don't be late to our next meeting. You do as I command, remember?'

As He pulled away, Hunter bit His bottom lip; not hard enough to draw blood, but she knew He felt it. 'Master in the bedroom, but nowhere else,' she replied, licking her lips. 'Don't forget it, Dominus. My body is yours, do with me what you will. I submit completely. My soul, however, belongs to me.'

He looked at her seriously. 'I will remember.' He lifted her bag from the floor and handed it to her. 'Next week, then. You're mine.'

Hunter smiled. 'Always.'

He watched her leave, eyes locked on the door until it had closed completely. He took a deep breath, savouring the lingering scent of her, her perfume mingled with her ravaged body. He had her, he was sure. She was his. He trusted she would let no other man near her. There was something about a kindred spirit in this lifestyle, they knew the sanctity of what they were giving and what they received in return. Protector. Lord. Master. Lover. Eternal. He, in turn, would remain dedicated to her, for although he lived his life largely unencumbered by the desires and needs of others, the needs and desires of a submissive were his world when he chose her.

But there would need to be a clear separation between normal life and love. Experience had taught Him that it was too difficult, too complex and distracting, to try and combine the two. Introductions to parents and playing at 'happy families' were things that happened to other people.

This was what made Hunter perfect. Like him, she seemed to want a life that was entirely separate from his own.

With these thoughts occupying his mind, he left the hotel room and stepped back into the depressing outside world he was forced to occupy. The thought of Friday and having her all over again, of beginning their training as Dominant and Submissive, was the only thing keeping his attention sharp and spirits high.

*

Hunter drove straight from the hotel towards Edinburgh, where she was to meet her girlfriends for what would be an incredibly late lunch. Her muscles were exhausted, her entire body saturated with Him. She ached so much that she was barely able to change gear.

She drove more recklessly than usual, a huge grin plastered to her face as she felt the stickiness between her thighs with every push on the pedals. She couldn't wait to tell the girls what had happened. They had been in constant contact since The Hall, all fully aware of the obvious lust between Hunter and this erstwhile Lord Byron all weekend. She knew she would not be allowed to get away with not telling them every little detail.

The four women had a little wine bar down in Stockbridge where they would always meet when something momentous had happened in their lives. Despite incredibly busy work and relationship schedules, they made every possible effort to attend these soirées and remain faithful to one another in times of need or exultation. Today, happily, all three of Hunter's friends had managed to show. Indeed, they had already finished an entire bottle of Bollinger by the time she burst through the door.

Astrid, wearing an explosion of yellow satin with her hair gelled into spikes, was the easiest to spot. Tiffany was the quintessential American Housewife, her clothes more colourful and her jewellery far more dazzling than her more dowdy Edinburgh counterparts. Hunter was most surprised to find Darcey sitting in court shoes, sensible skirt, and crisp shirt. She must have just finished at the hospital. *How was it she could still look unruffled after doing a full nightshift? Did she ever sleep?*

Astrid was the first to spot the new arrival. 'Hunter!' she squealed, subtle as ever. 'Get over here and tell us all the juicy details. I can tell from how you're walking that it was quite the trip!'

'Jesus Astrid,' Darcey said. 'There are other people in this bar you know, and I do have to work around here.' Despite this remonstration, she wasn't too angry. She loved Astrid too much for that. In any case, after nearly ten years of friendship, she knew that it was out with the realms of possibility to expect her friend to modify her behaviour… or language… or volume.

Hunter kissed each of her friends on the cheek, before taking a seat at the table. The soft light from the modern glass sculpted chandeliers glinted off the granite bar and gave the place an understated contemporary style.

'Ok, so, tell us everything,' Tiffany said, deftly pouring champagne into a waiting glass for her friend. 'Have you finally found a man up to your standards or are we all going to be disappointed... again?'

'My god,' Hunter said. 'More champagne!? I've had quite a bit of this over the past forty-eight hours you know.'

'I bet that's not all you've had!' Astrid almost shouted. 'So, tell us! Is Mr. Gun-Toting Adventurer hung like a genetically-enhanced donkey after all?'

Darcey winced, once again, at her friend's unnecessary volume and crass vocabulary.

'Close enough, but can we not call Him Mr. Gun-Toting please,' she said, looking pointedly at Astrid. 'It's His hideous friend who's the arms dealer, remember?"

Astrid's head dropped in apology. 'I only meant the rifle episode.'
'Oh, right. Wow, that feels like years ago.'

'But you like him?' Tiffany asked. 'This Mr Dangerous, Lord Byron character?' When Hunter nodded, she clapped her hands in delight. 'My god, I can't believe I finally, *finally* brought a guy to The Hall that Hunter actually likes! Woo Hoo! That only took, oh about one hundred years.'

Hunter smiled. 'OK, "Mr Dangerous" is one that one I can live with. After all, he does delight in keeping me slightly off-balance.'

'And?' Darcey asked, grabbing her friend's hand impatiently. 'Was he really that good?'

Hunter raised an eyebrow suggestively. 'Better. I am in delicious sticky little pieces, ladies.'

Astrid clapped a hand against the table. 'Well, off balance or not, I cannot honestly remember when I've seen you look so happy, so it must be love!'

Hunter laughed. 'No ladies, it's everything I've been looking for. So absolutely not love.'

The ladies had what felt like a thousand different questions for Hunter. And the champagne had been flowing for some time when Hunter began to recount the finer details of the sex that had taken place. When she was finished, her three friends stared at her through wide eyes, their mouths open in disbelief.

'Are you serious?' Tiffany said, finally. 'You came, just like that? As soon as he was inside you??' Hunter shrugged, grinning naughtily. 'Well, Jesus fuck,' Tiffany squealed, 'he really *must* be good!'

Astrid was still unconvinced. 'It just seems a little... unbelievable.'

Tiffany laughed. 'Oh, come on Astrid, it's not unheard of. Compared to *Darcey's* party trick, it's almost nothing.'

Astrid looked to her friend with a blank stare. 'Party trick?' she asked.

'Oh, please,' Darcey said, looking unusually embarrassed. 'Do we really have to go over this again?'

'Obviously, we do.' Hunter replied, laughing. 'Astrid, Darcey's party trick is to make herself orgasm using just her muscles and some sort of breathing technique. She doesn't use her hands, a toy, anything.'

Astrid looked to Darcey, who acknowledged the fact with a small nod. 'Bloody hell!' Astrid said. 'Now *that* is a girl who's in control of herself! I am seriously jealous.'

Darcey shook her head wearily. 'God, I'm sorry I ever told you guys.'

'Well, you were pretty hammered when you did!'

Hunter bit back a joke about it being just as well she had such a fabulous trick up her sleeve, as Peter wasn't exactly Casanova in bed by all accounts. The cumulative effects of the champagne and lack of sleep had clearly caught up with her. As the laughter subsided, Tiffany turned the attention back to Hunter. 'So, you might have found the man to match you then.'

Hunter shrugged, grinning.

'Has he tied you up yet?'

'Not yet. We didn't really have time for any of that.'

'What – in two whole days?' Tiffany asked.

Hunter shook her head. 'But I don't mind. At one point I passed out under a chaise longue I just couldn't take any more pleasure. He was everything I expected and more. I am completely drunk on Him now. I would literally do anything He asked of me.'

'So, what's next, Hunter?' Darcey asked.

Hunter shrugged. 'Nothing. Not until next weekend, at least. Mr. Dangerous is leaving for Malaysia tomorrow. I'm good with that, though: I'll need the week to recover.'

'You going to talk on the phone?' Darcey asked.

Hunter laughed. 'God, no! I'm an all or nothing girl. I want it all when I want it and when I don't I want to be alone. Virginia Woolf was spot on; every woman should have A Room of One's Own in which to remain sane. Men should be summoned when required and dismissed when not.'

'Damn right!' her friends said in unison, before collapsing into laughter again.

'So, anyway, next weekend He's taking me to this place… hang on, I have the key in my bag.'

'He already gave you a key?' Tiffany said. 'Wow. That *is* organised.'

Darcey sniffed. 'Or presumptuous.'

Hunter tilted her head towards Darcey. 'Sweetheart, we both knew why I went to that hotel. There was no presumption required.'

Tiffany scrutinized the solid wooden fob that was attached to the key. It had an embossed golden windmill carved into it. 'I recognize this place,' she said. 'Richard took me once for an anniversary.' She looked back to Hunter. 'He's taking you all the way to Norfolk?'

Hunter stared at her friend, confused. 'Norfolk?' she said. 'Like, in England?' Tiffany nodded. Hunter could only continue to stare; His plan seemed far less impressive now she knew she'd have to get herself south for the weekend. But her travel plans would have to wait; right now, Tiffany had an announcement to make.

'Speaking of bonkers schemes and unnecessary decadence – Richard and I have set a date for our wedding! So, ladies, keep the fourth of May free.'

Her three friends all gaped at Tiffany in complete bafflement. It was some time before Hunter broke the silence. 'Sorry, but I think you'll find the marriage happened three years ago. Or did you and Richard forget?'

Tiffany grinned, enjoying her friends' obvious confusion. Then, excitedly, she yelled, 'I am finally getting my Story of O latex wedding! And...' She paused to take a dramatic breath '... I want you guys to be my latex bridesmaids!'

The three friends shrieked in unison, reaching over the table to pat Tiffany's hands and face (they were now well into their third bottle of Bollinger). There wasn't a doubt in any of their minds that they would be there to celebrate their friend's big day.

'OK,' Tiffany said. 'So, while we're all together; what colours would you like for your dresses?'
'Neon Yellow!' Astrid yelled, without a moment's pause.

Hunter laughed. 'No! Absolutely not. Vile.'

'Absolutely fine!' Tiffany cried. 'You can have whatever you want. I just want all my gals to be happy!'

'Lavender for me,' Darcey said. 'Or something similar.'

Tiffany beamed. 'Of course. Elegant, stylish, quintessential Darcey. And for you, Hunter?'

Hunter smiled. 'Red. Obviously.'

Tiffany looked to her friend; her eyes bright with happiness. 'What else?' she said. 'I feel that at this point "Hunter Red" should be, like, a legitimate pantone colour by now.'

'Hm. I like that. Perhaps a "Hunter Red" lipstick. Something that stains skin as well as it does a shirt collar.' The girls all laughed at this. Hunter, meanwhile, was imagining His entire body covered in her lipstick kisses.

'Careful ladies,' Warned Darcey, 'She's lost thinking about *him* again.' They all turned to look at Hunter who grinned unabashed. 'Well can you blame me? But no, enough of Him for now. I want to hear all about this wedding! Tiff, what are the plans so far?'

Glasses were re-filled, and wedding plans discussed, and Hunter basked in the warm glow and acceptance of her three favourite people in the world, as they got more and more excited planning the crazy, kinky fun they would have at Tiffany's Story of O Latex Wedding. Latex bridesmaids' dresses were only the beginning…

The Danger

"I am all in a sea of wonders. I doubt; I fear; I think
strange things which I dare not confess to my own soul."
Bram Stoker

The young receptionist smiled at Hunter, with only the
slightest hint of irony etched into his expression. An
immaculately dressed boy of no more than twenty, with a
light dusting of caramel stubble, a cheeky smile and
twinkling eyes peeking out from a slightly too-long blonde
fringe. He found this couple intriguing and amusing in
equal measure. Since he'd come on shift at the beginning
of the weekend, the pair had treated this hotel like a private
den of iniquity, seemingly unconcerned that there were
other guests in the vicinity. The receptionist had
immediately understood that they were clearly having some
sort of illicit affair. Probably the all-too-common CEO and
secretary routine. *Well, they're certainly going for it*, he
thought, a little jealously. 'What is he treating you to now,
then?' he asked.

Hunter returned his smile. 'Everything,' she answered
coolly.

He chuckled lightly in response, wondering if life would
ever take him on an adventure such as this. He certainly
hoped so, particularly as the man she was here with was
drop-dead gorgeous, just the kind of older man he could see
himself getting into some serious trouble with. If only the

universe would be so kind as to put one in his path. Unfortunately, most of the powerful men who came to stay at this hotel looked through what they considered 'the help.' *Well. One day, he would be the one checking into places such as this and you could be damn sure he'd be on the lookout for a bit of extra-curricular fun 'below-stairs.'* Shaking off these thoughts, he turned his attention back to Hunter. 'And how can I help you now?'

'Can you send up another ice bucket to the room please?' Hunter replied sweetly.

'We're here to serve,' the boy said with a smile. He liked this woman; had done from the moment she'd arrived in her nosebleed-inducing stilettos and exquisitely fitted smoke-grey dress. He remembered the way she had smiled at him over her Chanel sunglasses, and her obvious surprise when a glass of champagne had arrived at her side before she had even registered her name. Whoever her mysterious companion was, he was clearly in control and pulling out all the stops to impress her. Which made him even more intrigued about the woman herself.

'You do know you can call down,' the boy told her. 'There's no need for you to come all the way to reception.'

Hunter shrugged. 'I had to get something from my car anyway.'

Hunter could tell from the receptionist's expression that he was intrigued as to what that something could be. She had no doubt that, since their arrival at this tiny, isolated boutique hotel, they had been the subject of much speculation. Not least because the loud, athletic and above all kinkily obvious sex they had been having all over the place had clearly been overheard by everyone else there. Possibly, they'd even been overheard by some people in the next town.

The weekend had been an eye-opener, even by Hunter's elaborate standards. Their room comprised the whole windmill tower, and there was a small but beautifully appointed kitchen on the lower floor. The upper floor was reached by an ornate wooden ladder, and contained an enormous bed, with a claw foot bath at the window, which overlooked the stunning Norfolk coastline. There was nothing she had wanted that He had not given her. He had anticipated everything she could possibly have desired. She was not entirely unused to wealth and luxury, of course, but this place, and the level of comfort it offered, was something completely new to her. She was beginning to understand that this man was insanely rich, even by Richard's somewhat grand standards.

Nevertheless, Hunter was determined to be as much an equal to Him in their courtship as possible. While He paid for the ridiculously expensive hotels, she supplied the ridiculously expensive wine and any other titbits that featured on the menu for their sexual adventures. In this case, cherries.

He had told her that he loved the poems of Pablo Neruda, to her surprise and delight as she too was an avid fan. So, she had brought cherries in homage to Neruda's poem, XIV, and would have Him feed them to her in the bath when she returned to the room. She knew that there was a delicate balance between seduction and romance, but she fancied herself to be an expert in walking that particular tightrope, even in vertiginous heels.

In the past two weeks she had been struck more than once by the terrible thought that she might actually fall for this dangerous and enigmatic man. But, deep down, she knew it could never happen. He was far too aggressive for any girly notions of Shakespearian or chivalrous romance, and *she* was far too cynical for any of that Austen rubbish. It was the lust with which He attacked life that drew her to Him as inexorably as humanity to a 'Do Not Touch' sign. Historically they probably would have been called libertines, or bon vivants. Proving, if nothing else, that the French clearly knew how to enjoy themselves. Today, they were more likely just to be called trouble.

He was clearly as bored and unimpressed as she was by the quotidian nature of the life that most people either aspired or acquiesced to. The only slightly discordant note in the symphony of her erotic imaginings was just *how* bored with life He sometimes seemed to be. Where she was adventurous, *He* seemed to be downright reckless, and although she could feel the inevitable fascination with His cavalier nihilism, there was an equal concern that He had already sucked all the potential and enjoyment from His life. And if that were true, then what was left for Him? And by extension, regarding her dealings with Him, what was left for her?

So far, she had matched Him sexually, matched His appetite for debauchery and bacchanal. But if this was only the beginning, then what was coming next? She wondered about a 'real' relationship with this man and had the

101

disturbing thought that if she threw herself into Him in any real way, if she erased the distance that she had carefully constructed between them, she'd be dead within the year. It was undeniably dangerous to be a slave to someone who had already unravelled so much of life's rich tapestry.

The receptionist's voice brought her back from her musings. He was waiting at the bottom of the ornate staircase with the pewter ice-bucket she had requested. Shaking the last of the thoughts from her mind, she crossed the room towards him. He met her with an impish grin, before handing her the ice-bucket. 'Enjoy,' he said.

Hunter laughed. 'Oh, don't worry, we will.' She smiled and winked at him, licking her lips ever so slightly as she did so, before returning to her would-be Master. She turned away and thought she heard him say not quite under his breath, 'oh, I know.'

As she slowly ascended the curved mahogany staircase, she remembered another man she'd nearly fallen for, so many years ago. A man just as dangerous but in a very different way. He was a diplomat, also a bon viveur and libertine, but with a moral compass much more aligned to her own, in so much as he seemed to actually have one. He was also an alcoholic, although in this case, a real one. But he had a soul, it was just that it had been irrevocably tarnished by the lives he'd seen in the hellholes he'd worked in. She suspected that it wasn't completely destroyed, yet. He lived through the pain by alternatively marinating in too much alcohol or dangerous and inappropriate women, or both. Another kindred spirit she felt attracted to at a far more fundamental level than the purely sexual. She often thought that it was a shame that their paths had not converged in a more permanent or manageable way, but he wasn't for her in the end. He remained a dear friend though, but kept at a safe, comfortable distance.

*

In the early hours of the following morning, they stopped their ravenous consumption of each other to drink champagne and replenish some of their much-depleted energy. Hunter visited the bathroom, returning to find Him reclining on the enormous four-poster in nothing but the hotel's terrycloth robe. A platter of oysters lay on the bedside table next to him, the oysters cresting the mounds of ice as if thrown by reckless waves onto a frozen shore.

Hunter joined him at the foot of the bed, mirroring him, only with silk, not terrycloth. She was anticipating how divine the oysters would taste with the bottle of Perrier Jouët Belle Époque that was chilling next to two frosted glasses. *Is there nothing this man cannot supply?* she wondered. *Probably not*, she concluded. If she desired it, He would provide it for her. She would have to put that to the test she mused wickedly, imagining the outlandish things she could demand, purely for the enjoyment of seeing how He would manage to procure them.

'Do you know how many times I've been this close to death?' He asked her suddenly, inserting His knife into an oyster's slippery crevice.

The question took Hunter by surprise. 'I couldn't even begin to guess,' she replied, struggling to get a handle on the sudden change of tone, not quite sure whether He was teasing or not. 'Though… Tiffany mentioned you once had cerebral malaria, I think…' She trailed off uncertainly, watchful of the far-away, slightly sinister, look in his eyes.

She felt unsteady, like the solid stone of the windmill had started to pitch and roll like a ship in a coming squall. She braced herself for the inevitable storm. The weather had clearly picked up the mood of the place, as autumn had turned to winter and seemed to suddenly assail the windows with the scratching of leaves, and the methodical thunder of hail against the glass. It had been wonderful a mere two hours ago, they had drunk wine and He had, as she had requested, fed her cherries between sips as they luxuriated in yet another bath, listening to the weather rage outside had only served to outline their cosseted carnality. She had ruined the moment briefly when she put her champagne glass down behind her on the lip of the bath, only to miss completely and have it shatter comprehensively onto the floor. He had just laughed. It had made the bathroom floor look beautifully sparkly and given Him the excuse to throw her bodily from the bath onto the bed to avoid cutting herself. God he was strong.

'There was that,' He said, 'then there was the time I was hunting and was nearly gored by a pig.'

'A pig?' she repeated, nonplussed.

'It was in Malaysia; we were going to make jungle-curry. I never take much when I go into the wild there, we cook what we catch.' He balanced the oyster on the tip of the knife.

'Sounds a bit labour intensive just for dinner,' she said, attempting to lighten the mood.

'You think so?' He asked. Reaching forward, He slid his fingers into her hair and forced her head backwards. Before she could think to protest, He lifted the oyster to her lips and slid it into her mouth. Then, holding her gaze, he took a long draught of champagne and kissed it into her mouth in one forceful Machiavellian motion. She struggled to swallow as His tongue ravaged the inside of her willing mouth. But, god, it was delicious; almost as delicious as He was.

He leaned back on the bed, breaking the salty kiss. 'There's something primal and satisfying in hunting for yourself, even if it is just for oysters.'

'Fuck hunting, just give me that again,' Hunter replied, her eyes shining with desire.
'I knew you'd like that,' He said, with the same unbridled confidence Hunter had come to expect from Him. 'On your knees.'

Without a word, she slid off the bed and onto the floor, the satin of her champagne kimono pooling around her in a way that made her look like the pearl inside the centre of an oyster. He caught his breath at the beauty of the image. She seemed to float on the pale pink silk above the swirls of the gold and cream carpet, like some Botticelli Venus engorged from a briny fantasy. A siren sent to torment Him. He couldn't get enough of her.
Hunter knew she was attractive, and she made no apology for the knowledge, which He already loved about her. But

He also knew that she was not fully aware of the true extent of the sexual power she possessed. She could turn the banal into the bacchanal with nothing more than a look.

He needed to regain some control. He moved to the edge of the bed, the champagne and oysters still easily within reach. He sat up tall, parting his legs so that she kneeled between them in her satin pool. She looked up waiting, calm, almost serene in her expectation.

'We need to discuss terms,' He told her. 'We have delayed too long already... Open your mouth.'

She obeyed immediately and He delicately poured a sip of champagne into her.

'Right,' He said, holding an oyster ready for once she had given her response. 'Where do you stand on the most obvious point – Pain?'

'I don't like pain,' she said. She looked suddenly ethereal, as if she was speaking to him from another world. 'I like desire and possession, submission and control. But not pain. Never pain.'

He looked at her nervously. 'But... you begged me to tie you up the second we arrived here; those ropes left marks.' He could still see the bruises on her wrists as she kneeled in front of him.
'That's not pain,' she said, smirking at His mistake. 'There is a distinct difference between delighting in the sting of a leather belt and being beaten bloody with the buckle. I've had friends who liked that, but I could never see the appeal myself.'

'I see,' He said, relieved and secretly pleased that she was exactly what He had initially judged her to be. 'Well, you have nothing like that to fear from me. I will make you submit completely and unreservedly. But my desire to devour and devastate you is purely metaphorical.' Gently, He tipped another oyster into her open mouth. She swallowed it slowly, softly, her eyes locked on His. It was almost enough to send Him over the edge, but He managed to keep his composure. He continued. 'Tying you up is an obvious yes I assume?'

'For me it's essential. I ache inside just thinking about it. There are no restrictions there at all so long as I can breathe, and you don't leave me alone.'

'Done,' He said. 'Now, what about lashes, whips, floggers and so forth?'

'All of the above,' she said, smiling. 'But no canes; slight welts are fine but nothing that will split my skin.'
'I wouldn't dream of it,' He said. He could already picture the marks He would leave on her perfect body. 'This could take a considerable amount of time.'

'It could, so how about I just give you my hard passes and we can fine tune the details as we go along. I think it's fairly clear where my boundaries lie anyway.'

'I would agree. Let me give you a couple of scenarios to finish with just so that I am clear and don't overstep. You do something that displeases me, and I punish you with one of the agreed toys.'

'Yes.'

'I take you to dinner at The Hall on a leash in nothing but a corset and stilettoes.'

'Yes. I am yours to do with as you wish, within the boundaries we agreed of course, and no other man touches me but you. Ever.'

'That is an absolute. So, now that that is out of the way, more or less, do you trust me?'

'No.' She grinned.

'A good place to start.' He affirmed, smiling at her joke.

He heaved her upwards onto the bed, pulling the tie from her robe until it slid from the bed to the floor, and she straddled him, naked. She grinned at Him, eye-to-eye.

'Raise your arms.'

She did, and He tied her wrists together above her head, before fastening them into a hook he had screwed into the top of the hotel's four poster bed. She gasped, delighted.

'When did you…' she started, but before she could say more He kissed her hard, taking all the breath from her body and turning her insides to jelly. He spread her legs wide and pulled her down onto him, teasing her, refusing to give her all of Himself. She groaned in pleasure, as her eyes closed, and she tried to stretch herself down onto Him.

'Patience,' He said.

'Never.'

She writhed above Him, desperate to feel all of Him, her arousal heightened to fever pitch by the tie cutting into her wrists and the feel of Him sliding in and out of her, but never giving her everything. Within two minutes she was begging and pleading, spitting desire and hot frustration. Then, just when she was crying tears of need, He surged himself into her, groaning in equal pleasure. She bucked on top of Him faster and faster, as she ground her hips down onto Him with all her strength. Sweat slid between them, and His fingertips left bruises in the delicate flesh of her thighs. She could feel the orgasm building in her whole body. She was starting to shake, and He was quickly losing control. He sat up, hands in her hair, His mouth greedily taking hers. She wrapped her legs around His waist as she came, with her whole self, trembling and spasming all over Him, and He roared His release into her. They collapsed together, His head on her shoulder, hers against the bedpost, arms still tied. Their breathing came in raggedy gasps, as she cried tears of abject pleasure into His hair, and her muscles continued to sing.

*

It was hours later, and they were walking through the grounds of the hotel. Beautiful fir trees extended heavenward, giving the grounds the look of an enchanted forest. Bright red ivy adorned the outside of the windmill and the more traditional brick extension. There was even a maze made of hedges and a lake surrounded by carefully curated bridges.

He had insisted that they go mushroom picking on this, their final afternoon at the hotel. He wanted to cook for her; something that would complement the eye-wateringly expensive bottle of Russian River Valley Chardonnay she had brought, and which He had been very pleasantly surprised by. *His previous submissive must have had crap taste in wine,* she thought, as she picked her way between roots and foliage. Hunter was at a loss to understand why they were going to such lengths to *find* their dinner, though she suspected He wanted to show her the value of finding, as well as cooking, their own food. Hunter, for the most part, was unimpressed; she'd prefer to buy from her local organic farm than trudge through the woods digging in the dirt for what was essentially a rather attractive fungus. Still, it was nice to be out in the fresh air, and it made a snifter of whisky by the fire later that evening even more appealing.

After an hour or so, the basket He had brought with Him on the walk was overflowing with mushrooms. 'Right,' He said, clearly pleased with His find. 'These are perfect. Fry them in butter and garlic with a splash of wine, add to pasta and cream and you have a meal fit for the most obedient of slaves.'

'I'm flattered,' she replied.

He took a deep breath of fresh Norfolk air and looked out towards a small hill on the horizon. 'I need to get out into the wild as often as possible. I like luxury but I need wilderness.'

She was tempted to point out that the grounds of a five-star boutique hotel inside a windmill wasn't exactly roughing it, but didn't. In any case, she knew what He meant. It chimed with everything she'd been told about His exploits both in Scotland and overseas. He clearly liked to hunt, even if it was only for mushrooms.

'Come on,' He said, turning towards the hotel. 'We've got enough. Back to luxury.'

'Well, I have to say that is definitely more my natural milieu,' she said smiling, taking His arm as they turned back to the hotel. It was a stunning vista, the windmill silhouetted against the setting sun, and the Norfolk coastline in the distance. The breeze swirled around them, bringing colour to her cheeks, and ruffling His dark hair. The temperature was dropping with the sun, and she could smell rain on the air. She leaned a little closer into Him for warmth and decided that at least with this one, life would certainly not be boring.

*

'Well?' He asked, taking a sip of the wine that had accompanied the meal. 'How was it?'

Hunter looked down at her empty plate and gave a happy sigh. 'Absolutely delicious,' she replied, raising her glass in salute. 'Your slave approves.'

He nodded his thanks, then moved the plates to one side of the mahogany table, circumnavigating the tealight candles that peppered the surface like stars. It was at that moment she noticed that his knife had made a reappearance once again. *What is it about Him and that thing*, she wondered. She loved the sex play, and she particularly enjoyed it when He ran the tip over her naked and willing body. Never breaking the skin of course, but keeping her balanced on the very precipice of pain. Making her almost wish that He would mark her with it. But it was becoming a bit of a sinister sort of sexual talisman.

'If you were about to die, how would you want to go?' He asked softly, playing the blade against his palm.

She was completely caught off guard, once again. 'Well, the obvious answer,' she said, hesitantly, 'is in raptures beneath your powerful body.'

He held her eyes. 'I'm serious. You know I've experienced a few closer shaves than most. How would you go? Pass away in your sleep at ninety? Flying down route 101 in a Lamborghini?' He leaned forward on the table, regarding her in the candlelight. 'No,' he decided. 'They're both a bit too plebeian for you, aren't they. You would expect something a little more glamorous. Something exotic and unusual, but poignantly tragic as befits a woman of your grace and intrigue.'

Hunter wasn't sure if this was a very peculiar form of flattery or if perhaps the wine had finally gone to His head as much as it clearly had hers. In either case, the conversation had taken an odd and macabre turn.

'Glamorous yet tragic?' She said, almost to herself. 'God, I've no idea what that would be. Falling off a yacht into the ocean never to be seen again? Eating something dreadfully expensive and exotic only to find out too late that you were fatally allergic to it? It's a tough sell as there's nothing particularly glamorous about dying, no matter how you go. Look at poor Grace Kelly, or Ernest Hemmingway? Both glamorous almost to a fault but neither a car crash nor suicide by shotgun really has the same elegant ambiance about them. Perhaps it's just impossible to die how you live.'

Hunter locker her eyes on his. 'I honestly haven't thought,' she said. 'Something elegant and painless perhaps. Or do an Amelia Earhart and disappear in mysterious circumstances.'

He looked at her, the hint of a smile playing on His lips. 'They do say poisoning is an easy way to go.'

Hunter laughed. 'Not if it's strychnine. Those are some contortions you would not want the world to see. And as for the pain? No, thank you. In any case, poisoning is a woman's weapon. Perhaps it is *you* who should take care.' Holding His gaze through twinkling eyes, she emptied the remaining wine into their glasses and drank hers down in one gulp.

'My submissive would never have the temerity to do such a thing,' He assured her. 'You know you have to be very careful with poison, even everyday things can be potentially deadly.'

'Like you, you mean?' she teased, warming to the theme, running her foot up along the inside of His thigh.

'No,' he said. 'But take mushrooms, for example.' He gestured to the two empty plates, which sat in front of them like witnesses in a dock. 'You have to know what you're picking. If you don't know what you're doing, you die.'
She looked at Him questioningly. She wasn't sure if she was elated by what she assumed was a particularly morbid kind of foreplay, or terrified because part of her genuinely believed He might have chosen to poison her. If this was a

weird way of trying to glamorously and elegantly check-out of existence, like He had started off by saying, then she was damn sure she didn't want to go with Him. Also, the irony would be too much. After hunting dangerous animals for years in death-traps all over the world, He bows out with a mushroom? No. He would never let that happen. Would He?

The room suddenly felt very warm, the candles seemed to be burning more strongly. She placed a hand to her cheek. The dark wood panelling and the thin air seemed stifling. Her head was spinning. What *had* she just eaten? His face betrayed nothing, no malice, no humour, and no hint of a game. She felt close to panic at the thought that here, tonight, she had become His final stop on his crazy and nihilistic descent into hell.

But then, just as quickly as they had arrived, her worries fell away. Hunter looked to Him through fresh eyes, and immediately understood that she was safe. Of course, He hadn't poisoned them. He was playing with her, toying with her boundaries, making her unsteady, challenging her limits. He was her Master, and that was what Masters did for god's sake.

'Let's go,' He commanded suddenly, startling her, and causing her to gasp involuntarily. Without waiting for her reply, He picked her up bodily from the chair that she was sitting in, threw her over His shoulder, walked into the bedroom and threw her down on the bed to be defiled once again. 'If we're going to die,' He said, unbuckling his belt and kicking the door closed behind him. 'At least we'll go screaming.'

Hunter squealed in delight. Now, *this* was more like it…

*

She awoke with a thumping headache and the driest mouth that she could ever remember having suffered. Groaning, she reached over to the bedside table for a glass of water and drank it down in three gulps. She let her head fall back onto her pillow and sighed.

It was then that she noticed the blood. There was blood on her wrist, her breasts, her thighs. Panicking, she sprang into a seated position. Oh god. There was blood literally everywhere.

She glanced around, and was relieved to find Him asleep, for the moment at least. Terror scythed through her as she remembered their creepy discussion from the night before. What had He done to her? Was she cut? Why didn't she feel any pain? How had He done it without her waking up? Oh god, had He drugged her?

She was halfway towards a full-blown meltdown when something touched her right arm. Yelping, she looked round to find him awake and grinning like a Cheshire cat. 'Well, this is different,' He said.

She stared at Him, confused, and then, more carefully, looked at herself – no marks, apart from the bruises from the floggings and ropes and a bite mark on her inner thigh, which were par for the course. He seemed to be enjoying her discomfort as He propped himself up on an arm next to her. Turning back to Him, the fog in her brain finally began to clear, when the penny dropped, she relaxed immediately, her tension evaporating like steam from a cup of coffee. 'Oh please,' she said, laughing with relief. 'We both know you're no stranger to a little blood. You know what menstrual blood looks like. I'd be surprised if you didn't know how it tasted.'

'Well, let's see, shall we…' He said, pinning her arms by her sides and descending between her awaiting thighs.

*

Once again it was time to part ways, to return to their respective and 'respectable' lives. She was still reeling from his exploration of her bleeding body. He had been completely unfazed by anything. He was a most unusual man indeed.

He reclined in the room's single leather armchair watching her pack, taking delicate sips of an amber coloured single malt as He watched her. How He could drink so early after such a weekend of debauchery she had no idea. It would be at least a week before she could even manage a life-affirming Bloody Mary.
'By the way,' He said. 'The knife is yours.'

She looked at him, shocked. 'You're knife? But… you *love* that knife.'

'I want you to bring it to every one of our meetings. Think of it as a kind of kinky talisman.'

She continued to gape as she plucked the knife from His outstretched hand. She just hoped this 'talisman' wasn't a harbinger of more dangerous activities to come.

She knew He was showing off, but she was experienced enough to know that men liked to peacock, so she was not going to complain. In any case, she felt He was entitled to a little smugness, considering He had given her one of the most intense weekends of her life, again.

'I'll be seeing you at Astrid's little get together on Hogmanay,' He said. 'I'm afraid I shall be indisposed with work overseas before then.'

Indisposed with work? Well, he certainly liked to make Himself sound powerful and important. 'Astrid invited you?' she asked.

He shook his head. 'Richard did. Tiffany's overseeing absolutely everything, and limiting the number of loonies that Astrid knows to a two to one ratio of relatively sane people.'

'Oh? And which category do you fall into?' she said, waving the knife at Him in mock-admonishment.

'You're getting awfully provocative,' He cautioned. 'Careful or I'll have to punish you.'

'Oh, and wouldn't *that* be a tragedy,' she said playfully as she threw the last of her lingerie and heels into her overnight case. That done, she turned to Him, smiling naughtily. 'Alright, Master. I shall leave the arrangements up to you. But I will be at Astrid's party, so you can have me however you like.'

He stood from His chair and held her in a tight embrace before holding the door open for her and handing over her overnight bag. 'Until New Year then, my beautiful Huntress.'

She didn't reply, merely sashayed out of the oak doorway, blowing him a kiss over her shoulder as she did so. Once again, she left a hotel room and her Master, sated and sore and a little unbalanced, with a solitary discordant note ringing in her consciousness.

*

'Your man is magnificent,' the young receptionist said, his voice breaking slightly, to his horror and Hunter's delight. Hunter could see what he wanted to ask; writ large across his delicate young features. He was unsure of himself now that he'd engaged her beyond the professional level of receptionist and guest.

She took her jacket off, intentionally revealing the bruising and marks He had left beneath her clothes. Her eyes flashed, challenging him. 'If you think you can handle a man like Him, or a life like this, then get in touch and I'll introduce you around.'

'What's your name?' he asked, trying desperately to appear nonchalant.

'My name?' she asked, eyebrow raised. 'You don't have it on the reservation?'

'Well… no. Not unless you really are Mr and Mrs Smith…'

She burst into throaty laughter. 'No, no, we're not.'

'I didn't think you looked like a wife,' he said, smiling shyly.

Hunter laughed again. 'Honey I'm not, I'm…an arrangement. And it's Hunter, Hunter Blair.' With that she turned on her heel and began to walk away. Then, as an afterthought, she took His handkerchief from between her breasts and threw it to the surprised young man.

The receptionist stood rooted to the spot. The cloth in his hand had such a masculine scent that his cock immediately began to harden. This mysterious older man who was so clearly the property of this intriguing woman was a primal specimen. God, how he wanted a man like that for himself. His own Master, his own entrance into this world. Maybe even eventually, his own slave. He wasn't certain yet how he wanted to explore this world, but he knew he wanted more danger, more adventure than his current life offered him.

He was snapped from his reverie a moment later, by the ringing of the reception bell. He looked up to find the scent of the handkerchief made flesh. He was so startled to see his mysterious stranger standing by the desk, that he nearly dropped the handkerchief. Panicking, he stuffed it into his pocket and crept timidly towards the stranger. His face was that of a naughty little boy who's been caught with his hand somewhere it shouldn't be. 'Yes?' he asked.

'Checking out,' The man growled with a smile.

The receptionist went through the motions of checking out, trying very hard to behave normally. But the stranger's power was palpable. *Oh god,* he thought. *I'll definitely be picturing this man in my fantasies tonight. As for what I'll do with the hankie...* Forcing back the smile that had sprung, unbidden, to his lips, he slid the receipt into a linen envelope and handed it to the stranger. 'There you are... Sir.' Hunter would have been proud of the slight emphasis on 'Sir' - he was clearly learning already.

And with that, the stranger turned to go, leaving the receptionist to deal with the erection he was desperately trying to hide behind his desk.

The Hotel

"I, with a deeper instinct, choose a man who compels my strength, who makes enormous demands on me... who has the courage to treat me like a woman."

Anaïs Nin

It was Hogmanay. Or if you weren't Scottish, 'New Year's Eve'. Darcey had outdone herself. She had managed to get them all into Edinburgh Castle for the celebrations. It had helped that it was also Astrid's 30th birthday, as she had once had a brief fling with one of the Castle officials, back in her wilder days. Apparently, he had been very happy to okay the event, with only a little persuasion from Darcey.

Considering these gatherings were only permitted for serving military personnel, and that only Darcey among them held a commission, a party on the biggest night of the year, inside the barracks of one of the world's most iconic locations, was a truly major coup. For appearances sake, they'd all promised the Castle contact that they'd all tear off a perfect synchronised military salute should anyone vaguely official-looking turn up.

Hunter was packing her small case in the bedroom of her Edinburgh flat, her excitement already palpable. It was early evening, and from her window she could see the sun setting over the imposing silhouette of Edinburgh Castle, perched atop its rocky outcrop like a cat on a bar stool. She loved that view; it made her feel like she was living inside one of those old movies starring Marilyn Monroe or Sophia Loren. All she needed was a martini, a feathered peignoir and a dressing table mirror surrounded with lightbulbs. For now, though, a glass of red wine and an empty suitcase would have to do.

She smiled as she realised that in many ways it was actually much harder to dress for a ceilidh than it was for an orgy. What did you need for an orgy? Whatever you felt most sexual and attractive in. Usually something that could be easily removed with the very minimum of fuss. And it didn't matter how painful the heels that you wore were, due to the simple fact that you wouldn't ever be in them for that long. Or if you were, you certainly wouldn't be standing up.

Ceilidhs, meanwhile, might be ridiculously fun, but they were not for the faint hearted, and were known to leave even the most athletic patrons breathless and sweating. Choosing an outfit that was sufficiently elegant, sexy, *and* hard-wearing was no easy task. Shoes were a minefield for a start; you needed high heels, obviously, but choose heels that were too high, and you were at very serious risk of breaking an ankle. Hunter usually preferred Stiletto heels, but Stilettos and Scottish dances, with their high kicks and flying limbs, were a dangerous match. As for the dress? Well, you needed a dress that was stretchy enough to withstand all the crazy Highland flings, but if it was a fraction too loose, then you risked suffering a rather dramatic wardrobe malfunction. Hunter smiled as she remembered that Tiffany had found this out the hard way. Hunter would never forget Tiffany at their first university ceilidh, the look of abject horror on her face as she was lifted bodily off the floor by an over enthusiastic giant

Scotsman. Her strapless dress had fallen to her waist much to the delight of her dance partner and other guests in the room. Tiffany had been mortified; she had still been divesting herself of the last vestiges of her guilt-ridden religious upbringing at the time. The thought brought tears of amusement to Hunter's eyes even now. She remembered consoling a distraught Tiffany in the ladies' loos with a martini and drunken assurances that 'no-one had even noticed' when they clearly had.

Jewellery posed no less of a problem. If you chose to wear anything remotely valuable, then you did so at your own risk. Hunter had lost count of the number of earrings, bracelets, and necklaces she'd lost over the course of her lifetime ceilidh attendance. Even now, in her 'mature' adult years, she frequently left the dance halls minus at least one such trinket.

After much contemplation and a second glass of wine, Hunter finally settled on comfortable strappy high-heels that would remain securely on her feet, a halter-neck, and a ball dress with a fish-tail kick in the most decadent deep-red satin. The halter-neck would keep the dress in place, and the boning in the dress would keep *her* in place, no matter how energetically she was flung around. It was tight enough to show her curves but forgiving enough to give her room to breathe or – more likely – pant in exertion the longer the night wore on. All she needed now was a wrist strap, which would keep the swathe of fabric off the floor and allow her to flash just enough leg to be erotic at such a high-class event.

'Et voila!' she said, with a squeal of excitement. 'Job done.' She could already see herself arriving at the Castle, a puddle of red satin cascading behind her as she swept into the Great Hall.

She could not *wait* for the night to begin.

*

Their entire party was to spend the night in The Balmoral Hotel. Tiffany had chosen it, Hunter knew, because the bar at The Balmoral was an old haunt of theirs. It was also the place where she'd introduced Hunter to Richard all those years ago. It was also within walking distance of the Castle – very important on a night such as this, when all the main roads in the centre were closed off to traffic, including taxis.

Hunter had booked her own room in which to get ready. Although she would be on His arm tonight, this was her friend's birthday and therefore not an official assignation between them. Given His friendship with Richard, she supposed she would have to get used to this occasional blurring of the lines in their relationship. For the most part, however, their independent worlds were likely to remain entirely separate; their mutual friends and proclivities aside, they moved in very different circles.

Hunter had also chosen a separate room because she had a little surprise planned for Him. She knew that she would end up in His room after the event, but, for the moment, she wanted to play one of her very favourite games. Tonight, she would *force* Him to make her submit. She would fight as hard as she could, and for as *long* as she could, against the inevitable pain of her desire.

124

She was almost dizzy with anticipation. It was rare she ever got to play this game, as previously she had never sufficiently trusted the man involved. But she knew He wouldn't let her down, knew that He'd enjoy this game as much as she would. She sat on the edge of her bed, impatient for Him to arrive. When, finally, she heard the sound of a key in the door, she darted into the bathroom, leaving the stage set.

He walked in through the door and dropped His overnight bag on the back of a chair. He had been so eager to see her again that He'd come straight to her room from reception. The muscles shifted in His broad shoulders, betraying the stresses of the previous week. His work was taking more of a toll on him than usual. *He really would have to start doing more business in the UK.*

He picked up the whisky that had been left for Him, impressed that His submissive seemed to be learning His needs and demands. He was about to take a long pull of the rich amber liquid when He suddenly noticed there was something hooked coquettishly onto the side of the glass.

A mushroom.

He was momentarily incredulous until He realised what it meant; then a slow smile spread across His face. So, she wanted to play, did she?

He adored the fact that she had chosen to tease Him in this way. Now, He would have no choice but to put her in her proper place. He began to loosen his tie, which would come in handy later as part of her punishment, a punishment she would feel for days.

As if summoned by His insatiable desire, she walked in from the other room. Her movements were confident, slow, and deliberately sensuous, and they drove Him wild. The soft lighting played over her tanned skin. She wore an extravagant choker of black, rich leather and gold chains around her throat. She was dressed in 6-inch Louboutin heels, stockings, suspenders, a cut-away black thong, and stiff-boned corset which left her full breasts completely exposed. Her nipples were already betraying her desire, firm, hard and adorned with ornate gold jewellery that attached to her collar.

She walked past Him, ignoring Him, and poured herself a drink from the whisky decanter on the table. He watched her, uncertain what was going on; by rights, she should have been on her knees worshipping His cock already. She turned and locked eyes with Him, defiant and challenging, goading Him to react. Glaring at her through heated eyes, He laid His drink gently on the table and turned to face her. 'Did you enjoy it?' she asked, eyes sparkling, an amused smirk playing across her lips.

'You'll pay for that,' He said, nodding towards the mushroom that now sat in a napkin on the table beside Him.

She just laughed, 'Oh Master, you'll have to catch me first.'

Then, she ran.

Perhaps He should have seen it coming, but He was unused to such insubordination. He lunged for her wrist and missed, a grunt of frustration escaping His lips. Incensed, He leapt across the room and caught her by the hair as she reached for the handle of the door. He forced her hard against the wall and pinned her there with His body. Facing away from him, her nipples grazed the cold surface and stiffened. He was without a doubt the strongest lover she had ever had. She hated how much she wanted this man, how much power He had over her; already she could feel the wetness spreading down her thighs as she squirmed against the wall.

'You're mine now,' He growled into her ear. She could feel the satisfaction in His voice caressing her skin and enveloping her limbs.

'No,' she gasped. She fought back, hard, arms twisted behind her, her nails grazing His neck and raising a welt.

But she was no match for His strength. Her resistance only made Him want her even more. He could feel his cock throbbing for her, straining to tame her. He would dominate His insolent slave yet. Grabbing her scrabbling hands, He twisted them tightly behind her back and held her wrists fast. With His free hand, He removed his tie and bound her wrists firmly behind her back. No more scratches from her tonight.

'You can struggle all you like, but you know it won't do any good.' He traced his tongue slowly down her face, before gently biting her bottom lip.

'No!' she breathed, still challenging.

Vice

Her hands now bound tightly behind her, He swung her roughly around and forced her back against the wall, His face an inch from hers. She tried to turn from Him, but He held her by the collar and forced His tongue into her mouth, kissing her hard. He pressed His body against hers and felt Hunter shiver against His chest. He was enjoying every second of her struggle, this mock resistance. He knew how much she wanted him. He could smell it on her skin, taste it in her mouth. He squeezed her nipples roughly, eliciting a moan from her. She hated herself for enjoying this so much but could barely muster the strength to resist. Sensing his advantage, He ran his hand down the stiff material of her corset and slipped His finger inside her thong.

'No, no, no.' Hunter was panting now, barely able to breathe with His hand around her neck. He bit down hard on her bottom lip, murmuring, 'Yes, yes, yes. Wriggle all you like; it'll just feel all the better when I fuck you...'

He had known, as soon as He felt the hot, wet, slickness running down her thighs, that He couldn't play this game much longer. Neither, He knew, could Hunter. She could pretend she didn't want Him all she liked, but He knew He controlled her body better than she did. He knew just how to manipulate the inside of her, where to stroke and touch and tease. He pushed his fingers inside her and immediately found her sweet spot. He played with her, stroking the inside of her, building her to what He knew would be a truly explosive orgasm. He teased her, bringing her to the point of orgasm then cruelly stopping, letting her know that she was His toy, His slave. She cried and moaned, whimpering 'no' but pushing herself harder against His hand, kissing Him back ravenously.

Finally, she came, hard, shaking and gushing and convulsing all over His hand. He felt it, felt her clench around His fingers. Letting out an animal growl, He threw her face down onto the floor, her body still rocking with the power of her orgasm. He quickly loosed the knot at her wrists and then rebound her hands over her head, tying the other end of his tie to a table leg. She tried to resist even now, she tried to get to her knees, but the force of her orgasm had taken the strength out of her.

'You're mine now,' He growled. Pressing her harder against the floor, He threw off his belt and shirt like an assassin would ready his weapon - swift, aggressive, with the practiced ease of a professional at work. The crack of the leather reminiscent of bullets sliding into place. The action a deadly harbinger of the mortal eclipse that was inevitably to come.

Pressing a knee against her lower back, He looped His belt around His fist, keeping a tight hold of the buckle, as per their previous agreement. The sound of him undoing the buckle finally woke her from her post-orgasmic stupor. 'No!' she shouted, as He brought the leather down hard across her ass. 'No!' she yelled again, but she was betrayed by the look of delight on her face. He raised his hand again and again, and again. He loved watching her writhe and squeal beneath him, her ass turning redder and redder with every lash.

Finally, just as she thought she couldn't take any more, He dropped the belt and released His straining cock from its confinement; it was perfect, thick and throbbing with desire. He ripped off her thong, spread her legs and forced Himself inside of her. When she screamed, He ignored her.

He fucked her, as hard and as deep as He could, gently choking her with one hand and pulling her hair with the other.

'Try and fight it,' He said, forcing her onto His cock, stretching her around Him.

'I can't,' she gasped. And it was true. She was a slave for him. She couldn't get enough of him. She begged Him to fuck her harder, deeper, faster, to fill every willing inch of her. Nothing else mattered, nothing else existed except His cock inside of her. She wanted nothing else but to be used as a whore by this man, taken and abused again, and again, completely shackled and defiled. And He knew it.

He plunged into her harder and harder, and she started trembling around Him, screaming his name. Finally, she came so hard, her body squeezing around His cock so tightly that she forced the orgasm out of Him. He came even harder inside of her. Gushing hot, thick, sticky sperm deep inside of her body, claiming her. Still coming, He pulled his cock from her body and gushed all over her thighs, her ass, and her back, covering her body in His seed.

'You're mine, you hear me?' He said, as He collapsed on top of her twitching, sticky, spent body.

'Yes Master,' she replied breathless.

'Now get up,' He said, forcing himself onto his elbows and looking into her eyes. 'We have a party to get to. I'll be ready in an hour, and so will you. There's a chilled martini arriving for you in exactly five minutes, so I suggest you get off the floor so that the poor concierge doesn't suffer a spontaneous ejaculation when he enters the room.'

She moved to sit bolt upright, momentarily forgetting that she was tied face down on the floor to an immovable table leg. She yelped as she wrenched her shoulders and landed hard on her elbows. He was beside her in an instant, midway through putting on his shirt.

'Ssshhh,' He purred. 'Slowly, now…' With infinite care, He unwound the ties around her wrists and massaged some life back into them. The tie had been tight, and the grooves it left were obvious. He kissed her palm, before helping her slowly to her feet. She stood in front of him, hair dishevelled, corset gone, suspenders askew and the tie dangling from one wrist. She blinked slowly, coming back to herself as a lazy smile spread over her face and she stood swaying slightly, relishing the liquid stickiness that she could feel running down the back of her body. 'Two hours, you said?'

'One,' He replied, as he re-buckled His belt and pulled on His shirt. He paused, remembering something.

'Before you descend into full preparation, I have a gift for you.' Still somewhat ruffled from their games, He moved across the room to where His jacket had fallen and pulled a very expensive-looking box from His inside pocket.

She stretched languorously and perched, delightfully sticky, on the end of her still-made bed. He walked to her side and, almost sheepishly, handed her the box. She untied the matt black ribbon that held it together and then, opening the box, gasped in delight. Nestling among the folds of black satin was an ornate red snakeskin collar, with the word, 'Venatrix' embossed in gold lettering across the front. Her breath caught; she had never seen anything so beautiful. She looked up and saw that He held the matching gold chain-leash in His powerful hand. She looked up at Him, her eyes glistening with tears. 'Venatrix?' she asked.

'Well, the Latin isn't exactly right. A closer translation is 'Huntress'. My Huntress, and we can hunt the world together, Master and Slave. That is, if that is something you want?'

It was. She stared awestruck at the gift.

'Let me put it on you?'

'Of course,' she said, relieved to find her voice and a modicum of composure. Inside she was cursing her dress choice as there was no way she could wear the halter-neck now. She'd need to wear the emergency second she'd brought.

He carefully removed her black choker, which by some minor miracle had survived their exertions, and replaced it delicately with her new red snakeskin. The material was cool against her neck, and soothed where he had been holding her against the wall. He tightened it so that it constricted her only minutely, so that at no point could she forget that she was wearing it, but so that she could breathe and drink without having to modify her musculature. *He really is a Master*, she thought.

'Stunning,' He said, barely able to tear His eyes from her. She had a sudden desire for Him to have her again, with His muscled grace He was irresistible. She wanted Him to backhand her across the face and force her against the wall again, this time wrapping the chain around her throat. His eyes locked with hers and He could see her thoughts written in vivid red above her.

'Later, Venatrix. We have a party to get to.' He downed the last of the whisky she'd left in her glass, winked and was gone. Taking her chain with Him.

She sat for a second, completely overwhelmed, overjoyed by her gift. Then reality brought her back to earth; Tiffany would be here any second so that the two women could get ready together. She stood in the middle of the room, looking around blankly, having no idea where to start.

When the door knocked, she remained in her state of undress. Tiffany breezed into the room in a waft of sweet yet subtle perfume and a cloud of enthusiasm. 'Damn lady,' she laughed. 'You look like you've been ridden hard and put away wet!'

Tiffany handed Hunter the puddle of rose satin on the dressing table she was reaching for. Then, taking a closer look at her friend, her eyes widened. 'Holy shit,' she gasped. 'What is that on your neck?'

Hunter smiled softly, stroking her neck. 'Only the most exquisite gift that I have ever been given.'

'Good lord, it's embossed,' Tiffany said, peering closer. 'What does it mean?'

Hunter told her. She felt like she was walking on air, between the earth-shattering sex and the confirmation of everything she had ever wanted from life she felt like she had to be in a dream.

'So, you've had a delightful evening, then?' Tiffany asked.

'And the rest, He is a god among men.'

'So, I see,' Tiffany said, noticing the blush at her friend's throat and the obvious marks on her wrists. 'Right, you get in the shower, and I'll get the outfits organised. Drink?'

Right then, there was another, much crisper knock at the door. Hunter smiled. 'As if by magic.'

Tiffany raised an eyebrow, but opened the door as Hunter went to shower. An impeccably dressed concierge stepped into the room with two Harris crystal glasses filled to the brim with chilled martini, an olive in each one. His silver tray also contained a cocktail shaker and some snacks.

'Complements of the gentleman who just left,' he said, before exiting as professionally as he had arrived.

Well, thought Tiffany, *he certainly is a gentleman. And with impeccable taste to boot.* She busied herself laying out dresses, shoes, underwear, and make-up, and putting some appropriate party music on the room's speakers. When Hunter re-emerged, she was well-scrubbed, and her eyes were shining. When she sipped her drink, they shone even brighter. 'Oh my god, this martini is amazing!' she said.

Tiffany laughed. 'Sweetheart, you're on such a high, you could be drinking petrol and still enjoying it.'

'True.' Hunter grinned. She had applied the barest sweep of make up in the bathroom and was now stepping delicately into her red La Perla lingerie. Tiffany, meanwhile, was putting on a ridiculously ostentatious necklace.

'Oh my god, tell me those aren't real,' Hunter said, noting the oversized pink diamonds around her friend's throat.

Tiffany looked to Hunter with raised brows. 'What do you think?'

Hunter groaned and looked at her friend through wide eyes. 'You cannot wear those! One burl and you'll never see them again!'

'I know, I know, I tried to tell Richard, but he insisted. He's promised to be gentle.'

'Gentle? Richard? After half a bottle of finest single malt? You are going to end up on your ass again and you know it, and you'll lose those stunning diamonds under a table somewhere!'

Tiffany sighed; she knew her friend was right, but she also knew her husband's rule was law. She had to wear the diamonds, and if they got lost, they got lost. She'd just have to deal with it later. At least Richard never got angry about things like that. Unlike Peter. He was always so severe with Darcey, acting like she'd done something awful with every little mistake.

'Well, if they do come flying off, I can't promise I'll be crawling about under tables to help you find them,' Hunter said. 'This dress is held up by nothing but hope as it is!'

Both women were a hair's breadth from ready. Killer heels on, deliciously sexy underwear on. Red lace for Hunter, pale pink satin for Tiffany. Make-up and hair done to perfection. Every woman worth her salt knew, you put your heels and make-up on first, the dress was always last. Even more important when a man was watching you dress, you wanted to tantalise them right up to the last possible moment.

Hunter knocked back the last of her drink, and almost reverentially reaffixed her collar at her throat.

'You're wearing it to the party?' Tiffany asked, surprised. 'You know it's not just our set tonight?'

'I do. But He commanded and so I must. Plus, you know what most people are like, they'll think it's fashionable and not even notice the link to attach the chain.'

'Or the fact it's embossed?'

'Oh, I'm not worried about that. How many people do you know still read Latin?'

Tiffany pretended to consider the question. 'Um, Darcey?'

'Ha. True. But trust me, she won't give two hoots about my collar once she sees what Astrid is wearing tonight!' Both women laughed at this, knowing that in about five minutes they would all descend to the bar downstairs and Darcey would get her first look at Astrid's 30th birthday outfit. Astrid had wanted to get ready alone so that no one, not even her best friends, saw it in advance.

Tiffany smoothed down the satin of her cream ankle-length dress that was slit straight up the front to mid-thigh. 'You ready?' she asked.

Hunter smiled, trying to contain her ample cleavage in the low-cut red satin with the provocative slit up the side, this time very definitely cut to upper thigh. The collar complemented the outfit to perfection. 'Let's go.'

The two friends left the hotel room, one in cream and one in red, looking like heaven and hell made flesh.

The Fear

"But pleasures are like poppies spread,
You seize the flower, its bloom is shed."

Robert Burns

Walking into the Balmoral bar, Hunter was – as always – filled with a sense of wonder. The room was filled with plush jewel-coloured tartan chairs and curtains, while an entire wall was nothing but a floor to ceiling whisky display. There must have been hundreds of different bottles up there. Apparently, the Balmoral had the largest whisky collection anywhere in the world, and tonight Hunter was inclined to believe it. The dark Edinburgh night was kept at bay by a roaring log fire in an enormous stone fireplace, and the flames seemed to lick the whisky bottles and turn the room to burnished bronze.

Tonight, the room held an additional surprise in the form of Astrid, who was perched *on* the centre of the bar. Dressed in what looked like a one-outfit mash-up from the Rocky Horror Picture show, she couldn't have appeared more out of place if she had beamed directly down from Mars.

'Good Lord!' exclaimed Tiffany. 'She looks like a disco ball in boots!'

They crossed the room to join Darcey at the bar, where they continued to stare bemusedly at their silver-spiked and glitter-frosted friend.

138

'So…' Hunter enquired expectantly of Darcey.

Darcey turned around with an audible sigh, 'Honestly, I was expecting worse. At least this outfit covers some flesh.' She reached out and brushed a hand across Hunter's neck. 'What's this?'

Hunter grinned. 'Gorgeous, isn't it?'

'Oh yes,' Darcey said, with a grin. 'Only the finest for his pet.'

'Ouch. Still thorns on your stem I see. And here was me thinking it was Astrid who'd be getting the brunt of your disapproval tonight.' Hunter said raising an eyebrow.

'No, you're right, sorry, I was thinking about something else.' Darcey finished, waving her hands vaguely in front of her, as if to banish unwanted thoughts. Smiling in apology.

Hunter laughed and placed a hand on her friend's shoulder. 'We missed you upstairs, by the way. It's not the same getting ready without you and Astrid.'

'Thanks,' Darcey said. 'I missed you ladies too.'

Tiffany smiled, then clapped her hands together, taking charge of the situation. 'Right,' she yelled, over the clamour. 'Let's get this party started! Astrid gets your ass off the bar and get over here!'

Astrid hopped from the bar and began to push her way through the crowd. The girls watched her spiked hair bobbing through the sea of shoulders until, finally, she reached them.

'Hello, ladies!' she shouted, pushing a suspiciously alcoholic-looking tray towards her friends.

'Astrid!' Tiffany shouted. 'It's *your* birthday. *We* should be buying the drinks!'

Astrid grinned. 'I didn't pay a penny for these. Thanks to your husband, my tab is on him tonight.'

'Quite right too!' Tiffany agreed. 'So, what is this? Whisky?'

'Nope, Bonnie Prince Charlie's favourite tipple.'

'Ooh!' Hunter said immediately. 'Drambuie.'

Astrid stared at Hunter in surprise. 'For god's sake, how did you know that?'

'Oh, please,' Hunter replied. 'Anyway, it wasn't exactly Drambuie he drank, it was whisky mixed with honey and herbs, which later became Drambuie.'

Astrid furrowed her brow. 'For someone as hot as you are, you are a complete nerd sometimes.'

'Please don't get her started,' Darcey said laughing. 'I swear she wishes it was still the eighteenth century and she could actually be a Jacobite.'

'Or shag Bonnie Prince Charlie!' Astrid added, rather too loudly.

Hunter grinned. 'Charlie would have been far too effete for me. Give me one of the big, growling clan chiefs any day. Or William Wallace; he was at least six foot six!'

'OK, OK,' said Darcey, motioning for quiet. 'Getting back to business; here's to our fabulous Astrid on her thirtieth birthday. And to the best Hogmanay of our lives.'

They all whooped and then knocked back their shots of Drambuie. Astrid immediately refilled their glasses. 'Thank you, Darcey,' she beamed. 'And thank you for organising the party. I honestly had no idea what a big deal it was until I started inviting people. I swear some of them didn't even believe me until they saw the invites. So, seriously, thank you. You're a wonderful friend!'

The four friends were still wrapped in the afterglow of this exchange when Richard appeared at their side. The girls gasped; he had really gone for it, wearing the rich red of the Royal Stewart tartan, a classic choice for the evening, a full sash and even a badger-head sporran. Tiffany's cream dress complemented his impressive ensemble perfectly, they looked like bona fide Scottish royalty. Hunter suspected that that had been the idea all along. If Tiffany couldn't be an English princess, then she'd settle for being a Scottish Queen.

'Ok ladies,' Richard said. 'We'd best go if we want to get there on time.' He glanced nervously at their shoes but knew better than to ask if they would make it over the treacherous frozen cobbles in their heels.

141

Vice

'Let's do it!' Astrid yelled as, excitedly, they began to file past the doorman into the darkness of North Bridge.

Hunter gasped the second she stepped outside. The night was so cold that it almost literally sucked the breath from her lungs. She was still chastising herself for not wearing a larger coat when, suddenly, her shoulders were enveloped in the warmest and blackest fur she had ever seen. He appeared at her elbow, pulling it down over her shoulders. 'Another gift?' she asked smiling.

'I can't have my slave getting cold, now, can I?'

'Just please don't tell me what it is or where you got it,' she said, a tipsy giggle escaping her lips as she pulled it around herself and luxuriated in its marshmallow texture.
'If it helps, it's all my own work,' He assured her, clearly showing off his prowess with a weapon.

'I suspected as much,' she replied, smiling despite herself.

Hunter guessed that there were around thirty others making the journey to the Castle from the bar. All in all, Astrid was expecting about one hundred guests. Her thirtieth birthday would certainly be a night to remember. For more reasons than Hunter realised in that moment.

*

The steep walk to the Castle certainly proved an obstacle to the high-heeled guests, but it was well worth making the journey on foot. The city looked gorgeous as ice crystals shimmered and danced in the air, while fireworks had already started to colour the sky at various points on the

142

horizon. The streets themselves were packed. People who hadn't been able to get official tickets to the street party on Princes Street were simply having impromptu parties in all the other streets anyway, despite the freezing temperature. People danced, sang, drank, fell over, and started all over again, and it wasn't even nine o'clock.

After around five minutes, they arrived onto The Royal Mile. Suddenly, there was something very ancient about their city, with its cobbled streets and the imposing buildings that flanked them on either side like medieval sentries. Hunter was enjoying the strong arm at her waist and the fur around her shoulders. Sighing happily, she placed an arm to His stomach and nestled her head against His chest. The walk up The Royal Mile to the Castle never failed to make Hunter feel like she was walking through history. The effect was even more beautiful tonight. The streets were so dark, the only way of telling where you were was the punctuation of orange lights that erupted from each pub they passed, and on Edinburgh's Royal Mile, there was one about every six feet. It was then that she noticed the colouring of His kilt.

'Hang on,' she said, pulling Him towards the light of one of the many nearby bars. 'You're wearing the Hunter tartan.'

'You noticed?' He replied with a raised eyebrow and lupine smile.

Hunter was incredulous. 'But... you must know my last name is Blair?'

'Of course, I do, my prickly Scottish thistle. But I wouldn't presume to take your name. In any case, this seemed far more appropriate; after all, we both know who the hunter is going to be tonight.'

Hunter smiled mischievously. 'I'm only glad you've worn your kilt. That way, you'll be able to make use of this.' She pulled a small sheath from the inside of her evening bag, and almost shyly handed it to him.

He looked at the sheath, frowning. 'I told you to keep the knife remember?'

'This is not *our* knife. It's a Sgian Dubh, for your collection. You need one if you're going to wear full Highland Dress. I'm afraid those other knives of yours just won't cut it, if you'll excuse the pun.'

He unsheathed the blade. It was a perfect example of Scottish craftsmanship, beautifully made and with a wickedly sharp blade. But it was the handle that most impressed him. 'What *is* this,' he asked, holding it up to the light to get a better look. 'Some sort of lacquer?'

Hunter shook her head. 'Not even close. It is, in fact, compressed highland heather. So, you'll take a piece of Scotland with you wherever you go. Think of it as... the vegan option.'

His roar of laughter was enough to startle the whole group, who had walked on ahead, singing and shouting celebrations. She leaned into Him, as He continued chuckling.

'Thank you, my huntress,' He said, placing the blade in his kilt sock.

Hunter smiled. 'Call me Venatrix,' she said, softly.

*

Very soon, they reached the crest of The Royal Mile, and the Castle appeared to them through the darkness like something out of a bardic tale. Huge and imposing, it seemed to cling to the rock with invisible talons, glaring down at would-be intruders, protecting the city just as it had for centuries.

A wide cobbled drive led up to a stone drawbridge, and with the gate raised it reminded Hunter of an open mouth, sharp fangs protruding from the darkness. Torches taller than any member of their party lit the way to the entrance, and the smoke flavoured the air. There was no artificial light, no modern trappings. To enter the Castle was to step back in time.

There were audible gasps from some of their party. Hunter envied those first magical impressions, only possible through virgin eyes. Having lived so many years in Edinburgh, she could only imagine what it was like to see the Castle for the first time, steeped in darkness and bathed in fire.

As soon as they entered the Castle, stewards in evening dress took their coats, whilst others brought trays of cocktails. Astrid had chosen the drinks for tonight and her choice of negroni matched the surroundings perfectly. Smoky, strong and a little intimidating to the uninitiated.

The walls were carved from stone, naturally, but bedecked with traditional tapestry and thick carpets to combat the cold. Fires burned in every possible grate and candles were dotted all around like hundreds of twinkling stars. It was like being inside a Midwinter Night's Dream.

The stewards directed the party up a curved staircase and into a long room. Hunter could only guess at its original use, but for tonight it was Astrid's banquet hall, and it was magnificent.

The guests immediately began to take their seats at the long banquet-style tables.
The four women had been placed towards the head of the table, with Astrid, naturally, seated at the very top. Astrid had made the decision to place the male guests at a different table from their female counterparts, ostensibly so that they could talk without the inevitable sexual distractions, but mainly because she knew that Darcey would be desperately in need of a couple of hours away from her overbearing arse of a husband.

Watching Astrid as she made herself comfortable, Hunter couldn't help but laugh. Her friend looked like a black-haired Barbarella in the shimmering fire lights, her face emblazoned with sequinned lightning bolts in rainbow colours. It was then that Hunter noticed Astrid was also wearing her vibrator necklace. Without meaning to, she let out a delighted squeal; that *surely* put Astrid ahead in their debauched little game. She was about to congratulate her friend on her completely fuck-it attitude when she noticed another guest sweep into the room, and her mood changed completely.

'Astrid?' she barked. 'You seriously invited Morticia?'

Astrid looked at Hunter with genuine surprise. 'What, you don't like her?'

Hunter was too surprised to speak. 'She *hates* her,' Darcey said, in a whispered voice. 'I don't know many people Hunter actually hates, but *she* is definitely one of them.'

They all turned to not-so-discreetly watch the woman take her seat further down the table. She may have been invited, but she was not among the elite and had been seated well away from the guest of honour. They called her Morticia because she had black hair to her waist and was so pale that you could well believe she only came out at night. Her husband, known as 'Corpse', was by far the least pleasant of all Richard's acquaintances, and that was saying something. Their age difference was obvious in demeanour as well as appearance, Corpse looked like the Picture of Dorian Grey's epilogue; a rusted old rapier dipped in pitch. He also seemed to be deliberately ignoring his wife. *No love lost there*, Hunter thought. It was well known that their marriage was a particularly unhappy one.
'So, why do you dislike her so much?' Astrid asked, taking a big drink from the wine Darcey had just handed her.

Hunter couldn't quite explain. She knew that her distaste was completely irrational. She had barely spoken more than four sentences to the woman in her entire life. She'd only even seen her at The Hall twice and had successfully avoided her. But for some reason something about her just bothered Hunter on some fundamental level. It also didn't help that the woman intentionally gave the impression (inaccurately) that her brains wouldn't fill a cocktail olive, and that pissed Hunter off no end.

Tiffany, who was closer to Morticia than any of the others, leaned across the table and placed a hand on Hunter's. 'It's not her fault she's the way she is. She's had a tough life. You know that she was a real-life Las Vegas sex-worker, right? That's why she married Nicholas. He essentially *bought* her.'

Darcey stared at Tiffany. 'Are you sure?' she asked. 'She was a bona fide sex-worker? Maybe you got the wrong end of the stick. Maybe she was just a show girl or stripper or something.'

Astrid shook her head. 'No, it was definitely sex-work.'

Darcey's gaze shifted to Astrid, stunned. 'How do *you* know?'

Astrid shrugged. 'She told me all about it one night. I was with one of Richard's friends at a business thing and she told me the whole sordid story.'

'And that's how she met Corpse?' When Astrid nodded, Darcey seemed to deflate in her chair. 'I just don't believe it. It just seems so... cliché.'

Astrid took another gulp of wine. 'I can't imagine why she'd make it up. She's honestly a much better person than she might seem. I guess she's just so used to acting that way it's like she can't stop. It's like it's the only part she knows how to play anymore. She was even flirting with me before I said I just wanted to have a drink and chat.'

'Ok, so that is a bit sad.' Hunter conceded.

'As for her husband,' Darcey interrupted, 'This bit I know because Peter mentioned him once. His real name might be Nicholas, but everyone who works with him calls him 'Old Nick' because, by all accounts, he is pretty much the devil.'

'Well, that makes complete sense,' Astrid said.

'Why?' Hunter and Darcey asked in unison. Tiffany grimaced; she obviously knew what Astrid was referring to.

'He's kind of like the smart and evil version of Trigger,' Astrid said.

'Oh, great,' Hunter said sarcastically. 'I like her even more now that I know she's married to an arms dealer.'

'Well, perhaps not arms dealing,' Astrid said. 'But he's definitely one of those super shady characters, even by *their* standards.' At this, the women's eyes turned to Richard and the group of incredibly dubious men who surrounded him. Although Hunter knew that Tiffany believed wholeheartedly that all of her husband's business affairs were completely legitimate, Hunter did not. And neither, she knew, did Darcey, who was even more sceptical than Hunter.

Vice

What the women *did* agree on, however, was the fact that some of the people Richard knew were very, very bad people indeed. It seemed that 'Old Nick' was one of the worst. Hunter couldn't help but wonder where her man fit into the picture, because judging by the itinerant company, no one was entirely squeaky clean.

'Anyway, that's beside the point,' Astrid continued. She motioned for her friends to lean in closer; immediately, the atmosphere changed from cheery gossip girls to Halloween slumber party.

'She was a sex-worker, obviously,' Astrid continued. 'And a high-class one. It was all champagne and hotel suites, not street corners and dirty needles. So, one day she and one of the girls she worked with were given to Nick by the hotel he was staying in.'

'What do you mean *given*,' Hunter asked.

Astrid took a quick sip of wine before continuing. 'I don't know the precise ins and outs, but they were handed to him when he signed into his suite and were his to 'use' for the week in any way he saw fit.'

'Jesus what a prick!' Darcey exclaimed, with rancour.

'No different to what Frank Sinatra did back in the day, sadly.' Hunter added with a sigh.

'Oh, it gets worse,' Astrid said; she was obviously enjoying telling the sordid little tale. 'Stephanie – oh, that's Morticia's real name, by the way – Stephanie and this girl were treated like shit from the start. Apparently, he called

150

them 1 and 2. Even wrote it on their faces in sharpie, so he could address the one he wanted at any given moment without having to treat them as people.'

Hunter shook her head in wonder. 'I just can't believe it.'

Astrid nodded. 'And you thought Trigger was bad. Well, this guy is the actual worst.'

'And yet, apparently, marriage material,' Hunter said, incredulous. 'Do you know, if someone did that to me, I'd kill him in his sleep.'

'I believe you.' Darcey said.

Astrid raised an eyebrow. 'I'm not even finished yet.'

'There's *more*?' Darcey exclaimed.

'Yup. So, the week went on and the women did, well, what they were paid to do. Old Nick ordered them to do whatever and then ignored them like they were objects. But then, for some reason, he forgot himself completely and began to speak to Stephanie like... well, like an actual human being. By the end of the week, he'd even decided he liked her enough to take her with him when he left Vegas.'

'Good lord. Where?' asked Darcey.

'Oh, fuck knows,' Astrid said. 'But he did. That was something like five years ago. They got married in Mexico last year. Her family and his all there, the whole shebang, very legit.'

Staring numbly at Astrid, the three friends fell back into their chairs. Astrid offered a sympathetic smile. 'So, as you see, she's not exactly living a fairy tale existence.'

Darcey was the first of the three to find her voice. 'I wonder – does she love him? Or is that the world's stupidest question?'

'She didn't say,' Astrid replied sadly. 'But can you love someone after all that?'

Hunter knew her answer. And as the dinner continued, she just couldn't shake the image of a roughly outlined '1' on the skin of a pale white cheek from her mind.

*

Revelations aside, the evening continued in high spirits. The women quickly forgot their conversations and concentrated on the exquisite meal, the fabulous speeches, and the amazing whiskies. A new dram of single malt seemed to arrive with each course. By the time the cranachan dessert was served they were all tipsy and laughing.

By the time they rose from their seats, everyone was suitably sozzled, and it was almost time for the firework display to see out the old year. Tiffany had secured bottles of champagne for the bells, so they were currently milling around and chatting happily.

It was incredibly unfortunate therefore that, at that moment, who should decide to come and mingle in their midst but

Morticia herself. She seemed, for some unfathomable reason, to want to talk to Hunter. Exchanging glances, the other three women shifted far enough away for decorum but not so far that they couldn't hear what was going on.

'Hello Hunter,' Morticia said with her version of a smile.

'Hi. I love your dress,' Hunter said, even though she thought it was a bit on the severe side. The skin-tight black dress did in fact make her look like the Addams Family matriarch. Although Hunter couldn't imagine that this was the look that she had been going for.

'I hear you've become one of us then?' Morticia asked softly.

Hunter immediately bridled, certain that she was not one of anything that Morticia was. 'One of what?' she asked. She searched desperately for a polite excuse to extricate herself from the conversation, but her glass was full and there was no chance to visit the toilets so soon before the stewards arrived to usher the party outside.

Morticia laughed languorously. Everything about this woman seemed to be vaguely languorous. *Maybe she's on Valium*, Hunter thought. *If I had to sleep with Corpse every night, I'd have to be on something, too.*
'A slave my dear,' Morticia said. 'I hear you belong to Trigger's comrade in arms these days.'

This attempt to throw Hunter in with Trigger and his arms dealing friends was yet another statement designed to irritate Hunter. She swallowed down her anger and smiled

153

sweetly. 'I assume it was the collar that gave me away,' she said, scoring a point for herself by pointing out her lavish declaration of ownership.

Morticia's mouth bent into something resembling a smile. 'Well, good luck,' she said, somehow managing to crowbar hitherto undiscovered levels of insincerity into the simple statement. 'I hope you fare better than his last one. She was a very dear friend of mine, you know. My best friend, really, if I'm honest.'

Hunter rolled her eyes. 'I'm sure she was heartbroken. But then, she'll live, won't she.'

'No,' said Morticia. 'No, I'm afraid she won't, not anymore.' Her voice was tinged with what seemed like genuine sadness. But there was something else; something far more sinister and unpleasant.

All Hunter wanted to do was turn her back against this insufferable witch and get on with a truly fabulous party. But Morticia had her; she knew it, and so did Morticia. She had to know what it was that she had to say. 'Alright, Stephanie,' she said, rolling her eyes. 'You're just dying to tell me something. So, spit it out and let's get it bloody over with.'

And then, she told her.

The Confrontation

"Abandon all hope, ye who enter here."

Dante

'Ladies and gentlemen!' the chief steward announced. 'Please, take your places outside, it's almost midnight!'

Stephanie smiled at Hunter a final time, then turned and breezed away, a haze of opium sickness made flesh. Hunter watched her slim figure, black and unyielding like lacquer, disappear into the throng of revellers. The girls, who, had overheard everything that had been said, rushed to comfort Hunter. When they saw the devastation on her face, they took her arm and led her outside onto the Castle wall and away from the other guests. They stood on the Chemins de ronde (a pretentious name Hunter had always thought for what was essentially a stone walkway around a castle wall) bathed in light from a moon so perfect it seemed to be mocking them.

Hunter was crushed. She couldn't get her thoughts straight. It was like a darkness had descended on her. She couldn't believe what she'd just heard. But if it was real, then her great libertine had turned out to have no soul after all. Her glorious, enlightened, delicious Jacques Casanova had become the irredeemable and abhorrent Marquis de Sade. Her disappointment was palpable. The beauty of sexual abandonment and exploration was what she lived for, but she could do without it being tainted with hyper masculine dirt and demand. There were some hells into which even Hunter refused to venture.

155

'You must have known he'd had other submissives,' Darcey said, gently.

'Yes. Yes of course,' Hunter said. She pressed a hand to her forehead, trying to get her thoughts straight. 'Of course, I knew. You aren't that good at something without having practiced. But that's... that's not the fucking point. The point is that she died. She *died*. Covered in marks made from that fucking knife.'

Hunter felt like she'd been punched in the solar plexus. She wanted to throw up, and for a moment she feared that she might. But the feeling passed, and was replaced with cold, hard rage. So much easier to feel rage than hurt, disappointment, or fear.

Already in her head, Hunter was trying desperately to disentangle her emotions, to convince herself that she didn't care. To complete a character assassination that would ensure that she could endure the sudden pain of what she had lost. She had to stay away from him. Immediately. She couldn't deny it had been a wild ride, but no more. This man was a true monster, and she would not offer herself up as his next sacrifice.

But why? Why had he done it? She guessed that she knew. When you have everything, all the money and all the power in the world to do whatever you want, what *is* left? There was really only one thing, something that money couldn't buy. A way of creating risk and excitement, to try and regain some of the wonder that life had ceased to offer.

And why murder? How could he have done it? Well, Hunter thought she knew that, too. When your life was meaningless what did someone else's matter? Especially someone who had willingly become a slave, dwindled to nothing. Reduced to a toy, an object. Hunter had never seen it that way before and it had certainly never been that way for her. She had never felt small or diminished or objectified. Not once. It was a lifestyle, a contract, an adventure, a *choice*. A way of playing with control, boundaries, and power. But if you already *possessed* that power completely, then maybe it wasn't enough.

Her friends continued to rally around her, trying desperately to make her feel better, to convince her she'd had a lucky escape, that she didn't need him. These, the usual trite phrases trotted out by girlfriends when a relationship goes bad, were useless at the best of times, but never more so than in the case of such a huge catastrophe.

'He's not *worth* it,' said Darcey, her own bitterness raising its head above the parapet of alcohol and self-control. 'Believe me when I say that *none* of them are worth it. Sure, the fairy tales all tell us that we'll all find our perfect prince, but that's a load of bollocks. Even if you do manage to find one, they soon turn into the frogs they really are. Problem is, of course, that you're stuck by then. It's too late. You're committed, you're a partnership, you're... you're fucking *married*, for Christ's sake, and there's no way to escape the hurt. It hurts you to leave, it hurts you to stay. So, you see? Whatever you do, the frogs win. Because as soon as you give yourself to someone, you lose a little piece of yourself, and you can never get it back.'

Vice

The girls stared open mouthed at Darcey. This was the closest their friend had ever come to admitting how unhappy she was with Peter. They had long suspected as much, of course, but it was a genuine shock to hear her speak like this.

'God, Darcey, I'm so sorry.' Said Tiffany.
Darcey's eyes fell to the ground. 'I'm just saying, Hunter. He is not worth it. Forget him. Find another one you can play with. It doesn't matter.'

'Looks like we're all fucked, then,' Astrid said, in the tone of someone delivering a great truth. Perhaps she was. Right at that moment, it was certainly hard to argue with her.

'Listen,' said Darcey, grabbing Hunter's shoulder. 'I've told you about that secret society thing Peter and I are members of, haven't I? The Libertine Society?'

'Only after a few bottles of wine!' Tiffany said, in a last, desperate attempt to cheer everyone up. She really was a cheerleader to the end.

'Well, I really think you'd love it. The events are ridiculously glamourous, and the people you meet are just... well, there are some unforgettable characters. I've been meaning to ask you for ages, and what better time than now; would you go with me?'

Hunter wasn't convinced. 'Sex with complete strangers isn't really my thing.'

'Oh, come on Hunter,' Astrid yelled. 'Hell, I'll even chum you along. I'd bloody love to get a glimpse of what goes on in that place.'

Darcey shrugged. 'You can come too, Astrid. And you Tiffany. It's well worth it, especially if it will help Hunter forget this whole episode.'

Tiffany grinned. 'Fuck it; I'm in! Let's do the opulent sex party thing for real down in London.'
Darcey touched Hunter's arm. 'Honestly, it's way more refined than sex with random strangers. Come along next weekend and you'll see.'

Before Hunter could answer, there was an explosion so loud that it knocked Astrid off her heels and onto the stone. Immediately, the city erupted with the cheers and singing of the half million or more revellers who had made the journey to share in this incredible moment with them.

'Jesus!' Astrid cried, pressing a hand to her chest. 'What the fuck was that noise?'

'That was the One O'clock Gun,' Darcey laughed. 'New Year is the only other time it's ever fired. Wait another few seconds and... oh! There they are. Fireworks.'

Hunter smiled despite herself, and as Darcey helped Astrid up, they all gasped as the sky burst into a hundred thousand colours. All four women had seen the display countless times before, and they knew that people as far away as Australia, San Francisco and Singapore would be watching it online at this very moment. After all, it was the most

Vice

famous night of the year, and this was the most famous
party of all. But whilst the fireworks had always been
impressive, the women had never known what it was like
to be *inside* the display. The fireworks went off above them
but cascaded down in front of them like a waterfall. The
effect was magical. The colours amazing. Each new blast
of colour was reflected in the eyes of the women opened
wide in amazement and wonder.

Hunter was already close to tears. But when the first notes
of Auld Lang Syne came bursting from the military band,
real tears began to stream down her face. She had had a
Master; she had been his. But she couldn't go back to him
now. Her life was too valuable and there were some games
that even she would not play. The price was too high.

*

Hunter had left her friends, despite their many protestations
that she should not be on her own, nor should she
necessarily go looking for a murderer alone in the dark.
Darcey had practically body-checked her when she had first
tried to leave. But Hunter had explained that she had to
confront him, she couldn't just disappear, he'd come
looking for her. More than that, he knew everyone here, he
was Richard's friend. Tiffany had made a point of insisting
that she and Richard had had no idea about his past. Hunter
believed her.

Hunter knew she'd be safe, even if she couldn't say exactly
why. Besides, he knew where she lived and if she offered
no explanation at all, he'd simply persist until she gave him
one. Although she had to admit she was now incredibly
frightened of this man on some deep fundamental level, she

160

wasn't afraid of what he would do to her *tonight*. He wasn't some homicidal maniac, a calculated risk had obviously gone very, very wrong. But it was a risk that she was unwilling to take. She had to make that clear, and she had to do it now.

Hunter walked the Castle walls as if in a dream, or in this case, a nightmare. With each step another barrier fell into place over her heart as she dismantled her submission and built a defence against him instead. The man who, as it turned out, hadn't been toying with her all this time, but threatening her. She was too numb to feel the emotions that she knew were seething inside her, they would come later. Now she had to find him, find him, and leave him. Before it was too late.

She shivered and turned a corner, her arm brushing the cold stone, though she barely felt it. He was shrouded in darkness, outside in the dark and leaning against the Castle wall, waiting, although for what she had no idea. He was too far away to have witnessed the firework display. *Waiting for her?* There were no candles here, only the cold moonlight reflected on the walls.

Nothing felt real, it was like she was tethered to the earth with string, and if it was cut, she'd simply float away.

He turned, his smile turning to ice on his lips when he saw her expression. For the first time she noticed the implicit threat in his stance and the terrifying strength of his hands. He wasn't a master; he was a monster.

He took a step towards her; she flinched back with a gasp. His eyes were uncomprehending, searching her face for some sort of answer, or explanation.

'We're over.' She said coldly. Two words that descended over them like a shroud. He made to move forward once more but she held up both hands, and for the first time, looked him straight in the eyes. Although she saw no violence there, she knew it lurked somewhere in his darkness, hidden by his games and his power.

'What…' He began, but before he could continue, she lunged forward and slapped him, hard, right across the side of his face. Despite their difference in size, the force of the blow had caught him completely off guard, and he was knocked backwards. He turned back to face her, and she saw a drop of blood run down his cheek. A mere hour ago she would have lapped at it hungrily, but now it turned her stomach. Replaced in her mind with a picture of a hundred bleeding wounds.
'Never again.' She spat, turning away, and running back to her friends.

He stood looking after her, not knowing what had changed her mind so definitively, but understanding that whatever bond they had shared, she had severed it, and there was nothing that he could do about it. With a sigh, he turned on his heel and descended the Castle wall, disappearing into the Edinburgh night.

The Society

"Let not light see my black and deep desires."
William Shakespeare

It was an enchanting, snow-filled evening in London, the entire city shining in contrasting tones of black and white. Flashes of silver light glinted off the Thames, and even the normal orange-hued streetlight was powdered with a dusting of elegant white powder. *What would he have called it?* She wondered. *A chiaroscuro sky, probably.* She would have loved to be on his arm tonight, or at the very least on his leash. All eyes on them. They would have been like royalty here. She winced as she thought of the exquisite collar that he had given her, the gift that she would never wear again.

She shook the images of him from her mind, cursing herself for thinking about him on her first foray into the sexual underbelly without being on his leash. She would not think about him again, she promised herself, even as she accepted that he would probably be on her mind for a long time yet.

The cool air caressed her skin as she looked up at the imposing building above her. The most modern of modern apartments, right on the water's edge. As she gazed up at the lights of the penthouse that was to be her stage for the evening, she imagined she could already hear the throaty moans and clinking champagne flutes. She approached the entranceway, which was flanked by an impressive looking

163

doorman, his untidy dreadlocks at odds with his crisp tuxedo. He looked like he'd been drafted from the Samoan international rugby team, and somewhat incongruously, introduced himself simply as 'Brian.'

'Good evening,' she said.

'Password?' he inquired with a polite inclination of his head and a wicked smile. Clearly, he knew exactly what was going on upstairs.

'Duchess,' she replied. She was surprised to note a slight tremble in her voice. Before her encounter with him, she would have strutted in there as if they had been waiting for her arrival for the party to start. She could tell herself that it was because he had knocked her confidence, but that would have been a lie. She was just sad and missed his presence.

The obliging Brian pulled back the scarlet rope reminiscent of too many tacky nightclubs and pointed her towards the lift that would lead her to her destination. The lift slid skyward with the briefest of whispers, and then the doors opened into a small but perfectly appointed vestibule. Stepping out of the lift, Hunter realised she was more nervous than she would like to admit. However, she was immediately reminded of the rules that Darcey had explained before they set out.

Rule 1. NEVER use your real name. There were some VERY important people at these events, from politicians to celebrities. Anonymity was guaranteed, and because of this, was ruthlessly protected. Which brought her neatly on to rule two-

Rule 2. ALWAYS be masked. Never remove your mask no matter what you're doing.
Rule 3. Safe sex is non-negotiable.

Rule 4. Women were in charge. 'No' meant 'No,' and if anyone decided to wilfully misinterpret this particular rule then they would have to deal with the Incredible-Hulk downstairs.

Darcey had explained that the whole scenario was always completely safe and run by the mysterious 'Duchess.' Nobody that Darcey knew had ever seen the Duchess before. There were many patrons who thought she didn't even exist, and that the events were simply run by one of the regular partygoers who were considered the Duchess's underlings. In any case, Hunter could see why these evenings appealed so intensely to Darcey. This place may have been like the Marquis de Sade's pied-à-terre, but it was both aristocratic and ruthlessly controlled.

At that moment, a perfectly chiselled naked man in a simple black mask appeared at her elbow with a tray of Champagne. 'Someone will be with you shortly,' he said.

Hunter sipped on the delicious champagne, steeling herself for what was to come next. She couldn't deny that part of her desire to fit into this world was a reaction to the revelations about him. She was going to be the most sexually desired and liberated person at the party, and he could go and fuck himself for disappointing her so hard. In any case, she was not going to let the lack of his presence ruin her night. She was here with Darcey, and she was going to enjoy herself no matter what.

'The Duchess bids you welcome,' a Venetian-masked woman purred into her ear, causing Hunter to jump in surprise. Thankfully her shocked expression was hidden beneath her own mask. She had gone for something slightly unusual when choosing her mask for the evening. It was cut in the Venetian style, that was true, but it was as black as oil and shimmered in the same manner. It was delicately sculpted from fine mesh wire, as if someone had fashioned a spider's web from the most delicate black iron threads.

'I'm the Marchesa,' the woman continued. Second to The Duchess, but you can call me M. And you are?'

She'd practiced this part. 'Lady Diana. A friend of Lady Helen and Lord Paris.' Lady Helen and Lord Paris were the aliases Darcey and Peter used whenever they attended these parties. Hunter suspected that these had been Darcey's choice, as she knew the story of Helen of Troy only too well.

The reason for her own name was simple. She had been brought up on Latin and had completed her Masters in ancient history at university. So, she had chosen Diana, the Roman goddess often depicted as a huntress in ancient mythology.

'Welcome,' M said. 'I am at your service if there is anything you need. As it is after midnight you must undress, but there is an *un*-dressing room at the end of the hallway. I hope you came prepared.'

'I have,' Hunter said, a little shyly, before making her way through the curtain-covered doorway at the end of the hall. There had been something familiar about 'M,' but she wasn't entirely sure what it was. In any case, there was no space in her head to think about it; she was too excited about the adventures that lay ahead, and eager to catch up with Darcey, who she was sure was somewhere running the show, and in complete control of whatever scenario she was involved in.

The *un*-dressing room already showed evidence of multiple female occupations – an overturned champagne flute, lipstick-stained glasses, and more stilettoes and lingerie than Paris fashion week – but no actual women. Glancing at her watch, she realised she was even later to the party than she had intended. She quickly unbuckled her (somewhat trite she had to admit, but nonetheless effective) ankle-length black trench-coat and slipped it off her shoulders to reveal a leather and lace ensemble that would have made Dita Von-Teese herself seethe with jealousy.

She might have looked the part, but she was too apprehensive to entirely *feel* it. Until this afternoon, she had imagined stepping out into the party with her four best friends, but Astrid and Tiffany had both been forced to cancel at the last minute, and Darcey had chosen to arrive some hours earlier than Hunter, for some unknown reason. So, here she was, negotiating her way into the shadowy underworld alone. 'Confidence, confidence,' she repeated to herself like a mantra. Then, with the deepest of breaths, she stepped out of the room and into what lay ahead.

The scene that she almost literally stumbled into was reminiscent of Giotto's descent into hell in the Scrovegni chapel, although admittedly without the corpulent blue devil biting everyone's heads off. It was both beautiful and disturbing, and everything she had imagined in the darkest depths of desirous nights. She placed a delicately stilettoed foot on the richly carpeted floor, careful to avoid the chaos of tawny curls that spilled onto the carpet from an ivy-corseted Botticelli Venus, who lay in raptures at her feet as a Michelangelo-sculpted god of a man languorously licked her nipples. Hunter looked around the room in wonder; she had previously thought that The Stables was the standard of debauchery, but that standard was being redefined tonight.

There were bodies intertwined everywhere, in various stages of undress, and various levels of congress. The bodies belonged to some of the most beautiful and erotically dressed people Hunter had ever seen. Stilettoes spiked the air and lingerie littered the carpeted floor. Sweat glistened on bodies in the candlelight as women rode men, pegged men, and enjoyed each other, and men writhed atop women and caressed anybody, and any body, within reach. It was a spectacular tableau of sexual liberation and celebration. Some of the women, who were universally gorgeous, were still wearing corsets, extravagant bras, or suspender belts, but with so much copulating taking place there was little room for anything else.

It was incredibly exciting to see the assortment of masks on display. Regardless of their positions, both socially and sexually, not a single face in the room was unmasked. Clearly people respected the protocols. This was good. Hunter began to feel more comfortable and began to simultaneously search out Darcey.

In a quieter corner of the room, Hunter was surprised to find several guests involved in nothing more debauched than drinking champagne and making small talk, as if they were at any old cocktail party. She was pretty sure on her approach that she heard the words 'portfolio' and 'hedge fund-manager.' *As long as no one mentions their bloody golf club,* she thought with a smile.

Included in this group was a rather dapper-looking young man with a military physique wearing sock suspenders with his stylish black Tom Ford underwear. Some would find that naff, she knew, but Hunter was a complete sucker for anything reminiscent of a bygone era; anything from the 1920s to about the 1950s and she was hooked.

Suddenly, through the fug of sex and lust, she spotted Darcey through the arched doorway of the adjoining living room. She made her way through the sweaty throng and greeted her friend warmly.

'Darcey, I can't believe it took me so long to come here! It's incredible.' Then, looking around; 'Where's Peter?'

Darcey sighed. 'Oh, he's around here somewhere. He always manages to find people to suit his particular tastes.'

'Oh? What tastes are those?'

Darcey cursed herself for this rare display of indiscretion. She did not want to go into details of why she came to these events. Namely, so that Peter could find some other obliging girl to fuck him up the arse and give her a night

Vice

off. Thankfully, she wasn't required to think of a way to brush off Hunter's question, because right then the Marchesa appeared, like a kinky pseudo-saviour, and addressed the room.

'Ok ladies,' she said. 'If we could have you all in the main salon now, please.'

Not everyone followed M's command – some were too engrossed in their own vices to notice she'd even made one – but Hunter and Darcey complied immediately. When they were halfway across the room, Hunter noticed the Botticelli Venus extricating herself from the multi-limbed mêlée in which she was entangled and stumble, giggling, to her feet.

The 'salon,' when they reached it, was bathed in low light, and filled with a deep, throbbing bass that echoed around the room at a volume where speech was possible, but which made it more comfortable not to speak at all, which was clearly the idea. The room had been cleared of furniture to make way for two rows of office chairs, which faced out from one another as in a game of musical chairs. But the games tonight were to be far less innocent, for each of the chairs held a blindfolded man clad in nothing but underwear and a pair of cuffs that bound his hands tightly behind his back. Hunter had to admit, whoever the Duchess was, she had truly fantastic attention to detail, and she clearly knew what she was doing.

'I think it's fairly obvious ladies, but if you will indulge me for just a minute,' the Marchesa entreated of the women, who were all lined up around the room, salivating over the veritable smorgasbord of masculinity on offer. 'Each of these men has given one hundred percent consent to be the toy of any and all of the women here. When you see one you like you can do whatever you wish with them. There are only two rules; neither their handcuffs nor their blindfolds may be removed. They will never know who was responsible for their pleasure tonight. You are completely in control ladies.' And with a final flourish she left the women to make their choices.

Hunter grabbed Darcey's hand in jubilation. 'This is freaking fabulous!' she squealed. Darcey smiled. 'I figured you'd enjoy it. And I'm sure you can see now why I'm so comfortable here. I could have a patient or a colleague, but with the masks and a bit of care no one need know or acknowledge anything.'

'And, more importantly, we have gorgeous men that we can use and abuse at will,' Hunter said.

Darcey laughed. 'Fair point. I do enjoy that we're in charge here.'

'Is Peter ok with you… indulging?' Hunter didn't want to spoil the mood but at the same time she wanted to make sure she didn't overstep on Darcey's behalf and cause any unnecessary marital angst.

'Oh yes, he's fine with this, ironically. As long as he finds women to indulge his particular proclivity, I get the night off. So to speak.'

Hunter narrowed her eyes towards her friend. 'You mentioned this before. What procliv –'

Vice

'Anyway,' Darcey said, cutting her friend off mid-sentence. 'We'd best get involved before all the best ones are taken.' And with that, she marched off towards an imposing man on the far left of the group. Sighing deeply, Hunter placed her drink on the table next to her and swayed over to her chosen prey. The beautiful young man she'd spotted earlier in the Tom Ford underwear.

She stood in front of the bound and blindfolded man and appraised him thoroughly. He wasn't as visually arresting as her previous lover, but he was nonetheless a fine specimen of manhood. Taught muscles, a light dusting of chest hair, and thick stubble on a strong jaw, not to mention that delicious pair of sock suspenders, which were really why she'd chosen him in the first place. He was younger and more innocent than she would usually go for, but on the other hand, she did so love corrupting the pure. It was one of her favourite pastimes.

She remained silently in front of him until he began to sense her presence. After a few moments, he shifted in his chair. 'Hello?' he asked, his voice small.

So sweet, Hunter thought. He was much younger than she'd first assumed, perhaps only just out of his teens. This was going to be *fun.* She moved forward slowly, until she knew that he could smell her perfume and feel her breath on his cheek. He laughed nervously.

'You almost expect to be drilled for name, rank and number.' he continued, clearly very, very nervous.

AHA! she thought. *So, he is an army guy after all.* It certainly explained his physique, and how he might have

172

found himself here alone. Single men were not allowed unless they were vouched for or served a particular purpose. Like being a fuck toy for a voracious and insatiable older woman. In London, if you're looking for fit and healthy specimens who are likely to be gentlemen, you go to the armed forces.

Still, she waited, breathing slowly onto his neck, not touching, just teasing. She noted approvingly that a bulge was beginning to appear in his boxers. Lord, men were easy. She sighed into his ear and heard a responding groan. His muscles started to tighten against his restraints.

She slowly, delicately, dragged her nails down his biceps and over his forearms, admiring how claw-like her black nails looked against his muscled skin. She stopped at the handcuffs and held his wrists with her fingers. He moaned again. So much power, even in just one fingernail. She ran her nails back up to his shoulders and rested them around his neck, then she gently straddled him. She pushed her breasts towards his face, allowing them to graze his jaw. He strained forward, opening his mouth, looking for something, anything, to kiss, bite or suck.

She slowly sank onto his lap, wrapping her thighs around his waist until her spiked stilettoes were on the floor behind him. She pushed herself into him, his erection insistent beneath her. With an aching slowness, she began to nibble on his bottom lip, pulling away the more insistent he became. She gently sucked his tongue, all the while dragging her nails down his broad shoulders and back, and almost imperceptivity rocking against his groin. He was barely able to contain himself.

She kissed down his neck and along his collar bone. She teased his nipple and increased her rocking against him. 'Please,' he begged. 'Please, please. Touch it. Please. I can't take it. Please, please.'

She really was enjoying this. She moved against him, knowing that he could feel the bite of the thick brass buckles of her suspender belt against his thighs. She snapped the elastic taught over her thigh as she gently bit his nipple.

He groaned, straining against her. He was probably the most frustrated man she'd ever had the pleasure of torturing. Full sensory overload. He pulled against his bonds and leaned into her, his mouth searching for hers. She allowed her hair to fall over his face, felt him breathe her in. She hooked her index fingers into the elastic of his boxers just below his hip bones and tugged down just enough to release his straining erection. It was crying with desire.

She ran her tongue along his face and then, in one smooth motion, stood in front of him, her hands resting high on his thighs, fingers still holding his underwear ever so slightly down. She bent forward with exaggerated slowness. She kissed his cheek as she descended, then his neck, his collar bone, and his stomach. She grazed a nipple then continued down, her hair electrifying his skin as it tumbled over him. She was bent almost double, her silhouette impressively poised. She breathed over his cock as she lowered her head further. He was almost inconsolable.

In one motion she extended her tongue as far out of her mouth as she could and then languidly licked his cock from the base, slowly, slowly, until she reached the tip where she gave it an aggressive flick. Then she turned on her perfect stilettoes and stalked away, the imagined applause of the other women ringing in her ears.

Hunter walked towards the doorway she saw Darcey grinning back at her, holding a glass of champagne for her friend in her outstretched hand. Darcey was evidently also finished with whomever she had been playing with, content to observe the ongoing debauchery. *Darcey was always standing on thresholds,* Hunter thought as she approached her friend. She also noticed that Peter was still conspicuous by his absence. Poor Darcey, abandoned at an orgy of all places. Few men would leave their wives unattended in a bar, never mind somewhere like this, and yet, Darcey stood alone. Unselfconsciously so though, presumably if you can save the lives of the unconscious, the curious glances of the unclothed are nothing to write home about.

'So, you like the army now do you?' Darcey questioned, passing Hunter the champagne.
'Wait, how did *you* know he was army?' Hunter replied, taking a long sip, and clearly enjoying the cool crisp taste that cleansed her tongue of the night's activities.
'Peter brought him,' Darcey explained.
'Ah, that explains his solo presence. Bit young, isn't he?'
'Oh, he's somebody Peter's mentoring or training or something. I think he used this is a sort of test. You know, if you're man enough to be seconded to the RAF then you're definitely man enough to come here, or some such

rubbish. You know how each of the forces likes to wind up the others.'

'Bloody hell, god knows what the boy will be expecting back at his squadron now!' They both laughed at the idea of the boy returning to his army base somewhat more of a man than when he left. And how he wouldn't be allowed to tell anyone about it. Not that anyone would believe him even if he did. It was at that moment that Peter emerged from a nearby throng. Darcey waved over, smiled at Hunter, then went to join her husband in whatever it was he was up to.

*

Hunter left the party feeling elated and subdued all at once. She had brought the most powerful specimen in the room to his knees. Not once had she uttered a word. He would have no idea who had reduced him to the quivering, twitching mess of desire when he was once again capable of coherent thought. On one hand, she had enjoyed the sense of power and control. But it wasn't enough. It had been too easy. She needed the opposition, the force exerted over *her*. To control a man was child's play. To have one control her was harder. Because she herself had to let go, had to hand over that control.

She couldn't deny it – she missed him. She missed the hours they had shared, the control he had wielded over her with such incredible ease. But at the same time, loneliness had its own seductive charms. There was something undeniably romantic about the feeling of longing. It also gave her a vague sense of superiority. It kept her apart from the picket-fence and picnic population that she did everything to keep herself separate from.

Maybe it's better this way, she thought, as she walked along the Thames towards Embankment, heels clicking on the stone. Maybe it's better to be alone, to save men only for the days and nights I'm in need of a sexual distraction. That way, my life will always be my own, and I'll never have to compromise my own desires and ambitions for anyone.

Yes, she thought, taking a deep breath of fresh, early morning air. *It's better this way. Better to be my own woman than a slave to conformity.*

These were liberating thoughts, indeed.

She only wished she could believe them.

The Garden

"It is only by way of pain one arrives at pleasure."

Marquis De Sade

On her return from London, as well as the usual tedium, Hunter's work had brought with it an unexpected and pleasant surprise; a feeling of safety. The revelations about him had scared her more than she liked to admit to herself. But being back in her wine dungeon, in the vaults under Edinburgh's South Bridge, calmed her bruised soul. Considering the vaults were supposedly haunted, this was perhaps a little ironic. On the other hand, there was something of the dark and the dangerous that had always appealed to Hunter on some visceral level. Which was what had led her to fall for his dubious charms in the first place.

Her wine cellar was the place where she was in complete control. The owner of the cellar lived in France, and trusted Hunter to manage the place as she saw fit, so the only person she was accountable to on a daily basis was herself.

It didn't hurt that if things got particularly bad there was always a chilled bottle of her favourite Meursault on hand. Darcey had also been conspicuous by her presence. Hunter would appear from the storage cellars to find Darcey sitting at one of the tasting tables or perusing the shelves. As busy as she was, and as unpredictable as Hunter knew her shift patterns to be, Darcey had visited at least twice a week, and had done so since their return from London. She always bought some bottle or other, but Hunter knew that was a pretence, she was really there to check-up on her. Tiffany had even popped in on her way back from some sort of agricultural event in the Borders. It was clear that the women were determined to help Hunter got over her crisis in any way they could.

In many ways London had been the perfect distraction. Hunter had returned feeling partially like her old self again. The same spark of challenge and fire in her, the same sexual desire. But it had been short-lived. As time progressed the spark had dwindled to barely an ember, and Hunter had found entire days going by without really remembering what had happened. She knew she was selling a lot of wine. She just couldn't have told you what it was. She was also not entirely sure that she hadn't shipped a case of Cotes Du Rhone instead of Cotes Du Beaune to the University of Edinburgh Alumni party. No one had complained, but she would have struggled to care even if they had.

Hunter realised that she had been staring at the shelf in front of her for a full twenty minutes, and she still hadn't switched the music in the cellar back on. She frowned; she couldn't even remember which bottle it was that she was actually looking for. *I have got to get a fucking grip,* she thought.

She may have wanted to be ready to move on, but deep down she knew it was going to take a lot more time. Until she felt herself completely released from him, she had to get on with the rest of her life. She had to continue to create her own adventures, and distance herself from the life they had shared. She needed distractions, *lots* of distractions. London had done the job but that had been weeks ago now. She needed something new, something to throw herself into and get completely lost in. What she needed was The Garden.

*

'Why is Glasgow always so freaking cold?' Tiffany complained, as the four friends shivered in a seemingly endless queue outside of the club. Everyone was wrapped in enormous coats, but their destination was easily deduced by the latex and leather that peaked out at ankle and wrist.
'It will be worth it once we're in,' Hunter assured her friend, blowing warm air into her hands.
'Oh, I know, I just can't wait! The cold isn't helping but I am so excited to see what they have in store this time.'
'If Astrid's outfit is anything to go by, it's going to be pretty spectacular,' Darcey said nodding in Astrid's direction.
'Damn straight,' Astrid said, slightly muffled.
'Thank god!' Hunter said, as they were finally ushered inside by an intimidatingly tall man wearing a full latex nun's habit. As they filed past him, heads bowed in mock reverence, he blessed each of them in turn with the thick wooden crucifix he was holding.

The club, if you could call it that, was an ad-hoc arrangement in a disused warehouse somewhere on the outskirts of Glasgow. While many, many people would undoubtedly view it as seedy or disgusting, to Hunter it was absolutely glorious. She had never seen so many perverts, or such a variety of fetishes and proclivities, in one place. Every gender and sexual orientation were represented in glorious technicolour: strapping six-foot body builders in head-to-toe rubber being led around on leashes by weedy pale Scottish accountants in tutus; people so intricately and completely tattooed that you barely noticed they were entirely naked; latex, leather, and PVC; body glitter and feathers; and some quite spectacular and painful looking piercings.

What was even more wonderful was the simple joy on the faces of the participants. This arena lacked the raw intensity of The Libertine Society, but it seemed altogether gentler and more accepting. It was officially called 'Tartarus' but was affectionately referred to by participants and party goers as 'The Garden of Evil.' Whatever your kink, you could express it here with no fear of judgment or reprisal.

Hunter had come dressed for burlesque in her pride and joy – a genuine vintage Las Vegas show-girl outfit that had once been worn on stage by Lisa Malouf Medford herself. The detailing was exquisite. The bodice was comprised of thousands of Swarovski crystals woven into mesh that sparkled on the skin like miniature fireworks. The rich ostrich feather train made her look like she was floating on marshmallow cream. Hunter had opted to leave the headdress at home tonight, so she was freer to enjoy the delights on offer; those headdresses were heavier than they looked. Headdress or not, however, Hunter was radiant. Standing beneath the faux chandeliers and mock moulin-rouge decor she looked like a divine bird of paradise, profoundly happy in its gilded cage.

Some of the more outlandish outfits were pretty shocking. Take Astrid, for example, who was currently busting moves on the dancefloor while wearing a life-sized leather horse's head. The silken black mane of which stood proudly like a roman legionnaire's helmet. This feat was made even more impressive by... well, her feet, which had been forced into ballerina points by the pair of hooves she had had custommade for the occasion. By rights, the hooves should have been supported by a pair of enormous heels, but where there should have been heel there was only space. What kept Astrid upright was some killer core strength and a quite spectacular work of physics, which was probably not exactly what Newton had had in mind when he formulated his laws of gravity and motion. The costume was finished off with one of the tightest black body suits Hunter had ever seen. How Astrid was going to compete in the pole dance competition whilst wearing the ensemble was anyone's guess.

The overall erotic effect of the place was only slightly spoilt by a somewhat shabby gentleman dressed in only a lace-up leather vest wanking sadly by the corner of the bar.

'Are you joking?' Hunter said, her lip curled in distaste. 'He can do that at home watching porn. Doing it here is just... creepy. He's clearly getting off on someone in this room, and they're none the wiser.'

Despite this, Tiffany couldn't help but feel just a teensy bit sorry for the old fella. But then, she had a heart big enough for even the saddest of individuals. 'At least he's happy?' she said.

'Yeah, well, I just hope it's not *us* he's finding pleasure in,' Darcey said.

Suddenly, the look of pity vanished from Tiffany's face. 'I hadn't thought of that,' she said. Then, as an afterthought, 'Yuk.'

Hunter burst out laughing. 'No need to worry, Tiff. His focus is on the gimp-mask crowd over by the medical instruments. Which, let's face it, is a worry in itself.'

'What are you talking about?' Darcey asked.

Hunter gave an involuntary shudder. 'I can't understand how any woman who has suffered the indignity of a smear test would ever, *ever*, want to submit to the same again for *pleasure's* sake.'

'Don't knock it until you've tried it.' Tiffany said. She was definitely into more serious hardware than Hunter. Where Hunter preferred the delicate and elegant, Tiffany preferred the industrial and obvious. Hunter had often teased her that this was the difference between her British class and Tiffany's American brass.

'So, what are you here for if not *that*?' Darcey asked, with a nod towards the sex doctors, who were squatting and prodding, happy as clams, behind a slightly sinister hospital curtain.

'I am here to forget,' Hunter said. 'To get lost. To indulge. So, anything, really, though I won't do *that*.'

Tiffany gave a teasing smile. 'Alright, Meatloaf. Calm down.'

Hunter rolled her eyes, but she had to smile. 'Ha ha.'

Tiffany reached over, gave Hunter's shoulder a gentle squeeze. 'You know I'm only joking. It's just hard to know what to say when you're looking so... sad.'

'I am?'

Tiffany nodded, her face steeped in sympathy. 'He... He really got to you, didn't he?'

Hunter looked miserably to the ground. 'He did. I have no idea how I let it get so far so fast. I mean, we only saw each other a handful of times.'

'But it wasn't like you were meeting up for a spot of coffee,' Darcey pointed out. 'Your times together were completely intense.'

'I know, and you're right. These sort of arrangements speed everything up somehow. All of your emotions and vulnerabilities. I'm normally better at keeping a barrier up. Keeping a little bit of myself separate. I don't know what happened, but I gave him everything.'

'I know honey. But maybe that's what made it so amazing... and you'll always have that, even after, you know...' Tiffany trailed off smiling wanly.

'Well,' Darcey said. 'On a slightly happier note, there's a guy over there who can't seem to take his eyes off you, and he's standing next to some pretty impressive hardware.'

Hunter turned to look at the man in question. He was definitely attractive, tall and muscled, with a sweep of blonde hair and a cocky smile that promised all manner of illicit pleasures. 'Right,' she said. 'This is it – time to get a bloody grip. Time to forget about *him* and the whole sordid situation once and for all.' She fluffed her hair and fanned out her feathered train. 'I'll go and introduce myself.'

*

'Have you ever had the pleasure of a St. Andrews' Cross before?' he enquired, licking his full lips, and sliding the suede flogger from the belt loop of his leather trousers. Which were the only item of clothing he was wearing. The sinews on his forearms shifted as he gripped the flogger tight and ran the thick leather falls through his fingers, all the while holding Hunter's gaze with his piercing blue eyes.

Hunter had never been on a St. Andrew's cross before, but it looked like the perfect way to lose herself for an evening, to forget the pain and distract herself in pleasure. The Cross, to the uninitiated, looked a bit like a large wooden crucifix, but, while it was certainly large enough to crucify a person on, its real purpose was far more pleasurable. Rather than being placed in a T shape, it rested on two legs in an X, and rather than being attached to it by nails, the 'victim' would be spread-eagled and tied up by their wrists and ankles, usually with leather straps. What happened from there depended entirely on the participants' imagination.

'Are you interested?' he pursued, as Hunter looked it over hungrily.

'God yes,' she breathed. 'Do your worst.'

The leather straps were heavy and insistent against her wrists and ankles and made any movement almost impossible. The smell of the leather was reminiscent of the

twist of smoke through the privileged air of an old boys'
club. She was losing herself in the sensations already. She
wanted to feel and not to think. Take the mental pain away,
by inflicting the very edge of pain on her body. The French
called it 'La Douleur Exquise' exquisite pain, and it really
was. There were many more extreme variations, she knew;
they had already walked past a room full of medical
equipment that Darcey had legitimately wanted to go in and
sterilise. But after the revelations about him, Hunter was
determined to play things a little more gently, for now.

The man with the suede cat-o-nine-tails was taking it easy
on her, she knew. To be fair to the poor chap they had only
just met, and consent was everything at these events.
Hunter knew that he would not want to overstep. She
winked at him and said, 'I'm a big girl, gorgeous, and I can
take a lot more than that.'

'As you wish,' he said.

By this point, as was common at this kind of event, a small
crowd of appreciative onlookers had begun to form. That
was fine by Hunter; let them look, let them imagine. The
man began by stroking the tails of the whip all over her
body, from one ankle to the opposite wrist, and then he
repeated the same motion down the other side. This awoke
her skin to the stronger sensations to come. He was clearly
an expert in the use of the implement and handled it with
easy grace.

Once he had aroused her sufficiently, he brought the lash
down suddenly onto the wood just to the right of her face.
It made her gasp in surprise, and instinctively she pulled on
her restraints. What a delightful fright he had given

her. *Clever boy.* The shock had even brought a few gasps from the fascinated audience.

The next lash connected with her upper thigh. The sting sent a surge of pleasure through her and forced a gasp from her lips, and a wetness from her centre. Before she had recovered, he had cracked the whip again, this time against the inside of her thigh. She could see how much he was delighting in toying with her. She, in turn, was delighting in the release the physical sensations brought her. She thought of nothing except when the next lash would fall. The crowd looked on appreciatively. Hunter slowly slid into the sensations of anticipation and shock, as she closed her eyes and surrendered to her tormentor's darkest desires.

*

Sometime later, not long after the end of Hunter's impromptu BDSM show, Astrid found Darcey standing contentedly by the centre bar. Darcey was sipping some surprisingly good champagne from a goblet-styled flute, more relaxed than she had been in months. Astrid, meanwhile, had only just returned from the stage, having put in a stunning performance on the pole only a few minutes earlier. Divested of her horse's head, she was now shaking out her hair into its signature black spikes and checking her smudged eye make-up in a hand mirror.

'It's nice to see Tiffany enjoying herself,' Darcey said, with a smile.

Astrid turned to see Tiffany stroking the arm of a gorgeous raven-haired girl wearing a PVC corset and matching hot pants in stunning indigo. 'Oh my god,' she said. 'That girl is magnificent.'

'Astrid. That magnificent girl has a penis.'

'What?' Astrid leaned forward, squinting her eyes to get a better look at the girl's hot pants. 'Are you sure?' she asked.

Darcey laughed. 'I'm a doctor, I know what a penis looks like. Oh my god just look will you, it's fairly bloody obvious.'

It really was. 'God, that's wild!' Astrid said. 'Do you think Tiffany knows?'

'Well considering Tiffany currently has her hand gripped around it, I'm going to go with 'yes' she knows.'

Astrid grinned mischievously. 'Wow, well I knew she liked girls too… Hey! Maybe this is the perfect person for her.'

'Well, she had better be careful.'

'Why?' Astrid asked. 'Because of Richard? But… he *loves* it when Tiffany brings girls home.'

'Yes, but Richard's at least fifty. He may be liberal, but he's still from a different generation. Besides, he might not like Tiffany having fun with another penis.'

Astrid looked stunned. 'I never thought of that,' she said. Darcey tried to hide her smile. Astrid's assumption that everyone was as accepting of other people's proclivities was as endearing as it was misguided. Darcey, on the other hand, was significantly warier, and arguably, more realistic. 'Well, people are very singular, I mean there's everything under the sun -' Darcey began, when, as if to prove her point, an enormous and hirsute gentleman squeezed past them wearing a pale pink floral sundress, wide brimmed hat, and lipstick. He also carried a small lemon-yellow clutch bag. It looked like a Staffordshire bull terrier had dressed-up as child's doll but bless-him. He was clearly having the time of his life. 'But that means everyone has different boundaries. And ironically if ever there was a man that would have a fit about something so niche, it would be Richard.

'Huh. Well, at least that's Tiffany accounted for,' Astrid said, looking thoughtful. 'Now, where's Hunter?'

Darcey grinned. 'Over there, getting a foot massage from someone who clearly has a fetish.'

Astrid turned to see her friend, who was evidently having a wonderful evening. She was lying back on a chaise longue, ostrich-feather tail fanned out behind her, as a man delicately removed her sparkling bejewelled stiletto and ran his tongue along her toes with very obvious delight.

'Wow, if I had known this is what people with foot-fetishes enjoy, I'd have found myself one a long time ago,' Astrid said.

'Hmmm, I wouldn't,' Darcey said. 'Do you know the kind of bacteria that are on the soles of your feet? And that's *before* you've spent the night in a fetish club.'

'Oh, Darcey,' Astrid laughed. 'What would we do without you? Hunter's obviously not too worried.'

'She's not the one with the foot in her mouth, dummy!' Darcey replied good naturedly. Both women turned to see the man take as much of Hunter's foot into his mouth as he could and suck with obvious appreciation.

Hunter caught their eye and waved. She looked like a peacock queen. After her ministrations on the cross, this was the perfect way to wind down. She sipped her martini and felt the electrifying sting from the tongue of the lash recede from her skin. She knew most of the marks would be gone by the morning – she had never been into hardcore branding – but she hoped that some would remain, a secret reminder of a perfect evening to get her through the inevitable boredom of another day of work in the wine cellar. She often fantasised turning the place into her own mini dungeon when she was down there selecting a particular bottle of Bordeaux. Slipping her wrists through the metal bottle holders and having someone take her right there and then pinned amongst the bottles.

Hunter smiled at the fantasy and slid her hand between her legs, ready to increase her enjoyment to its conclusion. The man caught her wrist and smiled. He kissed her palm and laid her arm back across the chaise. He then slid further up between her legs, letting her feet drop either side of him, and rolled Hunter's crystal thong to the floor. He bent his head to her and began to explore every crease and fold. Hunter moaned. He increased his rhythm and flicked his tongue over her most sensitive spot. Hunter could feel her orgasm building.

It was then that Hunter's mind returned to him. She cursed herself, trying to shake him from her thoughts, but it was no use; it was him that she wished for at this moment of ecstasy. With every lick, caress and nibble she pictured him. His powerful shoulders forcing her legs apart and his arms beneath her. And when she came, throatily, abandoning herself to the sensations that powered through her body, it was him that she saw.

The Masquerade

"What is life, without an orgy now and then."

Agatha Christie

Hunter's friends had continued to be amazing. Although their trips to her wine cellar were fewer, they instead ensured that there was always the next adventure for Hunter to look forward to. They understood how powerful a distraction these trips could be; what to wear, what to bring, who to fuck, the possibilities were endless.

With that in mind, Darcey had booked flights for all four of them to London for the next Libertine Society event as soon as she and Hunter had received their formal invitations.

The next event was scheduled for a month's time, and although it still felt interminably long for Hunter, things were improving. She had begun to notice that she was actively looking for delightfully debauched distractions. Her trip to The Garden had given Hunter the boost of confidence that she had been desperately needing since losing him. The timing, therefore, could not have been better.

Hunter noticed him as soon as he strode into the wine cellar. The same languorous movements, the same strong forearms. He was confident bordering on cocky with an easy smile and a mischievous twinkle in his eye, all the more noticeable each time he swept his blonde fringe back from his face. It was her tormentor with the flogger from The Garden the week before. In fact, it was picturing a flogger hanging from his belt that had made the connection in Hunter's mind. She couldn't believe her luck. Darcey, she knew, dreaded an accidental meeting with a participant from one of the fetish events, but Hunter relished this blurring of the erotic and the everyday. It was like possessing a sexy secret that only she knew.

He arrived in the company of three other men. The appointment was for a tasting to choose the wines for a law society dinner at Parliament Square. *Lawyers,* Hunter thought, as she watched them perusing the shelves. *Oh, this is going to be fun.* She straightened her outfit, undid her top button, and sashayed across the room to greet them.

They turned as one to the sound of her heels clicking across the floor. Her smile of welcome was reciprocated by three of the men, but from the fourth she received a look of abject panic, before he recovered himself sufficiently to formally shake her hand.

'Such a gentleman,' she purred, as he blushed a deep, dark red.

'God Charles, calm down, I'm sure you've seen a beautiful woman before,' one of the men said, giving 'Charles' a good-natured poke in the ribs. They were obviously friends in the firm, or whatever it was, Hunter noted. And 'Charles' was now clearly on the back foot. *How delightful.*
Hunter smiled again at the four men, and began talking them through some of their options, all the while letting her

eyes linger on Charles for moments too long. He was beginning to shift nervously from foot to foot. Hunter was enjoying making him squirm. She would never betray someone else's sexual confidences, but he didn't know that. Hunter found his obvious unease endlessly entertaining.

The men had selected a few wines to try, so Hunter set them up at the tasting table. The four men were sitting facing her on high bar stools as Hunter stood on the other side of the table pouring out measures of various vintages. Charles had clearly chosen the bar stool furthest away from Hunter.

After talking through the merits of each one, she let them chat for a while comparing the various wines. Each time she looked at Charles, she imagined him knocking the glasses to the floor, taking her in his arms and fucking her right there bent over the table. She imagined him curling her hair around his fist and holding her pinned beneath him. She was sure he could read her thoughts. The colour had risen in her cheeks, and she had her hands on her hips as she swayed almost imperceptibly. He caught her eye, and she mimed biting him. He immediately dropped his eyes and stared fixedly into his glass.

'Bloody hell mate, it looks like you want to fight it not drink it.'

The rest of the men laughed as Hunter poured herself a tasting measure from the next bottle that she had lined up for them.

She licked the top of her glass to stop her lipstick from sticking to the rim, and watched Charles' lips part involuntarily. She could tell from their body language that his three friends knew Charles was interested in her. *Oh, if only you knew why,* she thought lasciviously, as one of them not-so-subtly winked at Charles whilst motioning towards Hunter.

'So, this one,' she began, 'is quite a daring little vintage from the Puglian region of Italy.'

They began to smell and then slowly sip the wine, following her lead. Charles was demonstrably ignoring her.

'Delicious.'

'God, that's good. Powerful, isn't it?' One of them commented.

'Oh yes,' Hunter agreed, 'a lot of people find it a bit overpowering, but I myself enjoy a solid mouthfeel.'

Charles choked on his mouthful of red and sprayed his colleague with a liberal mist of Nero Di Troia.

'Jesus Charles!' His slightly damp colleague complained, as Charles tried and failed to regain his composure, repeatedly coughing and gasping in his rush to recover himself.

Hunter laughed, 'don't worry gentlemen, it happens all the time.' She passed a cloth over to the dripping lawyer.

'I bet it does,' one of the men chipped in with a grin.

'At least you're wearing a black shirt,' Hunter smiled.

'Thank heaven for small mercies that's for sure,' he said as he took the cloth from Hunter and cleaned the wine from his clothes. 'You daft twat.'

Vice

'Agreed. Sorry,' Charles said, clearly mortified.

'No harm done mate. So shall we go for all Italian then?'
'I always feel that old world wines have a certain elegance about them, even the powerful varietals. To me old world wines seduce you, but new world wines fuck you.' Hunter offered a sweet smile as all four of the men's mouths dropped open.

'Shall I put the order through then gentlemen?'

*

Hunter practically burst through the door to her flat. She had to actively tell herself to calm down she was so turned on. She threw her bag onto the kitchen counter and hung her coat on the back of a chair. She then set about creating the perfect evening in for herself. She had had so much fun torturing Charles at the wine cellar that she could barely contain her excitement.

First, she opened a bottle of Montepulciano D'Abruzzo to allow it to breathe. She then turned the lights down throughout her flat and proceeded to light every candle in her bedroom, which took some time, because something that Hunter had in abundance, were candles.

She then ran herself a bath, making sure to add a rich scented oil to the running water. Finally, she approached her sex toy cabinet. Hunter had had this little box of delights specially made to display all of her favourite toys. It looked like a very large, black lacquer jewellery box, and it was lined inside with red satin.

It was so large in fact, that it took up almost all of her bedside table, but Hunter loved it, not only was the box itself beautiful, but it was another physical embodiment of Hunter's lust for the debauched and the decadent. The doors opened outwards to reveal an imaginative assortment of toys; all manner of vibrators, nipple clamps, arousal gels and lotions, pinwheels, thin Shibari ropes and leather restraints… If there was something that Hunter had more of than candles, it was sex paraphernalia. She selected her favourite waterproof vibrator and nipple clamps, laying them on the table next to her claw-foot bath.

She kept imagining the ripple of muscles in Charles' forearms as he brought the whip down hard against her skin. Reliving the fantasy she'd had of him fucking her over her tasting table. Her breath caught as she felt the familiar pull between her legs. She retrieved her glass of wine from the kitchen, and headed for her bath, shedding clothes as she went.

*

The following morning Hunter awoke with a smile on her face for the first time in over a month. She was actually looking forward to a day in the wine dungeon. *Who might come in today? Perhaps the soldier from London, or the foot fetishist from The Garden?* She made coffee as she imagined all of the different ways she could play with them if they did. As unlikely as a repeat of the previous days' coincidence was, nothing could dampen the flutter of excitement she felt when fantasising about it.

What yesterday had proven to her, was that she *didn't* need him, she was still the same Hunter. The same woman who was more sexually adventurous than most, and who struggled to take 'real life' too seriously. God, she felt like a weight had been lifted from her chest. She sighed in relief, and as she stood in her kitchen, she took a deep breath of the coffee as it dripped through her percolator, her mouth parting in appreciation. *In fact,* Hunter thought, as she poured her coffee into her travel mug, *I know what I can do to make today more fun.* She tipped the remainder into an espresso cup, knocked it back, screwed the lid on her travel mug, and strode into her bedroom.

She spotted what she was looking for on her bedside table, left from the previous evening's activities. She lifted her skirt and slid her thong down, just over the tops of her seamed stockings. She then picked up the little pot of arousal gel and applied a generous daub to her clitoris. She was about to re-screw the lid and slide her thong back on when she paused. The amount she'd applied was definitely enough to make work uncomfortable, she could feel the heat starting to prickle already. But she wanted more than uncomfortable, she wanted unbearable.

She wanted to be so uncontrollably frustrated that if the right man came in, she'd make him take her right then and there on the cellar floor. She slid her hand between her legs once more and finished the job. Suitably slick, and already feeling the delicious tingling, she quickly fingered her nipples inside her bra for extra torture. She straightened her clothes, picked up her vibrator necklace from where it hung on her jewellery stand, and dashed out the door, forgetting all about her coffee. All she could think about was her next adventure, and what sexual mischief she could get up to before her trip down to London with the girls.

*

Hunter stepped onto the plane with a barely concealed shiver of excitement. She absolutely adored flying, loved everything about the ritual of travel, and she was determined to make the most of this short flight to London. She sighed back into her seat, filled with the same anticipation she had felt ever since the invitation had dropped through her door the month before.

She had been standing in her hallway in a kimono, trying to balance a coffee in one hand as she sorted through the day's mail. By rights she should have already been getting ready for work, but one envelope, which had arrived complete with wax seal and calligraphed address, had captured her attention. She stared at it a full minute before carefully breaking the seal and reaching inside.

Dear Lady Diana,

Congratulations,

You have been chosen because you are smart, beautiful, and naughty, traits the Libertine Society adore.

The privilege bestowed upon you is an important one. It is your duty as Privé to share with us your naughtiest, most glamorous friends. Invite them to a party and put them forward for membership.

LS thrives through word of mouth. It is how we grow and remain as exclusive as we are.

D

After she read the card, Hunter had squealed so violently that she almost spilled her coffee. She was shocked, not only by the invitation itself, but by the fact that Darcey, the most modest of all four girls, should have already risen to the rank of Baroness in the Duchess' inner circle. She said a silent thank you to her friend for introducing her to the Society and promised herself she would bear the same moniker before long.

She was already aware of the steps she would need to take to be made Baroness. The Duchess used a complicated hierarchy of women (exclusively women) to ensure the survival of the Libertine Society. Those chosen would help recruit others and ensure that only the most select were accepted. It guaranteed that the event remained in female control, which was essential, but also that there was an air of privilege and intrigue about the entire organisation. It elevated it from simply another seedy sex party to a secret society of the most depraved. Something the Marquis de Sade or Casanova himself would have attended in centuries past.

It was evident that Darcey was relatively advanced in the hierarchy as she and Peter had obviously been attending for years. Hunter was new, of course, but she had clearly made quite an impression on the Duchess' second-in-command, the Marchesa, and had been given the honour of Privé already. She was determined to enjoy the honour as much as she possibly could, and of course, she already had two other fabulous women to bring to the next party.
Hunter was aware that she was throwing herself into this new pastime as a way of distracting herself from thinking about him. But if she was to traverse this world of decadence and debauchery alone, then she was determined to thrive. And the Society was, without a doubt, the best place to start.

The nights wouldn't be the same without him, of course, but she would adapt. The military man she had enjoyed at her first such soirée had certainly not disappointed. She loved that she had no idea of his name, loved that she could walk past him on the street and there would be the thrill of a sexual secret that the more quotidian and pedestrian members of society were completely oblivious to.

Hunter had immediately let Astrid and Tiffany know that they would be coming as *her* guests to the next party. She knew that Darcey was as excited as she was to have the whole group there together. Darcey had wanted to invite them herself for years, but Peter, the prick, had wanted to keep their attendance 'just for them.' Well, no worries; they were all to be together now, complete with bespoke masks and the aliases they had excitedly devised for themselves over the past few weeks.

Hunter had arrived at Edinburgh airport after the final wine tasting on the Friday evening without incident, where she had met her three partners in decadence and debauchery in the British Airway's Lounge for champagne before their flight.

Tiffany was some obscene tier in the executive club, despite not actually flying that much, but at Richard's discretion of course. They never flew anywhere in anything other than First or at an absolute push, Business Class, so Tiffany always made sure that the classes of her three friends' tickets matched hers. It wasn't usually necessary as they actually rarely travelled together. Their lives outside of their alternative lifestyle were so different that they often ended up arriving at places separately, even when holidaying together. Like when they had gone to Las Vegas for Tiffany's Hen Party. They had all been doing such disparate things at the time, that none of them had actually travelled there together. Tiffany had flown from Edinburgh via London of course. Hunter had been on a wine tour with work in Cataluña, so had come straight from Barcelona. Darcey had been competing in the Royal Air Force Skiing championships (as if she didn't have enough to do in her day job) and Astrid, unusually, had been visiting her extended family with her parents in Kerala, so had flown direct from there. That particular reunion had been truly spectacular. In this case, they were all making the Edinburgh to Heathrow trip together, and Tiffany would have been abhorred if one of them was stuck in economy.

To be fair, Darcey had family money and Hunter had an astonishingly effective way of living a champagne lifestyle on a lemonade budget, but Astrid was occasionally strapped for cash. She was used to the stripping lifestyle of having huge amounts of disposable income but sporadically. She had gone into permanent work only recently and while she was hardly the secretary, she still had to adequately prove herself in the corporate world before any real money would be coming her way.

One thing that genuinely irked Astrid, and there were very, very, few things that actually penetrated her normally impervious exterior, as she was almost pathologically easy going, was the advantage that men were given over women in the corporate environment. She loathed seeing those less qualified and hard-working than her being promoted more readily for the simple reason that they had a functioning cock, and 'looked the part'.

Sadly, even in this day and age, parts of the corporate world remained the vestige of an old boys' club.

Astrid knew that she was further hampered by demonstrably not looking the way that she was 'supposed' to. She was too quirky and unique, and this was reflected in her wardrobe, and sometimes that was all people saw. She was also painfully aware that as a younger woman of Indian-Scottish heritage, she further did not fit the mould, that seemed almost exclusively reserved for mediocre, balding middle-class white men, or at the absolute outside, severe middle-class white women. Maybe she should have stuck to the sequined not-quite-glamour of stripping, at least in that environment her personality and looks were a considerable asset.

The four friends had all worn their vibrator necklaces onto the plane and, as usual, no one appeared to notice. So, this round had been declared a draw. They had stowed their carry-on luggage over their heads, exchanging conspiratorial glances as they did so. It always added a frisson of excitement carrying so much leather and lace, as well as Astrid's butt-plugs and ball-gags, through security. Hunter imagined the looks on the agents' faces if they ever had to open any of their suitcases. She almost wished it would happen just for the amusement it would bring her.

Hunter leaned back, enjoying the roar as the engines engaged for take-off. She always equated this moment, this unleashing of incredible power, to that of an orgasm. She loved the surge, the rush as the plane left the tarmac, as if it couldn't be confined to the earth anymore. Tiffany, meanwhile, had taken a Valium with her pre-flight

3

champagne and was now metaphorically breathing into a paper bag. Tiffany hated to fly with a capital H, and detested every second she spent in the air. Both Hunter and Darcey had tried in vain to convince her that she was perfectly safe, but Tiffany was having none of it. Even the assertion that their pilot was a woman had failed to ease Tiffany's anxious mind.

Flying business class, the four women were handed flutes of champagne the moment the plane reached its cruising altitude, and thanks to the stewardesses' enthusiastic and almost fanatical refilling of glasses, they were soon giggling like they were back at the postgraduate club in their student days.

'So, what about your military man?' Astrid asked from across the aisle, leaning over a limp Tiffany. 'Will he be there tomorrow?'

'Are you kidding?' I couldn't pick him out of a line-up. Literally. And that's fine with me. I don't want a puppy. Anyway, the point of these things is to meet new people, not pick up old ones.'

'Old ones?' laughed Darcey. 'Jesus, the guy was about nineteen.'

'Very true,' Tiffany said, with a drunken smile.

'Tiffany, you weren't even there,' Darcey said.
Tiffany nodded. 'Very true,' she said, with a drunken smile.

'It doesn't matter how old they are anyway,' Hunter said, a slight edge to her voice. 'You know as well as I do that most men are a raging disappointment. They might start out well, but it's never long before they get too attached or become overly demanding. I don't have time for someone else's emotional needs and demands right now.'

There was a moment's silence, in which Darcey and Astrid exchanged glances; it was time, they knew, to change the subject. 'So, what's the plan for this weekend?' Astrid asked. 'And what's the deal with The Duchess? Have you met her?'

Darcey shook her head. 'Apparently, no one has. There are those who feel certain that she must attend the gatherings – after all, it's *her* society, and she'll want to make sure everything runs as smoothly as possible. But if she does attend, she clearly does an excellent job of blending in with the crowd.'

'Whoever she is, she's an absolute genius,' Hunter said. 'The whole thing is run with military precision. The masks, the aliases, the hierarchy; serious attention has clearly been paid to the details.'

'It's true,' Darcey said, with a far-off look in her eye. 'Her events are just perfect. They're so... mysterious. So clandestine, and... Oh! That's a point – you still haven't told me and *Lady Diana* here what your names are going to be for the next 48 hours.'

'Oh yes!' Astrid squealed, startling the stewardess who was refilling glasses in the next aisle. 'As of now, I shall only answer to...' She paused for dramatic effect. 'Cleopatra.'

Hunter and Darcey clapped her choice. 'Perfect Astrid,' Hunter said. 'Very you. And you, Tiff?'

Tiffany's eyes moved, heavily but happily, to her friends. 'Juliet,' she slurred, with a goofy smile. 'Lady Juliet.'

More applause. 'Equally fabulous,' Astrid said, rubbing her friend's back gently.

Hunter turned towards Darcey. 'Is Peter OK that you're going without him?'

'Oh, he's fine,' Darcey said. 'He trusts me. He knows that sex with faceless strangers isn't my thing. I'm there for the atmosphere, really. He's still fucking jealous, mind you, but I'm fine with that. I'm just so happy that we're all together again. It's funny, it's been feeling more and more like our old Glasgow days recently.'

Hunter smiled. 'Amen,' she said. Then, leaning back in her seat, she allowed herself to wonder what pleasures tomorrow evening's gathering would bring.

*

Dionysus, Greek god of wine, was known as 'The Releaser,' releasing all of man's inhibitions, and allowing unfettered access to debauchery and ritual madness. Hunter had always known this. She loved facts about the ancient world. But there's often a difference between *knowing* a fact and *understanding* it, and that was the case here. Hunter had known for twenty years that Dionysus and The Releaser were one and the same, but it was only during her second visit to the Libertine Society that she fully appreciated *why* Dionysus had earned his moniker. When the four women arrived, everyone had seemed a little awkward, trying that little bit too hard to please, desperate to project how incredibly happy and comfortable they were despite the general sense of discomfort that pervaded the room. But now the wine had been flowing for two hours, and every inhibition under the sun seemed to have been released. As she surveyed her surroundings, Hunter couldn't imagine that old Dionysus had ever put in a better shift.

The setting was almost exactly as before, an interchangeable penthouse hotel suite with rooms full of people in various stages of undress, inevitably masked and glamorous. An absolute giant of a man was crawling at the feet of an obvious dominatrix, he had clearly been naughty as Hunter could see the static bursts on his collar as his mistress shocked him in punishment. He didn't seem too upset by this treatment however, as he was barking like a dog through his canine mask and wagging his very convincing butt-plug tail in enjoyment. On the couch behind those two was an orgy of naked female bodies writhing and slipping over each other, their moans of pleasure threading through the atmosphere. Hunter smiled as two beautiful women brushed past her wearing matching fairy masks, gauze wings, nipple jewels and nothing else. It was certainly promising to be another absolutely fabulous evening.

The ladies had arrived significantly earlier than last time so as not to miss a single minute. Their punctuality had been rewarded with participation in a delightful opening ceremony, the likes of which Hunter had missed last time.

The guests had assembled in a circle, the palpable expectation of ritual tingling in the air. Then the Marchesa had entered, wearing a bejewelled ivory corset ensemble so striking that it drew appreciative gasps from the assembled guests. The Marchesa's mask, A Phantom of the Opera tribute with ruby teardrops falling from one eye, was so delicate it looked like it had been carved from bone. With her thick chestnut curls tumbling behind her she looked exquisite. Hunter noticed, with some confusion, that the Marchesa was holding an ornate teapot in her right hand and a China cup in her left, as though she had just walked out of a Mad Hatter's tea party. Hunter winked through her peacock mask at her friends, though she felt as nervous as anyone else in the room. Her nerves only increased when the Marchesa immediately strode over to her side, pinning her in place with the force of her gaze. 'Do you wish to embark on a night of depravity with us?' she asked.

An expectant shiver coursed through Hunter's body. 'I do,' she answered.

Still holding Hunter's gaze, the Marchesa nodded once, and poured some vivid red liquid into her cup from the teapot. Then, with exaggerated ceremony, she took a long deliberate drink and, leaning forward, kissed the liquid into Hunter's mouth.

Hunter was surprised and thrilled. The liquid was sweet and alcoholic, strong and cool over her tongue. She drank it down greedily, delighting in the feel of the Marchesa's tongue slathering her own.

The Marchesa gave a little bow and moved on to Astrid, who already had her mouth open. Hunter was glad of

Darcey's earlier advice to fix her mask to her face with double-sided tape. It negated the need for ties around the head that could come undone in the throes of passion, and would prevent masks from slipping whilst being kissed by exquisite fantasy characters.

When her turn came, Darcey hesitated over the liquid. Hunter knew it was the liquid and not the kiss that bothered her. Her friend was wary of putting anything into her body that she wasn't one hundred percent certain of, especially at an event like this, where there could be literally anything from absinthe to amphetamine in there.

Tiffany's kiss lasted significantly longer than any of the other women, to the delight of many of the other onlookers, some of which were showing obvious priapic appreciation. As the Marchesa continued around the circle, people began to move away from the group and into various side rooms and positions.

Astrid, unsurprisingly, was the first of the women to join the orgy, practically diving into the mêlée that was being launched on a large couch by the main archway.

Tiffany grinned. 'On that note, I think I want to play with the Marchesa. But, oh! Wait... that's allowed right?'

Darcey laughed. 'Of course. She's the biggest libertine here, trust me.'

'What about you, Darcey?' Hunter asked, when Tiffany was gone. 'What will you get up to?'

'For the moment, I'm happy standing here with my martini. What about you?'

It was a good question, to which Hunter had just found the answer. It came in a tall, dark, and incredibly muscular form. He wore the other half of the Phantom of the Opera mask, so Hunter concluded he must be something to do with either the Marchesa or the society itself. He was dressed in an opera cloak, dress trousers, and nothing else. Hunter smiled. Now *this* was her kind of man.

As Hunter began crossing the room towards him, she noticed that he was carrying something in his hands. Something large. Hunter paused, squinting to get a better look at the mystery object. Her Phantom caught the movement and turned to find her staring. A slow smile spread across his lips. 'Do you want to play?' he asked, his voice a deep sensual rumble.

'Always.'

'On the bed. Face-up.'

Hunter obliged.

Her skin was electrified, literally. Hunter couldn't believe she'd never had the pleasure of this machine before. A smooth glass orb at the end of what looked like a very large vibrator crackled with light and colour. It reminded her of the Van-De-Graff generators they had played with in high school, although this was definitely not a PG version.

As the Phantom slid the orb along Hunter's body, she felt like she was being lit up with some kind of sexual fire. The room they had chosen was sparsely occupied, and the various sexual encounters that *were* happening were taking place in the most distant corners of the room. Hunter suspected it was her consort's intimidating presence that ensured this minimum of privacy.

He wielded the wand like a weapon. Along her collar bone, her breasts, her stomach. She was gasping in pleasure. Every spark of electricity left a mark etched into her golden skin. Done with skill such as his, she suspected he could trace an intricate and deliberate design all over her body, like a type of brand. Already, her arms looked like a gorgeous desert landscape. The marks were patchwork, almost cracked, like a shattered mirror before the glass left the frame. And they were beautiful.

When he had finished with the front of her body, he turned her over and left his marks on her back, her thighs and her ass. Then, just as Hunter thought she could take no more, he bowed, kissed her hand, and helped her from the bed. Hunter stepped dreamily from the room, dazed and delighted. Her skin still prickled, her eyes sparkled, and she was breathing heavily. She needed one of these toys. She would make it her mission to get her hands on one as soon as she could. *Easier,* she thought, *than finding a man worthy enough to wield it.*

'He'll want something for that later, you know.' Hunter jumped and swung round to find Darcey standing by her shoulder with a drink and a smile. Darcey reached out to touch the ends of Hunter's hair, which followed her fingers in static attraction.

'Let him want,' Hunter replied, still in raptures. 'He'll take what I give him, if I choose to give him anything at all.'

*

The night continued with many more debauched delights for all four women, but as the sky outside began to grow unmistakably lighter, both Hunter and Darcey decided that it was probably time to call it a night, or day. They found Tiffany lying along a chaise longue, half-propped up sleepily against a wall, at least one colour of lipstick liberally smeared over her face. Her breasts were covered in what, for a horrified moment, Hunter thought were pinpricks of blood, though soon enough she realised it was more of the alcohol they had all drunk at the start of the night.

'Good night, then?' Hunter asked, teasing.

Tiffany was delightfully drunk. 'Wonderful,' she purred. 'M is delicious. Mmmmmmm.'

Darcey and Hunter exchanged an amused glance.

'Do you want to stay, or…' Hunter didn't even finish.

'No, I need to sleep. But I can sleep here…'

'Don't be ridiculous!' Hunter said. 'I'm sated and I know Darcey wants to get Astrid out of here before she's impregnated by someone.'

Tiffany's drunken gaze had fixed itself on the fine spider web of raised red welts that covered Hunter's body. 'What's all this?' she slurred.

Hunter grinned. 'It's my new toy. I'll tell you all about it tomorrow. So, I am very happy to adjourn downstairs.'
It was Darcey who eventually found Astrid, breathless and entirely naked beneath a sea of entangled limbs and grinding bodies. It was impossible to discern how many people she was currently fucking, but Hunter figured it had to be at least two. The three women looked at each other, wondering how best to interrupt the orgy to enquire whether or not their friend wanted to go home. To their relief, though, Astrid soon spotted them. 'Righto!' she shouted. 'I'll be done in a minute!'

'Dear lord,' Darcey groaned. 'Done with what?'

'Best not to speculate.' Laughed Hunter, still gently supporting Tiffany, who was getting closer and closer to just sliding down onto the floor.

Astrid appeared out of the sweaty amorphous throng, unselfconsciously naked, breathless, wearing one shoe, but miraculously with her Harley Quinn mask still intact. Darcey couldn't help but feel a little smug – her double-sided tape trick really *did* work wonders.

Ten minutes later, Hunter, Tiffany and Darcey were waiting in the main foyer of the suite when Astrid appeared, wearing a man's coat, and liberally decorated with various different people's bodily fluids. Even her spiked black hair had not been spared.

'Well.' Astrid announced breathlessly, as they negotiated their way into the lift. 'That… was… bloody *fantastic*! Not quite like the movies, though.'

'What's not like the movies?' Darcey asked, though she really, really wasn't sure she wanted to know.
'An orgy,' Astrid replied, matter of fact. Her friends stared at her blankly. 'Oh, come on,' she said, as the doors closed firmly in front of them, hiding the rest of the debauchery from their now very tired eyes. 'You know the ones I mean. 'Eyes Wide Shut' and all that.'

Darcey shrugged, 'Never seen it.'

'Well, it was only OK. But that's what I mean isn't it? In the movies it's all so glamorous.'

Hunter laughed. '*That* wasn't glamorous?'

Astrid considered this. 'Well, yeah,' she said. 'It's just… well, I mean there are a *lot* more naked butts in the real-life version, aren't there.'

Hunter burst out laughing. She was hoping this image wouldn't be the one she fixated on whenever she looked at a similar sea of debauchery in future. 'God damn it, Astrid!'

'Hey!' Astrid said, struck by a sudden thought. 'What if we added masks to our latex ensembles for the wedding?'
Darcey frowned. 'Astrid, latex masks would be unbelievable uncomfortable. God, our hair! Ouch.'

'Yeah,' Astrid said, momentarily deflated. 'You're probably right. I'll just need to go to more parties that have a mask requirement.'

'Well, you're welcome here for every event.' Hunter winked. By now, she was almost having to hold Tiffany up. *God this lift is taking its time,* she thought, as she watched Darcey trying not to come in to contact with the stains on Astrid's coat.

'I have to admit,' said Darcey. 'At times, it looked like you were hosting the party single handed.'

'I try,' Astrid replied, fanning her coat tails in a curtsey, and voguing unnecessarily into the mirror of the lift.

'Can you believe that there is only a month to go?' Tiffany suddenly squeaked. Clearly, she had heard only bits of the previous exchange through her drunken haze, and the talk of her wedding was the bit that stuck.

'I know,' Hunter said, patting her arm. 'We are all so excited for you, sweetie!'

'Did the dresses arrive yet?'

'Yes. Last week. We already told you.'

'Yay,' Tiffany said, swaying against Hunter with the motion of the lift. 'They fit, OK?'

'Yes, honey. We told you that, too, remember?'

'Oh, yeah. Yep, yep, of course,' Tiffany said, sleepy and clueless.

Finally, the lift doors creaked open. 'Alright ladies,' Darcey said. 'Time for bed.' Her gaze flicked towards Astrid. 'And maybe… a bath.'

Hunter helped Tiffany out of the lift, full of genuine joy at the thought of Tiffany's upcoming ridiculous wedding and the memories of the amazing night she had just had with her fabulous friends. Things were good, and serious entanglements with men were clearly unnecessary. Enjoying them in brief pleasurable encounters was what Hunter needed for now. For all other things, she had her friends. *I'm going to be just fine,* she thought. *I'm going get myself one of those darling little electrical numbers, and I'm going to be just fine.*

The Anticipation

"Lovers and madmen have such seething brains, such shaping fantasies that apprehend, more than cool reason comprehends."

William Shakespeare

It was the morning before the wedding, and she was packing for what promised to be a truly memorable event, when she heard the postman drop a letter through her door. At the time, she was trying to decide how best to pack her latex outfit so that it wouldn't crease or get that weird matt sheen it sometimes did when incorrectly stored, but she could never leave post for a moment without checking what it contained. Placing her outfit back on the bed, she immediately padded down the hallway to retrieve the mystery letter.

When she saw what it was, she felt her heart skip a beat. For there on the back on the envelope was the unmistakable fleur-de-lys wax seal of the Libertine Society. Holding it unopened in her hand, she wasn't at all certain what to expect. There were no more events planned for the foreseeable future. Could it be an invitation to the next big event in the Autumn?

No. It was something even more exciting; a small, maroon velvet pouch. Confused, Hunter read the card that had come with it -

Dear Lady Diana,

Congratulations,

My most trusted Marchesa has spoken to me on more than one occasion of your poise, elegance, class and, above all, depravity. Consider this a personal gift and thank you from me, for maintaining the highest standards of The Libertine Society.

Wear it with reverence,

Yours,

D

She opened the pouch and tipped the contents into her palm. It was a thick strap of black velvet, which encased at its centre an exquisitely carved violet ceramic profile of a Victorian lady. Her eyes widened in shock as she suddenly realised - she had seen this exact same necklace before! And not just once before, but twice!

So, Marissa was a member of the Libertine Society, too! Marissa, who Hunter saw at The Hall at every party and dinner, and who had never said anything, never even hinted that she was involved in such things. What's more, she must have been to far more than one Society event to have received a gift such as this. There was no other way she could have the exact same necklace that Hunter was currently holding. Then it dawned on Hunter; it was also the exact same necklace the Marchesa had worn that first night at the Libertine Society! *Oh my god,* Hunter thought, *how did it take me so long to put those things together*!

Hunter was by turns amused and amazed that Marissa, too, had managed to find her way into the Society's guest list.

She was equally impressed that Marissa had worn this necklace in front of them all. She must have taken such pleasure in the fact that no one noticed her secret. But how had she found her way into the society? And why had she never said anything? *I will have to spend more time with Marissa from now on*, Hunter thought.

Something else occurred to Hunter, then. What about Darcey? Where was Darcey's necklace? She had clearly been going for years; she must have a jewellery box full of tokens. Why hadn't she mentioned them? And how had she failed to notice Marissa's necklace that night at The Hall? Had she ever seen Marissa at an event in the past? There were so many questions, and so few answers. But one thing was certain. The next time she saw Darcey, Hunter would pin her down, and this time she would ask her everything; The Libertine Society, her marriage, the works. Even if she had to cable-tie Darcey to a chair and drip feed her martini to get her to talk to her, she would.

It wasn't long before another even darker thought hit her. Had Marissa and Richard ever...? But no, he wouldn't. Richard worshipped Tiffany. Hunter had seen the physical manifestations of that worship on countless occasions. In any case, there was no *way* Tiffany would allow something like that to take place without her full participation and consent. And Tiffany would never consent to an affair with an employee; she was no snob, but she enjoyed playing 'Lady of the Manor' too much.

Hunter placed the Duchess' note next to Tiffany and Richard's wedding invitation, which had already been given pride of place on the mantle in Hunter's hallway.

Then she went back into her bedroom, where she slid open the panel to her wardrobe and resumed her attempts to shake the niggle of uncertainty about Richard from her mind.

The wardrobe was full to bursting. One day, when she could somehow afford it, she would have the most glamorous walk-in wardrobe imaginable, something that would have made the likes of Marilyn Monroe and Audrey Hepburn swoon with envy. Hunter had spent a lot of time fantasising about this wardrobe. To her, it was so much more than simply a place to store her outfits; it was a physical journal of her life. Someday, when this version of her life was over – and Hunter was smart enough to know that life, as it was now, would eventually have to end – she would be able to look back and delight in all the debauched and delicious things that she had worn over the years. She would remember everything; every character she had played, every adventure she'd had, every crazy sexy bacchanal that she had been a part of. And she would know that she had had a ball.

When that day dawned, when life as she knew it finally came to an end, Hunter knew that her latex bridesmaid dress – the dress she was at that very moment attempting to pack – would take pride of place in her wardrobe of glamorous and debauched memories. Thinking about it, she was surprised to realise that she could even add *Him* to this category now. She had reached the point where she could remember the pleasurable times they had shared without spiralling into the abyss. Still, she would need to be careful not to think of him too often. If she did, there was every chance the reminiscences would force her back towards breaking point.

220

She tried the necklace on. *Fabulous*, she thought. But she wouldn't wear it over the weekend. It was Tiffany's day, and she didn't want anything to distract from that. In any case, it wouldn't match her dress, the latex creation that greeted her lustful eyes. It was incredible, the effort that Tiffany and Richard had gone to in putting together the matching bridesmaid dresses. As requested, hers was red, while Darcey had eventually opted for an incredibly classy ice blue. Astrid had, somewhat unfortunately, followed through on her choice of acid yellow, which looked even more horrendous in real life than it had in Hunter's imagination. There was no way that Hunter would ever have allowed Astrid such a tacky choice to such a classy event. But Tiffany, she knew, just didn't care.

The dresses were all skin-tight, low-cut and halter-neck, and came just to the top of the thigh, barely enough to preserve modesty. Each dress was finished with cream detailing around the bust and at the neck and hem. They also had latex suspender belts, as well as latex stockings that stretched from their thighs to their ankles and went around their feet with a discrete strap. Add a pair of 6-inch spike heels to the mix and the look was complete. Hunter imagined that they would look a bit like an erotic ninja cabaret from a slightly suspect seventies B-movie. And she loved it.

Glancing towards her clock, Hunter was shocked to realise and how much time had passed since she had become lost in her thoughts. Immediately, she took a deep, determined breath and resumed her preparations for the event of the century.

Some miles north of Edinburgh, Marissa was no less busy in preparing for her employers' wedding. Hovering by her side was Tiffany, who found herself wondering, for the thousandth time, what she would do without this wonderful woman. She kept waiting for one of the events at The Hall to be just that bit too debauched or risqué for her housekeeper. She worried about the day that something would push Marissa over the edge and have her running for the door. Thankfully, it had not happened yet.

Tiffany was so excited she could hardly concentrate. She was more excited about the upcoming ceremony than she had been for her *actual* wedding. She'd loved marrying Richard of course, and it had been beautiful and classic. But it had also been contrived and conservative. They had been married back in Indiana, and try as she might to love her state, she really struggled with the narrow-minded, right-wing attitude of some people there. She knew that nowhere was perfect, and every country, including the one she currently lived in, had its problems. But she really thought that the 'Good Old' U. S. of A' took the biscuit for bigotry and wanton stupidity. And that was even before the hairy Cheeto with syphilitic dementia had been elected.

Oh, how things had changed for her since her move to Scotland. She had been so confident – so American! – back then. She'd just marched right up to people and clapped them on the shoulder wherever she happened to find herself. Luckily this had been in Glasgow, a city even more garrulous and gregarious than the USA. She'd hit it off with her three university 'mates' immediately.

Back then, she had been by far the most conservative of the four friends. Only hours after they had first met, Darcey had suggested they go for a drink together. But Tiffany had politely declined, saying she had to go and find her church, so that she knew where she could go to pray. It was a miracle they hadn't dropped her right there and then.

Although Tiffany was apt to complain about Scotland, she was perfectly aware that her life had become infinitely better since she arrived there. Not only had it introduced her to the three most perfect women in the world, but she had also been able to shake off the shackles of religion, choosing instead to worship at the altar of sex, wine, and fun. Dionysus himself would have been proud. Now, *now* the brash, goody-goody cheerleader was to have her very own 'Story of O' style latex wedding. *Screw you Indiana!* she thought, as she made her way to her bathroom to begin her transformation. *And Scotland? Who loves ya, baby.*

*

Following one of the longest days of her working life, Hunter finally arrived at The Hall around dusk. Even at that time in the evening the sweet spring air was like a rebirth. The scent of lilac floated on the air, and pollen swirled like confetti in the breeze – very appropriate, Hunter thought, given the upcoming wedding. It looked like they were going to be spectacularly lucky with the weather. There were contingencies in place, just in case it had tipped it down the whole weekend, but she was elated that it looked like nothing was going to spoil Tiffany's big day.

The Hall and the grounds were decorated to perfection. Pink and white flowers arranged in plinths everywhere, beautiful pastel satin ribbon trimmed pergolas shading numerous well-stocked and elegant bars, and a large ivory marquee which was visible towards the back of The Hall. The grounds were also dotted with various paraphernalia that hinted at some serious games for tomorrow. There were many walkways lined with unlit torches and the hot tub was in the process of being thoroughly cleaned by enthusiastic attendants.

Hunter carried her case inside and climbed the stairs to one of the many guest bedrooms. Her name had been calligraphed in pink lettering onto a sign on the door. That evening was intentionally informal – guests were welcome to arrive at any time from early afternoon – so wine had been left in ice buckets downstairs in the drawing room along with numerous canapés and sandwiches. Once the guests had settled into their rooms, the rest of the day was theirs to do as they pleased. The Hall's snooker room, the Stables' bar, the sauna on the grounds by the lake; all were open for business. Hunter, though, wasn't interested in any of these distractions; she simply wanted to find Tiffany and share in her anticipation of her big day.

Hunter heard Tiffany before she saw her, though this was hardly surprising as she had already been joined by the human foghorn that was Astrid. The two women were reclining on the four-poster in the enormous master bedroom, laughing uproariously. They were dressed in matching oyster-pink kimonos, the same one that she herself owned, and which she had worn at the hotel with him.

'Hunter!' Tiffany exclaimed, leaping from the bed to embrace her friend. The wine Hunter had brought from Edinburgh was clearly not going to be her friend's first drink of the evening. Everything about Tiffany seemed to sparkle, it was like someone had thrown a fine dusting of pink glitter into the air. She was a princess. Astrid, meanwhile, waved over to Hunter from the spot on the mattress; she was midway through painting her toenails a vivid purple.

'Well, here it is!' Hunter said, matching Tiffany's enthusiasm. 'Your most fabulous day. How do you feel?'

Tiffany squealed. 'Like I'm going to die with excitement!' She reached over to her desk and picked up a distinctive pink box wrapped in thick black ribbon. 'Before you sit down and get comfortable, this is for you.'

Hunter looked at her friend questioningly.

'I hope you don't mind,' Tiffany said. 'I just loved it when I saw you wearing it in the hotel at New Year.'

'A kimono?' Hunter asked. 'My god, of course I don't mind. But you really didn't need to get me another.'

'Ah but I did,' Tiffany said, beaming. 'Turn it around.'

Hunter did. And there on the back, handstitched in iridescent cream thread, were the words 'Lady Diana.'

'Oh my god,' Hunter said, grinning. She wriggled out of her skirt and blouse and threw on the robe with all the

225

flourish of a matador. 'These are fabulous!' she said. 'Oh, I can't wait to see Darcey in hers.'
Tiffany smiled slightly uneasily. 'Okay, so full disclosure there's someone -'

'It's okay,' Hunter said, cutting her off mid-sentence. 'I know what you're going to say. But it's fine. I knew he was going to be here, and I've prepared myself fully. So please, don't worry about me. This is *your* day, and you do *not* need to be thinking about anyone but yourself.'

'Where's Darcey?' Astrid asked. Nails painted, she had set about pouring Hunter's wine into three disturbingly large glasses. 'Shouldn't she be here by now?'

'Late surgery,' Hunter said. 'Last I heard she was not having a good day. Ripped a liver first thing this morning and then had two back-to-back something disgusting's this afternoon. But don't worry. She called me a couple of hours ago to let me know her dress has been packed and she'll be here by midnight at the latest.'

Astrid shook her head admiringly. 'I don't know how she does it,' she said. 'She must be permanently exhausted.'

'She's certainly a trooper,' Hunter agreed.

'Before I forget,' Tiffany said. 'You three will all have a few extra little parts to play in tomorrow's festivities. The main event notwithstanding of course.'

'Really?' Hunter asked, excited and nervous in equal measure. 'What will we be doing?'

Tiffany tapped the side of her nose. 'All will be revealed in due course,' she said. 'All I need is for you to follow the plans that will be in your rooms.'

'Plans?' Astrid asked. She looked to Hunter, who simply shrugged. 'I didn't see any plans in my room.'

'Don't worry, Richard's writing everything up now. You'll have your instructions by bedtime.'

Hunter had to laugh, then. 'Shouldn't the groom be doing something less administrative on his last night of freedom?' 'If only,' Tiffany said, rolling her eyes. 'He's treating this entire event like a full-on cinematic production. Believe me, he's leaving *nothing* to chance.'

'Well,' Astrid said, fluffing her hair. 'Now that the *admin's* out of the way, I am off to use my Trigger finger.'

'*Trigger's* here?' Hunter said. She hadn't meant to speak the thought aloud, but the mention of Richard's friend had hit her like a kick in the ass. 'Why on earth does that man keep getting invited to these things? I mean, I know he's Richard's friend but... ugh!'

Astrid looked to Hunter, tickled by her friend's disgust. 'Be nice,' she said.

'Indeed,' Tiffany said, giving a mock frown to Hunter. 'Trigger might not be your favourite person, but he's not all bad. He's like... I don't know, an over-excited Labrador or something. His heart is in the right place, even if he is a bit thick.'

'Well, it takes all sorts, I suppose,' Hunter said, though she didn't believe a word of it. 'Anyway, Tiffany, I'd best head off too. Unless you need me, of course?'

Tiffany shook her head. 'Off you go. Any more wine and I'll have a thick head for tomorrow.'
Astrid gave a yawn, and then a stretch. 'Should one of us maybe wait up for Darcey?' she asked, sleepily.
'No need,' Hunter said. 'Peter is here, and on 'high alert' or 'def con seven' or whatever the hell it is. I'm quite certain he'll wait for Darcey before heading off to bed himself.'

A fleeting look of unease, so quick that under any other circumstances Hunter would have sworn she hadn't seen it, skittered across Tiffany's features. Something was clearly afoot. Hunter hoped it was to do with Darcey being late, and not knowing about the extra wee surprises for the next day, and not something more serious, but she was not convinced.

'Well, good night, ladies,' Astrid said as she bounced out of the room and down the corridor to do unspeakable things to an unspeakable man. 'See you at the wedding.'

Hunter followed a moment later down the long hallway, the silk of her robe fanning out behind her like she was on a Parisian catwalk. Now and then, she heard a burst of laughter from behind one or another bedroom door. All the other guests had clearly arrived without incident.

As Hunter reached her own door, she wondered what else the weekend had in store for them all. She dearly hoped everyone would have a wonderful time, but the look she had seen pass over Tiffany's face a few moments ago had left an uneasy feeling in her mind. She took her phone from her pocket and sent Darcey a text to let her know her door would be open all night *if* she needed her. As she pressed 'send,' she said a silent prayer that her worries were all for nothing.

The Day

"I want to do to you what spring does to the cherry trees."

Pablo Neruda

The moment Hunter's eyes snapped open; she could feel the excitement vibrating through The Hall. The pre-emptive atmosphere of the day was akin to a graduation. Perhaps, more accurately, a passage into something more profound, like freedom. Many people would find this ironic for an S&M wedding, but not Hunter.

It certainly didn't feel like a wedding, more like a coming of age, a flowering. This, she reflected, as she rose and stretched, could be something to do with the flower garlands that they were all expected to wear for the first part of the ceremony. Hers was sitting on the overly-pink, overly-girly dressing table. The latex would come later; as evening descended the darker festivities would begin. The nymphs of light would become demons in the night. But the day, the day was to be a sun-filled celebration of innocence.

Hunter could barely contain her amusement at the intended irony of this; Richard was many things, but he was certainly not subtle. Regardless, the freedom and exuberance of the day promised to be enlivening. As she switched on the shower, Hunter looked out of the bathroom window and was pleased to note that the spring sunshine of the day before had not simply been a tease, but a satisfying seduction.

The Day

Hunter stepped out into the bright sunlight and squinted through her elegant Chanel sunglasses. She'd chosen white frames to complement her first required outfit of the day. All the women present had been specifically instructed to wear white diaphanous dresses. The prerequisite that they had to be floaty, sexy, and –above all – *cheap* had greatly amused Hunter. She suspected that she knew why. They wouldn't last the day, not unlike some of the guests.

The flower garland she had placed atop her head as the final flourish to her outfit was not her usual style, but this was Tiffany's day, and she would have turned up in a twinset and pearls if it would have made Tiffany happy. The party was to take place at the rear of The Hall in the private walled grounds, away from prying eyes. An open-sided marquee had been set up and was adorned with pale pink satin sashes, which were surprisingly subtle for Tiffany. Hunter could already see efficient white-tuxedoed waiters pouring pale rosé wine into crystal glasses and arranging stands of pink frosted cupcakes.

As she neared the marquee, Hunter caught sight of Steward. He was already having a ball, chatting up some gorgeous young waiter. But – Hunter did a double take – she *knew* that waiter, had spoken to him countless times over her weekend at the windmill with him. *My god*, she thought. *Clever boy.* Hunter smiled and shook her head in disbelief, though deep down she knew she shouldn't be *too* surprised. After all, people with their slightly twisted darkness usually gravitated towards one another in the end. She smiled and waved in greeting, which brought a reciprocal wave from Steward and a disbelieving gasp from the boy. Hunter laughed. This was going to be even more fun than she'd thought! And good for Steward; he deserved someone nice for a change.

She continued to wander around, determined to enjoy the beauty of her surroundings before the inevitable bacchanal destroyed it. It truly was a beautiful day; dandelion heads danced in the gentle breeze, the spring sunshine bathed her bare shoulders in a warm honey glow. She has just begun to debate with herself whether it was too early for Pimm's when a deep voice purred at her ear.

'Hello.'

The world froze. Hunter felt as though she'd been struck by lightning. She had known he was coming of course, had been preparing herself for this moment for weeks. In the end though, her preparations had amounted to precisely nothing. The breath left her lungs and an overwhelming feeling of regret flooded through her. No, not just regret, regret tinged at the edges, with fear.

Out of this internal maelstrom she managed a cool 'Hello' in response. She shivered as sadness settled over her like a fine mist.

Hunter's mind was reeling. Just one word from his mouth was enough to reignite the conflict within her. For all her distrust and even fear of him, she still wanted him, and she loathed that she did. Her mind screamed no, but her body sobbed yes.

She had barely collected herself to respond before he handed her a delicate China cup. Without thinking, she took it from him, and immediately hated herself for doing so.

The clear pink liquid that slid down her throat was offputtingly warm. She had expected wine. But no, it was some sort of... tea? She had put herself at risk without pause. *So much for fight or flight,* she thought, as she stared into the cup as if trying to conjure the contents back from the bottom.

'Delicious, isn't it? Our consummate hostess is serving a little pre-game hibiscus tea to help those less hardcore than *us* keep up with the drinking.' He had stressed the *us* with a smile. Hunter wasn't sure if it was a reference to the two of them or a joke at the expense of those outside the inner circle, who clearly didn't have the stamina.

Her gaze travelled inexorably and involuntarily downwards, and she almost drooled at the obvious bulge in his trousers. She remembered what his cock could to do to her. All the delicious ways it had tamed her. And that curve, that curve that touched places no other men ever had. But every time she thought about returning to him, she thought of the look on Morticia's face as she told her, and she imagined the pain the girl would have suffered. He was dangerous, and she had to remember that. She knew that she couldn't. Not ever. She felt sick.

He seemed to sense her thoughts.

'You're still mine. However, you fight it, you don't have the power to break the bond we forged.'

At this assumed arrogance, white hot rage scythed through her. She comprehended, suddenly, as she felt a flush in her face and between her legs, that he'd put something aphrodisiac in her tea. Unable to maintain her discipline, she let a gasp of realisation escape her lips. She knew by his smile that he had understood that she had guessed what he had done to her. Panic blossomed in her chest, as adrenalin surged thorough her body.

'How dare you.' She breathed, shaking with rage, fear, and although she would die before she would ever admit it, visceral lust. She knew she should be terrified, but although panic and fear seasoned her thoughts, the darkness that was part of her was fed by this uncertainty, by the possibility of torture and pain. She lived for these games.

'You see, you are mine. You love this life as much as I do. You need it. You drank that tea before you'd even had a chance to think. I could have put *anything* in there and you would have drunk it down willingly.'

However else she felt about him, he never failed to touch something inside her. But she couldn't have it and it broke her heart. Desire like this was a fucking curse. She looked straight at him, trying to seem in control. Breathing in and out slowly, trying to calm her nervous system. Something she often had to do when their games reached their apex. 'That's… not true,' Hunter gasped, but even as she said the words, she knew he was right. 'And I don't need *you*.' Though her body, as ever, betrayed her words, she so wanted to mean every single thing she had said.

If he had heard Hunter's words, he pretended not to. 'Enjoy the day, Venatrix,' He said in his low deep growl. And with that, he turned and walked leisurely away, a Lord surveying his grounds.

The Day

Hunter hated to admit it to herself, but even the sound and shape of his voice had been enough to make her thighs stick together. Her delicate La Perla thong was already ruined. And he had put an aphrodisiac in her tea? What a monster! But what a Master... Fuck knows where he had got something that genuinely worked. It was probably illegal and from one of his many trips to Asia. Provided it wasn't actually something like cantharidin, perhaps she would survive the day.

They didn't just swim in the same pool of depravity, they experienced the world in the same way. No. She had to put a stop to those thoughts right there. She would not let him know how he had affected her. Now that the initial unavoidable jolt of desire had come and gone, she would maintain better control of herself. She had to. She just had to think of some way to ignore the effects of the drug. She was strong and she could do this. And if all else failed, surely Darcey would have something she could use. *Did they make an anti-Viagra?* she wondered, as she walked, somewhat dizzily, in search of her friends.

*

One of Richard's favourite toys was an original seventeenth century cannon, which he liked to show off to anybody and everybody who visited The Hall. It was natural, then, that he had decided to kick off the wedding weekend by using the cannon to fire a piece of each guest's underwear over the walled garden. Unconventional, for sure, but this was an unconventional wedding. Only the usual suspects had been invited, and none of them were likely to be surprised

235

by such an eccentric start to the ceremony. In any case, it certainly beat a bloody hymn.

Still, that was a hell of a lot of underwear. It reminded Hunter of Tiffany's Hen Party in Las Vegas. They were booked in to see Tom Jones at the MGM Grand on their second night, and Hunter had purchased a beautiful thong specifically to toss at him. On the night, though, her throw had proved significantly weaker than she'd imagined it to be, and the thong had landed on the head of an enormous bald guy about four rows in front. Astrid had nearly burst a lung from laughing.

Hunter found Astrid and Darcey on the back lawn, where the guests were starting to congregate. With the women all in white and the men in pastel deck shorts and polo shirts, it looked like a bloody prep school reunion, although admittedly one of the more exclusive ones. Hunter was desperate to talk to Darcey, but she wanted to do so alone, and knew she'd have to wait until the break between the 'Day' and 'Night' events. Richard, she knew, had filled the next 24 hours far too full of ridiculous set pieces to allow for anything as inane as regular conversation to take place.

The moment Darcey set eyes on Hunter, she sighed. 'Hunter how is it you've managed to make a cheap white dress look like it was bloody made for you. I look like I've borrowed my big sister's muumuu.' Darcey tended to stick to severely tight clothing to show her minimal curves to the best of their advantage, but her day dress was leaning toward the baggy. Astrid, meanwhile, looked like a small white lampshade. She was also wearing the most enormous, oversized sunglasses Hunter had ever seen. Darcey was more stylishly attired in small, classy frames. Hunter had cheated a bit and gone for a dress which was sexily slinky, but it did have a skirt with a handkerchief hem that made it just diaphanous enough to pass.

'Darcey, you look great,' Hunter stated in a tone that brooked no argument.

Darcey rolled her eyes. 'I look like a parachute, Hunter. *You* look like the lovechild of Jessica Rabbit and Grace Kelly.'

Hunter laughed. 'Well, if I'm Grace Kelly, then you're our very own Audrey Hepburn.'

'And I'm Tempest Storm,' Astrid said excitedly with a giggle. 'And Tiffany obviously, has to be Marilyn.' And with that, she threw on a pout, and she struck Marilyn's famous 'holding down her dress' pose.

The friends were still laughing when the big double doors of The Hall opened to reveal the happy couple. Tiffany practically glided onto the lawn. Her dress was floaty and pastel pink, her long blonde hair loose and woven with flowers - Astrid's handiwork, Hunter was told in a proud half whisper. Richard was wearing a waistcoat in a matching pink and could not have looked more like the cat who got the cream if he'd arrived dressed as a furry. There was a general quietening of voices as the guests turned to where the couple were waiting.

'Good morning, everyone!' Richard boomed. 'And welcome to the wedding of the century. The more outrageous and ostentatious you can make today the better! Seriously, all bets are off this weekend, and we have engineered a good few surprises for everyone. So, unless you're specifically required in one of the ceremonies –'

One of? thought Hunter; in the same moment, she caught Richard throw a discreet wink towards Astrid.
'– you are welcome to be as depraved and imaginative as possible! So, on that note, and without further ado – underwear please!'
There was a ripple of laughter as people started pulling underwear from shirt pockets, purses and, in Astrid's case, her cleavage. One of the women across from them simply lifted her dress and removed the thong she was wearing, much to the delight of her escort.

Hunter took the opportunity to survey the rest of the guests. Her waiter from the weekend, and the current object of Steward's affections, appeared at her elbow with a silver tray. She smiled what she hoped was a reassuring hello, and he grinned back. Then he continued to make his way through the crowd, inviting the women to deposit their underwear on the tray.

The first burst of cannon fire drew gasps and whoops from the crowd, all of whom tried to catch the scraps of cotton, satin, and lace as they rained down on them. There was a lot of good-natured guesses as to whose scraps were whose. It took a good six blasts from Richard's cannon to get through all of it. Much to the amusement of the staff who dutifully collected the detritus from all over the lawn, to appreciative applause from the guests. What they must have been thinking Hunter could only guess.

After the underwear had been retrieved, it was time for the next event, the 'Ritual Sacrifice'. This part of the ceremony had 'Richard' written all over it. It was to take place at an old rock that sat in the very centre of the grounds at The Hall. Richard liked to have people believe it was akin to something from Stonehenge, but really it was just a large stone, too big and too ancient to be moved without a lot of fuss. Today, however, it was to be the setting for a bit of kinky entertainment.

For the sacrifice, Richard said, he required 'the four most beautiful Maenads present', and with that he invited the bride, Hunter, Astrid, and Darcey to join him by the rock. The four women were instructed to stand with their backs against the stone, and to lift their hands as high above their heads as possible. At this point, it became clear that Astrid was far too short to take part in the ritual. Almost immediately, another woman volunteered as sacrifice. Hunter noted that it was the same woman who had whipped her knickers off for the opening ceremony. *So naïve,* Hunter thought. She only suspected what would happen next, but she had enough experience at The Hall to realise their dresses were not long for this world.

The rock was roughly four sided, so each woman was facing outwards and towards around a quarter of the guests, who stood around them in a circle. The women's' wrists were firmly bound with beautiful Japanese silk rope. They were then tied to each other, before the master tie was hooked over the top of the rock itself. By now, there really was no escape.

Hunter had gasped in pleasure as she felt the rope slide across her skin like a satin kiss. And now she was getting more and more turned on by the second. Smiling, she closed her eyes and…

Oh no! Amidst all the excitement, she had completely forgotten to ask Darcey what could be done to counteract the drug he'd given her. And now it was too late. She could feel herself succumbing to even the smallest stimulus, her entire body tingling as though it was slipping into a warm liquid. This was going to be a nightmare. She was starting to tremble. *God girl. Get. It. Together.* She breathed deeply and repeated the mantra in her head even as her pulse increased, and her thighs began pressing together involuntarily. She looked up and found his eyes on her, as she knew they would be. Unsurprisingly, he was already enjoying the show. Their eyes locked, and the intensity of their attraction would have brought Hunter crashing to the floor, were it not for the silk restraining her, and the persistent warning in her head. Instead, her desire started to pulse between her legs.

Suddenly, Richard stepped forward with a showman's flourish. He bowed deeply to the women, and then turned and did the same to his guests.

'Jesus Christ,' Darcey whispered. She was on Hunter's left, and Tiffany was centre stage on the right. No Knickers was between Darcey and Tiffany, invisible to Hunter from her angle. 'What's that he's holding?'

'A bayonet,' Hunter whispered back, thankful to Darcey for the distraction.

'A *what*?'

'It's authentic,' Hunter said. 'A World War One original; he showed me once before. But don't worry. It's for Tiffany.'

'Of course it is…' Darcey said.

The two friends fell silent. Richard had just embarked on yet another little speech. God, if there ever a man who was in love with his own voice, it was him.

Darcey's eyes were riveted on the bayonet, obviously anticipating some sort of mishap. Although quite what she thought she could do in such an event was beyond Hunter, and she found herself giggling at the thought. Good god, was she drunk? What the hell was *in* that tea?

Finally, mercifully, Richard finished talking and turned slowly towards the women. He walked towards his wife, weapon outstretched. *Freud really would have a field day here,* Hunter thought and started giggling again. Her strapless dress was already starting to ride down because of the position she was in, and if she kept giggling it would be round her waist in no time. The thought made her imagine him striding through the throng of guests and sucking her nipples as she stood bound and helpless. She closed her eyes and tried to think of something else, *anything* else.

'My love,' Richard said. 'Do you submit to be my sacrifice?'

'I do,' Tiffany replied breathlessly.

With that, he took the bayonet above his head and in a quick but practiced movement, he cut Tiffany's dress from cleavage to ankle. It fell in two glorious puddles at her feet. The crowd were momentarily blinded; then, as one, they gasped. Tiffany was covered from head to toe in pink Swarovski crystals shining, iridescent, in the sun. The jewels kissed her naked skin in swirls, making stunning designs that centred around her amazing curves and spiralled into her nipples. She was magnificent. Richard kissed her deeply.

'Gentlemen!' Richard roared, gesturing towards the three other bound women with the bayonet. 'Volunteers?' Richard returned to caressing his wife as a waiter stepped forward with a tray holding three very sharp-looking Sgian Dubhs. Immediately, the men began jockeying for the privilege.

Despite herself, Hunter still wanted desperately for him to choose her. She wanted him to slice through every stitch of her dress, to watch as it pooled at her feet and she opened her legs to him. In her mind she was powerless to stop him. She imagined him plunging into her as he thrust her hard against the rock with an animal roar. She wanted to feel the stone cut into the skin of her back, to feel the bite of the rope on her wrists as he fucked her harder and harder. She imagined him holding his knife at her throat as he took her, his other hand gripping the flesh of her thigh hard enough to leave bruises. She could feel his rhythm in her mind, could feel the heat between her thighs. All it took to break down all of her defences was a cup of aphrodisiac tea and a look. Fear evaporated off her with each passing moment, replaced with white hot desire.

His eyes remained locked on hers. Hunter drank in every sinew of his body, her want so strong it practically thrummed in the air. She felt herself sinking down and might well have fallen if her wrists had not been so securely bound. It was all she could do not to cry.

Hunter's ardour was not lost on Steward. He was watching her and could clearly see how much she wanted him. He understood the desire, and the dynamic of the relationship Hunter so clearly needed. He dreamed of a relationship just like it, if only he could find a young man willing and eager to be his submissive. *Maybe one day*, he thought as he watched the spectacle unfold, pretending to himself he wasn't looking around for the waiter from earlier. He vowed that he'd find the object of Hunter's desire later in the evening and have it out with him. *Those two*, he knew, needed one another, and he felt certain that only something completely ridiculous or totally irrelevant was keeping them apart. Hunter's pride probably.

It was then that Steward realised that no one had moved to release Hunter from her shackles. Peter had been first through the throng, practically knocking people over to get to his wife. A little gauche, Steward felt, even in this setting. One of the other chaps, a bloke he'd met once or twice in Cambridge, was attending to Jessica. But Hunter was still tied up and completely clothed. *He's clearly not going to move*, Steward thought to himself, *well, I'm nothing if not a gentleman.*

Hunter was in agony. Not only was she hornier than she'd ever been in her entire life, she was also tied up and unable to do anything about it. He was clearly refusing to come to her rescue. He just stared at her, a wolverine smile playing on his lips. *Bastard.* She would not give him the satisfaction of requesting his help.

Damn. she thought, *how am I supposed to get out of this?* There was certainly no question of any other man coming to her rescue. Everyone else was keeping well away, probably assuming she still belonged to him. He was certainly imposing enough that no one would challenge him, or dream of approaching his woman. His ownership was always total.

With all of the guests either admiring Tiffany's spectacular body art or watching as the other two women were divested of their dresses, she was just about to whisper over to Richard for some assistance when Steward strode forward, brandishing the final knife from the tray. 'Not to worry sweetheart…your prince charming has arrived.'

'Oh, thank god!' she replied smiling. 'This is a first, though. Having my clothes ripped off by a gay man!'

Steward laughed. Then, reaching forward, he cut through Hunter's dress so skilfully that it fell in half around her. She looked like Botticelli's Venus emerging from her clam shell, a fact that was not lost on the guests, who applauded with appreciation.

Hunter took a couple of steps from the stone and kissed Steward on the cheek in heartfelt thanks. 'Well, that wasn't so bad,' she said playfully.

Hunter knew that he was still watching her. She had the sudden desire to stick her tongue out at him, but she refrained. She even found herself able to peel her eyes from him for more than a second at a time. *Ah-ha* she realised. *The aphrodisiac must be wearing off.* Thank the lord. Now at least she could enjoy the rest of the day without making a spectacle of herself by drooling all over him.

All four women had now been safely removed from their confinement. While Tiffany was literally sparking in the sun, a naked Jessica was loving every second of attention. Darcey, meanwhile, looked achingly elegant in a strapless white bathing suit. Even though she was dressed so demurely, Peter was still hovering protectively close, and he hadn't given the knife back either. He was failing so spectacularly in his bullying efforts to be the alpha male that Hunter almost felt sorry for him. Almost.

It took some time, but Richard finally managed to pry himself away from a breathless Tiffany. By then, Hunter noticed, more than a few of Tiffany's gems were stuck to the crotch of his shorts. He led his prisoners from the stone and towards a tray of champagne glasses. Steward held Hunter's glass decorously as she massaged some life back into her wrists.

'Spectacular as ever, my dear,' Steward said.

'Thanks.' As she took her glass of champagne, she looked over to Darcey and Peter, who were deep in animated conversation. Storm clouds were brewing over there. She was considering whether to interrupt them when Astrid came bounding over to her.

'Well, I'm bloody jealous that I missed out on that! Should have worn higher heels!'

'Next time honey. Wait, Astrid, you realise you're drinking a mocktail right?' Hunter asked, as she noticed the creamy pink creation in the hurricane glass.

'What? Really? Shit, I thought it was some sort of a Mai Tae.' She looked disappointedly down into her glass. Then she grinned.

'Why do they call them mocktails?'
'Oh, I don't know, because they're making a mockery of the sacred art of drinking?' Hunter said returning her smile.

'No, I mean clearly they should be called cock-teases not mocktails! Obviously. It's exactly what you want, but you just can't have it!'

Hunter and Steward both laughed.

'Oh well done dear! Cock-Tease it is. Yes, I will definitely be using that instead in the future.' Steward said with a grin.
'I'm sure you will!' Hunter winked back at him. 'So, what now? 'I'm sure there's plenty more fun in store for us.'

'You're rootin' tootin' right there is!' Astrid squealed. 'And this time it's all about me. Come on, you two – I'm the croquet!'

Steward and Hunter looked at each other with the same question in their eyes; *She's the croquet?*

As soon as they reached the croquet pitch, Hunter and Steward found the answer to their question. There, at its very centre, was Astrid, stripped to her underwear and being staked to the lawn at her wrists and ankles with croquet hoops.

'Well, this should be interesting,' Darcey said, as she appeared at Hunter's elbow.

'Fabulous,' Hunter laughed. 'But… what the hell?'

'She's the scoreboard,' Darcey explained. 'Look, you write on her with those Henna pens.'

'Henna? That's going to leave quite the mark.'
Darcey raised an eyebrow. 'I think that's the idea.'

'Well, this should be a good game,' Steward said. Then, with a small bow and a mumbled apology, he set off for the pitch. Darcey turned to Hunter. 'Fancy it?'

Hunter shook her head. 'I think I'll just enjoy the sun for a bit before the next game. In any case, I haven't a clue how to play. So, Darcey…?'
Hunter was just about to ask her friend about the Society and Marissa – who, come to think of it, was conspicuously absent today – and all the other thousand questions she had for her when, suddenly, she froze. For there, not ten yards away, and hanging off his arm, was her replacement. The air left her lungs, and it was all she could do not to drop to her knees on the ground. Stammering, she looked to

Darcey, but Darcey had already followed her gaze and was now staring, open mouthed, at the couple.

It was scant consolation that her replacement looked like an uninitiated's idea of a submissive. She was weak and girlish, almost waif-like. *He could break her with barely a word,* she thought as tears threatened. *But perhaps that was the appeal.* She thought the pain she had felt at New Year was the worst it could be. She had been wrong. The remains of the aphrodisiac, which had kept her buoyed for the past hour, instantly turned her insides cold. She turned around and vomited spectacularly into the shrubbery behind her.

Darcey immediately sprang to Hunter's side and drew her subtly away from the croquet pitch and the prying eyes of gossiping guests. Hunter's only consolation was that he didn't see her misery; he hadn't even noticed her watching him, just sailed past, oblivious to the wreckage in his wake.

'It's ok,' Darcey said, rubbing Hunter's back. 'Just breathe. Get it all out. Get everything out.' Hunter wasn't sure whether Darcey was referring to the residual contents of her stomach or any remaining feelings she still had for him. 'Come on,' Darcey said, gently. 'Look at me.'

Hunter did as she was asked. 'God,' she began, taking in a great lungful of air. 'I'm sorry. I don't know… I didn't…' 'You are fucking better than this,' Darcey shouted. Tears were threatening to fall from her own eyes as well. She glanced towards the croquet pitch, ready to shoo away any guests who were eager to join their little drama, but fortunately everybody's attention seemed to be on the match. Apparently, and unsurprisingly, this was the 'strip' version. Already, many of the men were shirtless and some were also short-less.

Hunter took a deep steadying breath. Darcey was right. She *was* better than this. She was also sick of this. Literally. She was tired of all the ridiculous back and forth, tired of the pathetic soap opera that their relationship had become. And the *games*! She was so, *so* over the games. And this latest game was the *worst*! To do what he had done to her, say what he had said, and the whole time he had brought someone else. *The sick bastard.*

'Okay, sweetie,' Darcey said. 'When are you next involved with the events?'

Hunter tried to think. 'Me? Oh, uh… not until this evening. I think… The big finale. I think all the afternoon stuff is down to the men now. But…'

Darcey considered this, then nodded resolutely. 'Okay.' She looked Hunter straight in the eye. 'You're coming upstairs with me. I'll get you an IV and we can spend a couple of hours just… being *us*.'

Hunter stared woozily at her friend. 'Did you say IV? As in hospital IV?'

Darcey nodded. 'I brought a few. Excellent for a hangover and I knew what today was going to be. Come on. Let's get you into a bath or something and I'll hook you up. Then you and I are going to get ready. I'm going to make sure you are so sparkling tonight that *nothing* can bring you down.'

Despite her pain, Hunter was thrilled that she and Darcey would get some proper time together this afternoon. 'But won't Peter mind?' she asked.

Darcey shut her eyes and sighed. 'Peter can go fuck himself.'

Oh, thought Hunter. *Yikes. Okay, so we'll forget about him for a while. By the sounds of things, we should probably start by talking about what's really going on in Darcey's marriage.*

Hunter was a little disappointed to be leaving the afternoon party so early, but she knew that Darcey was right. She would need her armour tonight. She was going to make sure she looked so fucking fabulous that no one could touch her.

The Night

"Certain souls may seem harsh to others, but it is just a way, beknownst only to them, of caring and feeling more deeply."

Marquis de Sade

Darcey had disappeared. She had put Hunter in the bath, hooked her up to the IV, given her a brandy to calm both her nerves and her stomach, and left. Hunter had even had to take the needle out of her arm herself once the IV had done its job. She knew something had happened, as there was no *way* that Darcey would just leave her there. She was disappointed, and not a little concerned.

Hunter was stuck. She wasn't sure whether she should try to find Darcey or go and find Astrid instead. Astrid, she presumed, was still outside with those revellers who had carried on partying beyond the day ceremony. She could hear them from her window, drinking and dancing and, from the sounds of things, even enjoying the occasional fuck. Yes, thought Hunter. Astrid would still be outside. There was no way she would want to miss out on the fun.

In the end, Hunter decided to remain in her room. Darcey was a big girl, and Hunter had every faith that she could look after herself. She would do as Darcey had said; take some time to relax and get ready. When the time came to go down for dinner, she was sure to find Darcey waiting for her.

251

Vice

*

At the same moment that Hunter was slipping into her dinner dress, Steward was on his way to confront Hunter's previous paramour. He was already dressed for dinner, in clothes that would have screamed the word 'dapper' had that not been incredibly crass, therefore whispered it discretely instead. He may be en route to fix his friend's love life, but he certainly wasn't going to attempt to do so badly dressed. Standards existed for a reason after all. He stepped outside of The Hall to find the torches lit, and the grounds wrapped in an ethereal glow that seemed to have been borrowed from 'A Midsummer Night's Dream'. By some small miracle the temperature had held, and the sun was still a little way from setting. The whole atmosphere could not have been more perfect.

Steward wasn't remotely sure where to begin his search, but he didn't take the man for a convivial pre-dinner whisky and snooker kind of chap and felt certain he'd have given The Stables a wide berth. However, Steward knew that another little bar had been set up in the wooded area towards the back of The Hall, which seemed to be far more his sort of thing. *It's as good a place as any, I suppose,* Steward thought. And with that, he set off.

Stewart was still puzzling over how he should broach the subject of Hunter with a rather intimidating man he barely knew, when he became aware of raised voices. Not wanting to commit a faux pas by trespassing into someone else's argument, he thought it best to announce himself, but something about the tone of the dominant voice held him back.

'I heard that, you stupid whore,' it said. 'Stop making it worse. In fact, just stop speaking.'

Steward had stopped, discretely hidden from their sight by the side of the bar he had been looking for. He could see that the bar was unstaffed, but some cocktails had been laid out and the ice was still solid, so he assumed the bartender wasn't far away.

'You told me not to tell anyone and I haven't,' said the second voice. 'But what if it happens again? I hate that woman, but if his bitches keep dying, someone's bound to notice eventually.'

Steward wasn't surprised to find that the voices belonged to Nicholas and Stephanie; after all, they had never been the happiest couple, and were both prone to fits of temper. What had surprised him was the sheer level of vitriol and loathing with which they were addressing one another. But what the hell were they talking about?

'I'm only thinking of you, darling,' Stephanie said. Her tone was suddenly sweet and almost plaintive. 'You're well-known associates in certain circles. This could damage you, too. After all, you were there, you even...'

Steward peeked around the side of the bar just in time to see Nicholas strike his wife hard across the face. Stephanie fell backwards and landed heavily in the grass, tearing her satin dress on the root of a tree. 'If you ever mention this again, you know what will happen,' Nicholas snarled. And with that, he turned on his heel and stalked off.

With the sound of the slap still ringing through the woods around them, Steward strode forward to Stephanie's aid.

'My goodness my dear, what on earth has happened?' he asked, all solicitation, giving no hint that he had heard the exchange.

Stephanie accepted his arm and allowed herself to be pulled up. 'That bastard,' she spat.

'Shall I speak to him, darling?'

'No! No. I knew what I was getting into when I married him. I will *not* give him the satisfaction.'

'My dear, no man has the right to do any such thing to you. Ever. Husband or no'

Stephanie looked to her appearance, setting the folds of her dress right. She looked so full of sadness and resignation that Steward, never known to be at a loss for words, suddenly found himself speechless.

'I chose this,' Stephanie continued more confidently, raising her eyes to his. 'I know what you're going to say and you're right, but I knew the price.'

Steward shook his head. 'It doesn't have to be this way. You have so many options. If you'll let me –'

'No.' She held up both of her hands.

Steward sighed sadly. He knew he could say nothing that would convince Stephanie to accept his help. The woman had a core of iron. 'Alright,' he said. 'I'm sorry. Can I at least get you a drink?'

He took two of the cocktails from the bar and handed one to Stephanie. 'Look, I'm not going to push, but I confess I heard a little of the argument that preceded Nicholas' disgrace. Please, what was it that happ –'
But Stephanie, he saw, had already closed herself off to all further questions. With an almost imperceptible shake of her head, she turned to walk away. He watched her go, the signature sashay belying the broken woman who hid beneath the Stygian black dress.

Steward decided right then that he would have to make his own enquiries. Something awful had happened, of that he was certain, but what it was and who was involved remained to be seen. He knew he would be able to find out; as an incredibly rich white aristocrat no doors were closed to him. He'd always been aware of his incredible privilege, but now he could put it to good use.

He had also always known that Nicholas was scum. They were of similar ages, and although their paths hadn't crossed when they were younger, the world of the upper-classes was notoriously small, and Steward had heard Nicholas called worse things than 'Corpse' or 'Old Nick' over the years. He had often wondered, alongside many others, why Richard had such a close association with such a man. Thinking about it now, he also began to wonder how Nicholas could possibly be friends with someone that Hunter had shared a relationship with, albeit an unconventional one. The plot was certainly thickening.

He checked his watch. Bugger – it was almost time for dinner. His search for answers would have to wait until later in the evening. As he set off from the scene of Nicholas' crime, he was aware of a movement on the other side of the tennis court. Squinting through the encroaching darkness, there was a brief flash of what looked like blue silk. A moment later, it was gone. *Oh well*, Steward thought. *There are more important things to deal with right now.*

*

Dinner had been fabulous, a decadent five course affair with everyone in evening wear, or lingerie. The split was about fifty/fifty. Hunter had attended in a stunning puddle of gold satin that set off the red tones in her hair perfectly. Richard and Tiffany had sat together at the head of the table. But while Peter had been present, Darcey had not. Even more mystifying, Astrid had been nowhere to be seen either, and she *never* missed an event. High, smashed, even naked, Astrid would turn up. She was more reliable than the Scottish rain.

There was something else. Steward had insisted on escorting her, even though the waiter he'd been eyeing up all day had been serving on the other side of the enormous table in the marquee. Hunter had expected him to make some sort of move, but instead he'd practically dragged her into the marquee as soon as she'd emerged from The Hall. He'd even picked their seats at the table.

Hunter had tried to work out who precisely he was trying to keep her away from. But she gave up as soon she realised there were almost as many empty seats as occupied ones. She had taken her seat with a palpable sense of disquiet, but

256

as the champagne flowed, she had decided that it was just the festivities making everyone a bit crazy. It certainly wasn't a normal occasion and the heady atmosphere mixed with sex and alcohol was bound to make people behave strangely.

*

Back in her room, Hunter was sliding into the most beautiful latex creation she had ever been privileged to wear. Hand-tailored to her impressive curves, she knew that she looked like Jessica Rabbit in her 'Hunter-red' dress. She'd put a slight wave into her auburn hair, and it gave her a leonine predatory sexiness that she knew would bring any man to his knees. She complemented the look with a thin red latex choker and those killer Louboutins, which she was determined to wear through the evening even if it killed her. Billie Eilish's 'Bad Guy' could have been written for the man-eating woman she saw in the mirror, and she was ecstatic.

She knew her part in the proceedings verbatim and even though she'd missed her friends at dinner she knew exactly where they'd be now. Similarly enjoying their reflections and just as thrilled with their appearances and the evening to come. The heady atmosphere that had seemed to hit everyone else earlier was finally penetrating Hunter's consciousness. Maybe she'd fuck a waiter tonight. Hell, maybe she'd fuck two. She smiled lasciviously at herself as she turned to join the ceremony, deliriously happy that for the first time in a long time, her desire hadn't automatically taken her thoughts to him. Perhaps she was finally free.

'Hunter, you look delectable,' Steward said as he took her arm at the bottom of the curved staircase.

Hunter smiled. 'Why, thank you. You look absolutely dashing yourself. Our friend in the crisp white waiter's jacket stands no chance tonight.'

A slight blush illuminated Steward's cheeks by the flickering of the torches. 'Well, I did actually have a brief encounter with him in the library after dinner...'

'The *library*?' Hunter laughed. 'God, it sounds like something from Cluedo. An encounter in the library, with a... oh god, don't tell me!'

'Alas my dear nothing like that, I had to dash off rather abruptly as I wanted to talk to Trigger.'

Hunter curled up her nose. 'Why on earth would you want to talk to Trigger? Actually, don't tell me – let's just focus on what happened with your waiter friend.'

Steward shrugged bashfully. 'Oh, nothing really. He caught me brooding, and I'm not certain but I felt like there was a bit of flirting going on. Well, I got a bit flustered, and then so did he. He even spilled one of the drinks. Well, you should have seen his face when I offered him my handkerchief to clean it. He looked absolutely delighted.'

Hunter burst out laughing, 'I bet he did!'

Steward looked at her curiously.

Hunter shook her head. 'Doesn't matter. Come on.'

Steward smiled and threw an arm through Hunter's. 'Let the games begin!' he shouted, mimicking Richard's booming tone.

Steward led Hunter past the small bar he'd visited earlier to the specially constructed cave that was to be the scene of the evening's denouement. The guests stood in eagerness all around the entrance, a cornucopia of latex, leather, and lace. The picture was spectacular. The light from the torches licked across the latex, leaving evocative shadows on the bodies of the guests. Everyone was holding a glass of champagne, and a few people were even masked. Most of the masks were in the Venetian style, and Hunter could see that some were clearly authentic. She and Steward took their places at the top of the 'reception line', but she nevertheless flinched when Richard appeared suddenly at her elbow. He was wearing nothing but a ringmaster's coat and a pair of latex shorts.

A hush descended on the crowd as the rattle of what sounded like a coach began to draw nearer. *Very apt,* Hunter thought. Tiffany delivered by a horse in full livery. However, as the sound came closer, she realised that the shape materialising from the darkness wasn't really a horse at all. *Oh my goodness,* Hunter thought, chuckling to herself. *No wonder Astrid wasn't at the dinner.*

The assembled guests whooped and whistled as Astrid rattled through the centre of the crowd, the most amazing plume of horsehair trailing from the crown of her leather horse mask. Many of the guests had been holding whips and they were now putting them to good use as Astrid cantered past. Hunter had no idea how Astrid was managing to run in those hooves of hers, or indeed where she had found the strength to pull Tiffany in a chariot, singlehandedly *and* in full leather horse regalia. She doubted that she had ever been more impressed by her friend.

As Astrid neared the top of the procession, Hunter got her first glimpse of Tiffany, and good god, she was magnificent. She was encased in candy pink latex from her crown to her toes. Her beautiful long blonde hair had been pulled up and through to create a mane like Astrid's, though much less tall. The tightness of the full-face latex mask pulled her lips into a pronounced pout and emphasized the sparkling blue of her eyes. The latex covered every inch of her skin, except for her breasts, which were displayed proudly through more strategic cut-outs, and Hunter knew there would be a fold or a zip or something concealed between her thighs, as there was no way Richard wasn't getting in there tonight. Astrid was a masterpiece and Tiffany was the pièce de résistance.

When the chariot reached the front of the cave, Astrid took an elaborate bow. Hunter could hear her panting and see the sweat through her blinkers, but she could also tell that Astrid was walking on air. The assembled guests were going crazy in their appreciation, some taking to whipping each other in their frenzy. The few clothes that people were wearing were already starting to come off.

Hunter leaned over and whispered in Richard's ear. 'Now *that* was an entrance.'

Richard turned and gave her a wide grin. 'Would you expect anything else?' he asked rhetorically. He walked over to Astrid, who turned in the shafts and presented her ass. 'Good work, pony,' he said, whipping the bared bottom appreciatively. She tossed her head, sending the mane flying skyward and being rewarded with even more appreciative oohs and aahs from the crowd. The torchlight caught the richness in her black horsehair and bathed the whole scene in an ebony shine.

The mouth of the cave was hidden by a swathe of black velvet, and slowly the guests began to disappear through it. Richard walked over to the chariot and helped Tiffany onto the grass, which was just as well as her latex bodysuit ended in vertiginous platformed spike stilettoes. That was the last Hunter saw before she excused herself from Steward and hurried into the cave. Astrid, released from her trap, trotted unsteadily after her, clearly exhausted by her exertions.

Once inside, the two women disappeared behind another thick black velvet curtain into a small dressing area that was lit only by candles. 'God damn Richard.' Hunter cursed. 'I mean, I understand sticking to the theme and everything, but he could have given us more than candles to get dressed by. This is going to be difficult.' Hunter was looking critically at Astrid and trying to work out the best way to get her out of her outfit and into another. 'No electricity remember,' Astrid replied, steadying herself against a wooden table.

'Oh. Of course. Sometimes I forget he doesn't actually control the universe!' Hunter said, faux slapping her forehead. Both the women laughed. 'I do note, however, that he's left us some champagne. Good man. I guess I can't fault him too much.' Hunter poured each of them a glass of champagne as Astrid took of her hooves. Then, between them, they divested Astrid of her amazing leather construction. Standing naked and glistening in the candlelight, Astrid's skin was still covered in the henna from earlier in the day. If Hunter had understood croquet, she could probably have worked out who had won just by examining the writing, but as things were she just stared at it uncomprehending. At moments like this Hunter always thought that Astrid was the most beautiful of them all. So muscled, so toned, still breathing heavily from her efforts, she was an athlete and sexy as hell for it. Especially with her olive skin and black hair spiked at odd angles and slick with sweat. A particularly lovely sprite sent to cause mischief in the night.

'Hey!' Astrid said, gesturing to where her dress hung on a rail. 'Stop perving and help. I've got about 30 seconds to get my sweaty ass into that latex and that's hard at the best of times.' They could hear the guests gathering, some sitting in velvet covered chairs, some hovering. The main 'room' was only separated by the velvet so, while there was *some* secrecy surrounding events, there really wasn't much of it.

The corner of their little space was filled with various implements, which Hunter was careful not to upset as she poured Astrid into the latex. Once the change was complete, they set themselves to gathering what they needed for the ceremony. It was only when they donned their velvet cloaks that Hunter realised Darcey's was missing.

'Oh, thank god,' Hunter breathed.

'What?'

'Darcey, her dress and cloak, she must have got dressed already.'

Astrid stared at Hunter, confused.

'It's just, she disappeared earlier,' Hunter explained. 'And, I mean, you *must* have noticed… she's been so…'

Astrid sighed. 'Yes, I know what you mean,' she said. 'Something's definitely up. She was supposed to help me earlier, but she never showed. I assumed she was with you. But you know Darcey. She's probably already sorted out whatever it was, you know?'

One look at Astrid convinced Hunter that her friend was as worried as she was. But there was no time to think about it now. They had a show to perform. 'Ok,' Hunter said, theatrically sweeping the velvet cowl over her head. 'Let's go.'

Hunter and Astrid slid unnoticed into the main chamber. The room was lit with candles, which offered enough light to see what was happening, but made it very difficult to pick out individual faces. Nevertheless, Hunter immediately saw him – it was as though she was destined to seek him out whether she wanted to or not. He was masked in a black phantom-of-the-opera style mask which covered half his features but still showed his predatory smile. Hunter looked him dead in the eye, licked her lips provocatively, and then shook her head defiantly. She felt certain she could handle him now. Tonight, she was in charge, and he was nothing.

The fourth of the morning's sacrificial victims was next to him, wearing a spectacular latex creation of interwoven crimson straps that complemented her feathered collar and left nothing to the imagination. The straps gave the impression of welts, as if she'd already been whipped. Squinting further into the crowd, Hunter even noticed Stephanie, looking as repellent as ever in head-to-toe black PVC. Corpse was behind her, in what appeared to be a tuxedo. Hunter shook her head. *No imagination*, she thought.

The guests were in a semi-circle, the submissives seated, their dominants standing behind. All eyes were locked on Tiffany, whose head was lying on a red satin pillow, and turned to the semi-circle of spectators. She was secured by ropes to a stone altar in the centre of the room, her ankles and wrists tied to iron rings that were laid into the feet of the altar. Hunter wondered where Richard had got it from. It looked like it had always been there, like it was from another time. But Hunter knew this wasn't true. This whole stage had been specifically created for tonight.

Hunter became aware of a throbbing bass coming through the ground beneath her feet. Slowly, the music began to build, though the vibrations remained stronger than the sound. A pre-emptive hush descended over the guests; their eyes still riveted on the altar. Hunter moved into position directly behind Tiffany's prone form. She knew Tiffany couldn't see her, so she leant forward unperceptively and squeezed her friend's hand, tracing an 'H' inside her friend's palm for reassurance. Tiffany squeezed back.

Astrid took her place to the right of the altar, and a moment later Darcey arrived on its left. She winked at Hunter and reached over to give her a quick squeeze. Immediately, relief flooded through Hunter like a shot of absinthe. She felt suddenly giddy and had to stop from laughing in relief.

Finally, Richard appeared from the darkness, and stood commandingly in front of the altar, excluding Tiffany from the view of the spectators. He began a short speech about the importance of obedience and honour in a submissive.

There was murmured assent and palpable excitement from the crowd. Submissives of all genders and none leaned forward in their chairs, and dominants either held them back on chains and leashes or encouraged them forward. They were practically salivating.

Hunter couldn't resist a quick glance towards his wrist. She might be in control, but she still had to know if the waif was on his leash. However, it was too dark to make anything out. A moment later, Richard finished speaking and, with a snap, he brought a flogger down on the stone next to Tiffany's face, missing her by practiced millimetres.

Now, as the music and the beat of the bass increased, the women knew what to do. As one, they threw their hands skywards and let their cloaks fall to the floor, revealing all their latex finery. Hunter the she-devil, Astrid the absinthe fairy and Darcey the ice-queen. They knew they were magnificent, and they held their arms high, clasping hands, standing with legs apart and wild smiles, staring a challenge into the crowd. Each had a colour-coordinated flogger in a holster in their latex suspender-belts. The crowd fell silent.

Richard turned to the women and gave an elaborate bow; he then moved behind his wife and miraculously pulled the latex dress from her back, exposing the flesh of her body to the night air. Hunter noticed goose bumps raised on Tiffany's skin, but she knew it wasn't from the cold.

Richard stood a step back, and Hunter, Darcey, and Astrid raised their floggers simultaneously, pausing to build the tension in the room, then brought them down as one across Tiffany's back. She caught her breath but didn't scream. Everyone else in the room remained motionless as the women repeated the ritual a further six times. By the seventh stroke Tiffany had reached her limit, the women knew, and just as quickly they desisted. The chamber was silent but for the sound of Tiffany's panting.

The ritual wasn't over yet, however. Darcey swapped places with Hunter, and Astrid slipped behind the curtain once more. When she returned, she was carrying a smoking brazier in one hand and what looked like a brass poker in the other. She re-took her place and then turned to Richard. He swung into action with a flourish. He threw off his ringmaster's coat to reveal a chest criss-crossed with chains, then took the brass poker from Astrid and plunged it theatrically into the brazier. The entire room gasped. Astrid may have been small, but she was strong, and she was steady, which was why, when the women had hatched this plan, she had been chosen to literally carry the fire.

Hunter, meanwhile, had moved round so that she was at Tiffany's head, and with Tiffany's arms pinned out flat in front of herself, Hunter draped her own arms over Tiffany's and then, turning from the crowd, placed her cheek against that of her friend. But this was Tiffany's moment; Hunter was only there to help keep her friend calm. Just because the moment was something Tiffany desperately wanted; did not mean she wouldn't suffer. Hunter was there to help her take the pain.

Everyone was leaning forward in their seats now; they had an idea what was going to happen, but at the same time, they couldn't quite believe it. Richard was performing for the crowd, while at his elbow, the surgeon readied her apparatus. Hunter was surprised at how Darcey had succeeding in making herself almost invisible, even despite the contrast of ice blue latex against a black velvet curtain. Finally, Richard finished his theatrics and pulled the poker from the red-hot brazier.

Hunter held Tiffany fast, stroking her hair, eyes fixed on the area at the top of Tiffany's left butt-cheek where the brand was going to land. When Richard raised the poker, she had her first glimpse of the intricate design that was about to be burned into her friend's skin, forever. She closed her eyes tightly.

Poker raised, Richard addressed his wife. 'Do you submit?' he asked.

A pause so pregnant with anticipation you could hear the crackle of the metal brand as it cooled slightly in the air. Then, 'Yes.'

In one motion, Richard laid the metal against her skin. This time Tiffany did scream. Hunter held her and tried to absorb some of the sensation for her. Within seconds, Richard wrenched the poker away. Then, in a heartbeat, Darcey was by her friend's side to sterilise and dress her wound. The previous excitement from the crowd had been nothing but foreplay, at that moment they truly went wild, screaming, dancing, kissing congratulations and pure exultation.

Released from her bindings, Tiffany got shakily to her feet and smiled wearily at the crowd. Richard was already by her side, massaging her wrists and ankles, and helping her out of the rest of her latex. She was going to spend the remainder of the evening in her loose silk kimono – Darcey's strict orders.

'Well, that went well, I thought,' Darcey said, as the three women stood near the altar, smiling at their friend.

'Oh, I should say so,' Hunter said, laughing. 'I'm just glad you made it. I was worried about you, you know.'

Darcey rolled her eyes theatrically. 'Oh, come on,' she said. 'As if I'd ever let something like *that* go unsterilized.'

After that, the party began to take on a life of its own. The curtains at the entrance of the cave were pulled back to reveal a makeshift dancefloor that had somehow been assembled by the cave entrance during the ceremony. More torches were lit, and waiters began circulating with some truly deadly-looking concoctions in cocktail glasses. Hunter knew absinthe was in at least one of them.

Guests had begun to either enjoy the bacchanal in the velvet room or to spill out for some less debauched fun on the dancefloor. Tiffany had headed outside with Richard for some much-needed fresh air, the pair of them glowingly happy. The other three women had remained inside, but they were soon joined by Peter, who was wearing a very smug look on his face. 'Well, Darcey,' he grinned. 'That could be you next, eh? How about it, Hunter? I'm sure you can brand with the best of them!' It took all of Hunter's self-control not to curl her lip.

Darcey rolled her eyes at Hunter and took Peter off to the dance floor. *Even at an orgy he still looks like a pillock*, Hunter thought, as she and Astrid watched him stumble off.

'Why does he always wear military gear?' Astrid asked. 'I mean, of all the times...' She gestured at the myriad examples of fetish wear circulating around them. 'I mean, it's fine, I guess, if that's your kink... but it feels a bit...'

'Predictable?' Hunter asked. They both laughed. Hunter was about to continue when Astrid gave her a rushed kiss on the cheek and practically bolted away. Hunter was about to call after her when she felt a soft breath land on the back of her neck.

'You're exquisite,' He growled into her ear. 'And that was a stunning performance. There's nothing I wouldn't give to do the same to you, although perhaps in a more, shall we say, *private* setting.'

Hunter turned, and he stared at her, never taking his eyes from hers. 'But, as it turns out,' He continued almost sadly, 'you're too good for me.'

'We're *all* too good for you,' she replied evenly. Then, reaching out as if to take his face in her hands, she slowly drew her fingernail along his jawline. She leaned into him and breathed into his mouth, before turning and disappearing behind the velvet curtain.

She had left him nailed in place by his own erection she knew, and the thought brought back the old sense of power. She had survived him after all. And she wasn't going to go there again.

She slowly pulled her knife, the knife he had given her, the knife she would never part with, out of her latex suspender. Then she placed it against her skin, just below her thumb, on the wrist of her right hand. She felt the blade slip into her skin and the sensation brought a rush of arousal through her entire body. She watched the blood trickle slowly from the wound and delicately licked it from her skin, all the while imagining it was him doing it. Then she held out her hand and admired the wound. Every time she raised a drink to her lips, she wanted to see it, to be reminded of their times together.

Pleasure like theirs had been worth this pain, she realised. She might never wear a brand, but she wasn't going to be ashamed of the joy they had shared, and she didn't want to forget anymore and pretend it hadn't happened. It had, and at the time, it had been everything. But it was over, and she had to just move on. For real this time. It was as simple as that.

She could hear the party descending into an orgy beyond the curtain. She smiled as she heard Astrid moan in ecstasy at the ministrations of some willing participant. But she didn't want to join in. She did not want to spoil the wave she was riding by becoming drunk and maudlin, or worse, confronting Darcey or Astrid about some imagined problem. She also did not want to see him with her replacement. Time to let go. To the pool she thought. If nothing else the cool water would calm her, and latex was waterproof anyway.

The Decision

"All the world's a stage, And all the men and women merely players."

William Shakespeare

As she looked up at the cavalcade of stars in the sky above her head, Hunter was, as always, amazed at how clear the sky was as soon as you left Scotland's cities. She was, all things considered, in relatively good shape. Despite the drinking of the day and the intensity of the ceremony, she still felt alert, almost too alert. Everything was in high focus, the fir trees at the edge of the grounds like dark fairy-tale monsters guarding the medieval walls surrounding the garden, the warm theatrical lighting from the house sparkling over the dew-covered grass like spilled champagne. She giggled as she realised she was back in a hot tub, remembering that misty afternoon shooting a few months earlier. God, it felt like a lifetime ago now.

The warm water sloshed around her as she tilted the champagne glass back and forth, squinting through the bubbles and admiring them as they danced around the stars above. It had been such a wonderful day, drama and intrigue notwithstanding. A wonderful night, too, though rather quiet, suddenly. Which made her wonder, just how late *was* it?

'May I join you?'

She smiled, knowing the voice without having to tear her gaze from the champagne starlight. It was the voice of a story teller, a comforting, rich hot-chocolate voice that slid over your aural pathways like a warm bath. *Wow, maybe I am drunk*, Hunter thought giggling.

'But of course, My Lord.'
'Oh please, none of that!' he chuckled, gingerly lowering himself into the hot tub.

'I hadn't expected to see you again until morning,' Hunter said with a teasing smile. 'What happened to our friend?'

Steward sighed, trying valiantly to light a cigar with damp hands. 'Just not the right time,' he said. 'But don't feel sorry for me. I've had a fabulous evening, nonetheless. No one cares, genuinely, if you're on old aristocrat, an internet millionaire, or the gamekeeper, provided you can keep up with the drink.'

'And the sex,' Hunter said, grinning. 'I'm only glad Richard and Tiffany have no neighbours. What would they think?'

Steward laughed, and took a puff on his cigar, now successfully lit. 'True. It's funny, I often forget that there are people who'd be downright horrified by what goes on here. It's just all so fun and silly.'

Hunter sighed. '*So* much fun. I only wish I could stay in this world forever. At least here I'm never judged for what I do.'

'They judge you?' Steward asked. 'In the real world, I mean? Who would dare do such a thing!' He smiled and winked at her.

'They see through us all the time. Even Darcey's been called out in 'real life' for being too racy or daring or just plain inappropriate. It's exhausting, and just... *so* frustrating! I just want to shake people and scream, who cares if I'm wearing nothing but nipple tassels and a suspender belt? It doesn't matter! But then, of course, it really *does*... to some people anyway.'

Steward smiled sympathetically. 'It's hard to believe what you say about Darcey. I always thought of her as the most conservative of all you girls.'

'Oh, she is,' Hunter agreed. 'Or at least she is *now*. She never used to be though. Back in the day, she was probably the most debauched of the four of us. But... Anyway, remember, it's all relative, and we're talking about the most conservative amongst a crowd who just participated in a 'Story of O' themed latex wedding.'

His laughter echoed around the garden. 'You have me there. I suppose she always gets involved, and she certainly seems as comfortable as the rest of us in the get-up. I just, I don't know, there was always something of the outsider about her. As though she was watching herself do this without really getting involved.' He sighed, shook his head. 'Anyway, not my place.'

'No, I see what you mean. But it's not because she's uncomfortable.'

'Ah yes,' Steward said, knowingly. 'The husband.' He put a slightly sinister inflection on the final word. All in all, Steward was sick of people's husbands today.

'You're not a fan?' Hunter asked.

'No!' Steward said, hotly. 'I'm not a fan of any man who desires a woman because she is free and uninhibited, and then puts limits on those inhibitions once he has her. It's not right, the way he keeps her in a box, performing only for him, doing the things that he, rather than she, wants. At least, that's how it seems from the outside.'

'I'd love to see her let go like she used to. She was spectacular, you know. The very best of us.' As she smiled at the memory, she became aware that he was regarding her closely. 'What is it?'

'You are completely unapologetic about who you are aren't you?'

Hunter shrugged. 'I honestly don't think I do *anything* that requires an apology.'

'Even a branding?' Steward asked, smiling. When Hunter tried to argue, he cut her off with a wave. 'Oh, don't think I didn't see that gleam in your eye when Richard left his mark on Tiffany tonight. I know you, and I know what you'd give for that Hercules of yours to do the same to you.'

'Perhaps I'm not interesting enough for a branding,' Hunter said, pointedly refusing to acknowledge Steward's mention of him.

275

Steward took the hint and retreated. 'I think you might be the most interesting person I've ever met, Hunter. You know who you are, and you just are. You're innate. Even here, so many people are still playing a part, pretending to be into things they're not so they don't get kicked out of the crowd, or else holding back in case they're ejected for going too far. People are so on guard. But not you. You really are just... you.'

Hunter raised her glass in salute. 'Thank you,' she replied. 'You know, you're the second person to call me innate this year.' Although she offered no explanation for her last comment, Steward suspected he knew to whom she was referring.

'Come with me to Venice,' he said suddenly. 'You'll love it, trust me. If you like this lot, you'll want to come and meet a friend of mine in Italy.'

Hunter was surprised by the sudden turn in conversation, but she had to admit she was intrigued. 'Why?'

Steward shrugged. 'Simple,' he said. 'What our darling friends here aspire to be, the society of which I am a member actually *is and* has been for oh... for centuries I should think.'

Hunter struggled to believe this. But then again, this was a man she'd known for years, and who she'd never known to tell a lie, or even exaggerate. And she shouldn't be surprised that Steward had secrets. Hunter knew from experience that those with the least to the prove were often the quietest, whereas ironically those with the most to prove, and who were the most insecure, were never done explaining their own importance and influence. An image of Peter flitted briefly through her consciousness, but she blinked it away as quickly as it had arrived. As for the invitation...

'You know what, Steward, I would *love* to come with you! Italy's just wonderful, and where better to dress up in all my erotic finery than Venice? Thank you,' she said. 'Thank you so much.'

Stewart puffed up a little then. Unable to hide his delight at Hunter's acceptance. 'Excellent,' he said, his eyes twinkling. 'Excellent. Oh, goodness, we'll have such a time. This isn't just Venice we're visiting; it's eighteenth-century Venice! Get ready to meet Casanova himself.'

Hunter wasn't exactly sure what he meant by any of this but was certain it would be a fabulous adventure. Suddenly, as if the universe was in happy symbiosis with their plans, the sun rose over the grounds at The Hall, and bathed everything in an ancient, golden glow.

The Adventure

"To burn with desire and keep quiet about it is the greatest
punishment we can bring to ourselves."

Federico Garcia Lorca

Hunter looked out of the aeroplane window as she sipped
her negroni and watched the mist of Edinburgh disappear
behind her. The bitter orange scent and strong alcohol taste
on her tongue always reminded her of Italy. She was on an
adventure, and she couldn't be happier. It was impromptu
experiences such as these that always reminded her that she
was alive. She hated knowing what each day was going to
bring.

Whether it was the alcohol or the fact she had now
completely relaxed, her thoughts took her back to him. A
sad smile played across her features. Five months on, she
now, finally, had enough distance to cope with the
memories of their times together. She felt immensely proud
of herself, not only for this, but also because she had proved
to herself that she valued her life, her desires, and her
integrity over any man. That she had had the maturity to
accept and act on that understanding was a pleasant
surprise. She had seen far too many 'acquaintances' give
themselves over to men and their whims, deprioritising
their own lives and ambitions. When she had been tested,
she hadn't even hesitated. She had chosen herself. And look
where it had got her; she was setting off on a fabulous
adventure, back to eighteenth century Italy. If ever proof

were needed that she had made the right choice, it was right there!

Hunter could feel the sense of excitement growing inside her with every moment that passed. By the time she caught her first glimpse of Venice through the window of the plane, she felt almost tearful with anticipation. Venice had been a place she had been desperate to visit for so long. Now, finally, the moment had arrived.

Steward had travelled on ahead of Hunter and left her with the address of their hotel and the order that she get a private water taxi into the city. She had assured him that the regular water taxi was more than suited to her needs, but he had insisted and paid for the service in advance.

In the event, Hunter was grateful he had. Within an hour of touchdown, she found herself in her very own water taxi, sipping an Aperol spritz and watching the sun sink low. Very few places were ever as you imagined them, but so far, Venice was more than living up to expectations.

Hunter knew that Steward had booked her flight for the afternoon so that she would see the city via boat at sunset. She loved such attentive care. He was another person who understood how important it was to make the most of every single moment in life. If he were straight and thirty years younger, he might have been in trouble.

'Enjoying yourself signora?' the boat pilot asked.

'Si, grazie, che bella cittá,' Hunter replied.

'Non bella come te,' he replied, kissing his fingertips appreciatively.

Hunter tossed her hair as she leaned back against the plush leather seat cushions and sipped her drink. God, she adored Italian men! Nowhere else in the world did men seem to adore women so completely. They managed to tread that line of exuberant vocal and physical appreciation without ever being threatening or creepy, in Hunter's experience anyway.

She breathed in deeply, tasting the salt in the air, watching the golden rays of sun glint off the water and illuminate the stunning buildings as they sped past in their little motorboat. She laughed when she saw the little pier-side petrol stations everywhere for the boats to refuel. This was *definitely* a city that lived on the water. She sighed, feeling utterly contented. Half an hour outside of the airport, she already felt like she was home.

The taxi slowed and Hunter gave a delightful little shiver as she felt the swell of the water beneath her. She looked up and gasped. They had pulled up at the jetty of her hotel – oh, how fabulous it was to pull up to a jetty and not a taxi rank! The building took her breath away. It looked like something straight out of the movies. Hunter wouldn't even have been surprised if Juliet had appeared at one of the many balconies and begun pining for her Romeo. She stood, shielding her eyes from the golden streaks of fading sunlight that lit up the frescoes on the façade. Pinks, golds, and greens depicting flowers and water scenes. Immediately, she understood what Steward had meant about taking her to eighteenth-century Venice.

Presently, a stunning concierge practically sprinted to her aide. Hunter tipped the boat pilot generously and was rewarded with a kiss on her hand and a declaration of eternal love to his 'Bella Rossa'. Hunter grinned; she was going to like it here.

She breezed into the lobby in her trademark heels and a bottle-green dress that hugged every curve. There wasn't a man in the hotel who failed to stand to attention as she passed them.

'Buona sera, signora,' the receptionist smiled.

'I'm a guest of Lord Steward,' Hunter replied.

'Oh, I know,' the receptionist said. 'He described you quite vividly.' His eyes travelling over Hunter's body appreciatively. 'We will deal with your luggage signora, but signor has asked me to send you straight to him.'

*

'Do you know my favourite thing about this trip so far?' Hunter asked, swivelling in her stool, and giving him a dazzling smile.
'You mean apart from the company?' Steward said with a grin. 'Well, if I had to guess, I'd say the old-school glamour of the city.'
'You're close,' Hunter said. 'But what's arguably even better than *that* is that everything in Italy comes with an Aperol spritz. Even the water-taxi.'
Steward laughed. 'You're right there, my dear. So, what do you think of my little bolt hole?'

They were sitting in a charmingly understated dive bar, right on the canal side, opposite a working chandlery. Hunter adored it and told him so.

'These little affairs are so much more authentic than all the tourist traps by the square,' Steward said. 'This place, for example, does the best crostini antipasti and local wine for two Euro a glass. You go anywhere near Piazza San Marco and it's all vinegar masquerading as wine and food you wouldn't feed to a dog.'

'Doesn't bode well for dinner,' Hunter said with a laugh.

'On the contrary my dear, you forget I'm *almost* a local. I'm taking you to the most authentic restaurant in the city. Just don't tell anyone about it when you get home.'

Hunter mimed locking her mouth with a key then crossed her heart. 'I have to say,' Hunter said, taking a delicate bite of an anchovy and red pepper crostini. 'Watching dusk descend over the water like this is magical. I already love it here.'

'I knew you would. Which brings me to our fun and games. Tonight, we'll have dinner and then make a quick stop at another favourite bar of mine. Then it's off to bed early as we're going to the costumiers in the morning!'

'Costumiers?' Hunter asked, frowning. 'But I'm sure I have something appropriate. I brought all my usual party clothes.'

'Not a chance my dear. Didn't I tell you we were going to eighteenth-century Venice?'

'I thought that was an allusion to our hotel.'

Steward laughed. 'Not a bit of it! And unless you have an authentic three-hundred-year-old dress in your bag, you're insufficiently prepared.'

Hunter was momentarily speechless. Steward refused to elaborate any further but told her to be prepared for a treat the next day. Hunter couldn't believe by how much Venice was already exceeding her expectations.

The rest of the evening passed in a bit of a blur. All Hunter could think about was the distinct possibility of getting to wear an actual antique dress the following day. What would it look like? How had Steward managed this? And more importantly, who had worn it originally? And to what event? It was almost too exciting to imagine.
'All in good time,' was all he would say on the matter.

*

They went straight from the bar to the restaurant. They only had two nights in the city and Steward did not want to waste a minute by going back to the hotel. Besides, he had known that Hunter would step off the plane better dressed than most people were when they were going to Michelin starred restaurants.

'Now this is where real Venetians eat. None of that tourist crap, which by the way gets worse and worse every year.

You do not book; you arrive and pray for deliverance. The menu is small but perfectly formed and you drink local Venetian wine by the carafe.' He said as he held open the door for her.

'Sounds like heaven to me.' Hunter assented.

'Oh, and whatever happens you must have the polpette.'

'Yes Sir! And what are they exactly?' She asked as she tore off a mock salute.

'Classic Italian meatballs. Seriously, they are legendary throughout the city.' He assured her.

The warmth from inside hit her immediately. It may not have been the eighteenth century, but it still managed to make Hunter feel that she was back in the past somewhere. If the Rat Pack had been sitting at the bar, they would have fitted in perfectly with the old school atmosphere. She was seriously beginning to lament the fact that Steward was both gay and far too old for her. Because he was the most attentively kind man she had ever met. They also clearly had similar tastes in almost everything, although definitely not men. Hunter liked hers dark and dangerous and Steward liked younger and pretty.

Steward was right about the polpette, however. They were delicious, and the softest, lightest ones that she had ever tasted. *They must be veal*, Hunter thought. The sauce was also to die for, and as ever, the local Italian wine was like ambrosia when paired with such delicious delicacies.

Hunter had managed to wangle a last-minute Saturday away from the dungeon with the promise she'd sample some Venetian wines and make connections with suppliers. She'd definitely be finding out which vineyard supplied this particular restaurant.

They left the restaurant in high spirits, which were soon dampened by the torrential down pour.

'Bugger.' Steward said as Hunter laughed, and they dashed from the restaurant to shelter under a nearby awning, Hunter's heels already splashing through an inch of water.

'Oh God.' Steward continued sadly.
'What? What?' Hunter asked looking at the almost biblical rain and laughing. 'We need to get there,' he said, motioning over not one, but two canals.
'Right, and how do we do that? I have never been somewhere where you can see exactly where you need to be, but you can't bloody get there!' Hunter said as they both laughed.

'You're right sweetheart, well if that's roughly the direction of the hotel,' He said pointing vaguely off to the left, 'if we get through that passage there, hopefully it will take us over that bridge…' he said motioning to a bridge behind them.

'Surely that's going the *wrong* way?' Hunter questioned, watching the rain cascade down like a waterfall in front of them.
'Well, only in every real and literal sense. You see, what you come to learn about Venice is that you have to suspend all notions of normal direction and even sometimes suspend the laws of time and space. Unless you fancy a canal swim.'
'I do not.' She said with force looking at the very dark and very deep water.

'I didn't think so. In that case, follow me. There's that very welcoming bar I was telling you about close by. Let's grab a nightcap, dry off and get proper directions.'
They both laughed again, and Hunter leaned into him as they quickened their pace over the bridge, heads down against the rain, aiming for the warm glow of welcoming bar lights.

'Oh my god!' Hunter exclaimed as they entered St. Mark's Square, which was already under at least a foot under water. 'What is happening? Is there a flood?'
'Not to worry, this happens all the time.'
'What?' Hunter asked incredulous looking at the lake that had once been one of the most famous Piazza's in the whole world.

'No, it's a good thing my dear, trust me.'
'How, how, is ruining my stilettoes good?' She replied laughing, kicking up great splashes of water. It had reached half way up her calves by this point so the shoes were definitely a foregone conclusion. 'Thank goodness I went for a shorter dress.' She mused.
'No seriously, you felt how muggy it was earlier yes? Apparently, the spring weather has been unbearable, it's why this downpour caused such a flood.'

'So I see!' Hunter couldn't help but smile. She had never known that flooding was such a common occurrence in St. Mark's Square. She couldn't help feeling privileged to have experienced it first-hand. Even if it had knackered her shoes. She was also appreciating the karma of her ruined shoes. She had been pretty acerbic about all of the tourists looking ridiculous in plastic gaiters when the, what she had assumed to be a brief shower, had started.

Now she knew that they weren't the tourists at all but the locals. They clearly knew exactly what to expect when the heavens disgorged over their already waterlogged city. 'It will be cooler tomorrow, which will make the entire event more pleasant. Remember what you're wearing my dear.' Steward said, motioning her back under the colonnades which ran around the perimeter of the square. 'Ah yes, the most opulent dress ever created. I hope!' she laughed.

Finally, they managed to locate the bar, through the almost wall of water around them. Steward pulled Hunter close, opened the door with one hand and ushered her into the welcome refuge of warmth and a very large brandy. 'A water taxi home I think my dear. Steward said, closing the door behind them to the sounds of great Italian merriment within.

*

When Hunter and Steward arrived at the costumiers the following morning, Hunter was shocked to find two footmen manning its oak-panelled doors. She stared, speechless, as the two men, dressed in powdered wigs, brocade silk waistcoats and stockings, bowed, and pushed the doors open for her. Then, as they reached the inner courtyard, a similarly dressed and similarly silent gentleman appeared at her elbow with a crystal glass full of champagne. She couldn't believe it; they looked as though they'd stumbled out of a Fairy Tale.

Steward was clearly delighted by Hunter's reaction. 'I shall leave you to it my dear,' he said. 'After all, I don't want to ruin the surprise of seeing you in full attire this evening. You remember where we're meeting?'

'I do,' Hunter said, with a smile. At the breakfast table that morning, Steward had refused to say how he planned to spend his day, but it was clearly something rather exciting. In any case, she would be pretty much on her own for the remainder of the day.

'Until tonight then,' he said, leaving her with Prince Charming's attendant. 'Enjoy.'

Hunter was led into an apartment overlooking the water, though in fairness, it was more of a challenge to find a room that *didn't* look over one canal or another in this floating city. The building's whole interior spoke of faded glory. It had clearly once been a place of grandeur, but those days were certainly well behind it. As far as Hunter was concerned, this only added to its charm. All around her, she could practically hear the sandaled feet dancing, smell the perfumed air, and hear the chatter of exquisite evenings of centuries past. She closed her eyes and spun around gaily, sipping her champagne, and feeling like she was finally exactly where she belonged.

Hunter had been enveloped in complete silence for the past couple of minutes, and so she jumped when the sound of a sharp clap issued behind her. She stopped spinning so abruptly that some of her champagne slopped over the rim of the glass and onto the floor; but she hardly noticed, for striding towards her was by far the most impeccably dressed woman she had ever seen. The woman, who stood no taller than four and a half feet, marched purposely forward, shouting a stream of Italian words at her bespectacled assistant, who was frantically taking notes and appraising Hunter like she planned on buying her. The small women could have been a convincing advertisement for some clandestine dominatrix dungeon, and her assistant was so obviously her submissive that Hunter almost laughed. She expected a ruler to rap across her knuckles or ass at any moment.

'Venga qui!' she barked at Hunter, without breaking her stride. Hunter was by no means fluent in Italian, but the woman's tone was enough to communicate that she should follow, and quickly. She did so, and three pairs of heels clicked through into a cavernous room which smelled like a theatre and was filled with the most exquisite antique dresses that Hunter had ever seen. Once again, Hunter found herself speechless. The collection was something that even Marie Antoinette would have envied. She couldn't resist touching some of them on her way past. Olive green silk, regnal purple, full skirts, and intricately embroidered bodices with actual gold thread. It was almost too wonderful to bear.

Hunter's little dress mistress, as she was coming to think of her, ushered her onto a small velvet-covered stool, and immediately her submissive began to undress her with all the care of an artist painting a masterpiece. Hunter, unselfconscious as ever, offered the woman a smile. She was so well trained, however, that she did not once meet Hunter's gaze. Hunter was impressed; this dominatrix must be quite something to inspire such obedience. The woman herself, who still hadn't properly acknowledged Hunter, began to examine every inch of her naked body.

'Rossa,' she began, casting her critical eye over Hunter's colouring. 'Non. Aspetta. Si. Rossa.'

The assistant disappeared into the sea of dresses, before reappearing seconds later with a dress the colour of the richest Primitivo wine that Hunter could imagine. This was no red, or wine red; it was the red that those colours aspired to be. Rich, dark, and so liquid that Hunter half believed she could fall into the fabric itself. It was like blood, not the bright red blood of a scratch, no, this was the blood of a fatal wound. *Oh yes*, Hunter thought, *this is definitely the dress for me.*

The mistress gave another brief clap, at which three professional historical costumiers suddenly appeared from nowhere. With infinite care, they began constructing the dress around her. As they laced her tightly into the bodice, she realised that whilst she could breathe, every breath was felt from her pelvis to her clavicle. She couldn't remember when she had been more excited.

'Look here,' one of the dressers said in heavily accented English. 'You will do this yourself later, yes?'

Hunter nodded.

'Then you must pay close attention. This will not be easy.'

Hunter was sure she was right. The dress had clearly been modified, but it was still going to take some effort to get back into it later that evening. Although Hunter knew that in a pinch, any of the hotel concierges from the day before would jump at the chance to help her.

'It is very heavy, yes?' the costumier asked. Hunter was taking some time getting to grips with standing straight and holding the weight of the skirts. Fortunately, the boning helped distribute the weight in the bottom half of the dress, and despite the constrained breathing, Hunter was surprised at how manoeuvrable it was. However, there was no doubt in her mind that she would, as she had expected, be passing sideways through doors.

'Heavy, but worth it,' Hunter replied. Gazing into the mirror one of the assistants had wheeled around, she looked like a ruby flecked with gold. Her hair was loose now, but tonight it would be piled high in the Venetian style. The light caught her auburn tones and between the dress and Hunter's natural beauty she looked like the kind of eighteenth-century courtesan who would have brought Casanova himself willingly to his knees.

Vice

The Revelation

"In the very depths of hell, do not demons love each other?"

Anne Rice

The only sound to penetrate the darkness was the swish of Hunter's silk gown and the staccato tap of her heels on the wet stones as she tried, ever more desperately, to find the well in the moonless night. *What time was it?* She wondered. *Midnight? Later?* Whatever time it was, she knew she shouldn't be out on the street on her own at this hour. She knew that if she ran into any trouble, it would be difficult to get away in what she was wearing. Women's historical attire was not well suited to a hasty escape.

Nevertheless, she pressed on, warm despite the chill of the alleyway. Her sense of unease had brought the blood to her cheeks and made her heart beat faster. The Venetian streets reminded her of an historical London, but not the London of Charles the Second and his glamorous courts. This, she thought, was the London of Jack the Ripper.

Fortunately, the fear that might otherwise have overwhelmed her was being kept at bay by the knowledge that she was about to be inducted into a society, into a life that she had always wanted, and that she was being done so as Steward's guest. She was determined to put on her most dazzling performance tonight, and to ensure that her friend's taste, judgement, and credibility could not be impugned on her behalf.

292

She stopped suddenly, convinced she could hear the tap-tapping of a cane against the chiselled Venetian stone. But then just as quickly, it was gone. She shivered, and not from the cold. If only it was lighter, but in this part of the city street lighting was patchy at best. Venice may be beautiful, but it was also strangely claustrophobic.

Where was that bloody well? By all accounts, she should have reached it ten minutes ago. And finding it shouldn't have been so hard. This might be Venice, a city so labyrinthine and twisted that one wrong turn left you feeling like a rat in a maze, but Steward's directions had been specific to the point of obsessive. They had seemed so simple; make for the well, take a right through the archway and continue for a couple of hundred yards along the canal front. Easy. Except it wasn't. She was hopelessly lost.

Hunter took a deep, steadying breath. *Stay calm*, she told herself. *Remember, this is all part of the experience. And all this fear and adrenaline are short-term issues that will become a long-term aphrodisiac as soon as you find the...* Oh! Squinting through the darkness and the mist, she saw that she had finally found her elusive marker. *An actual well in the middle of a cosmopolitan city,* she thought, with a smile. *Only in Venice!*

Calmer now, Hunter looked to her right and saw the archway Steward had described to her. She let out a deep breath of relief, which, considering her dress, was an achievement in itself. She threw her head back and walked confidently forward, the apprehension of moments earlier already forgotten.

A couple of hundred yards along the canal, Hunter came to a second archway. She stepped through it to find a courtyard that was filled with her wildest imaginings. The change once she stepped through the archway was palpable, almost physical. Candles and incense burned on every available surface, so brightly that you could almost believe the place was on fire. Immense stone walls loomed on all four sides of the courtyard, the sky above shrouding everything in mist, as if guarding a precious secret. The darkest ivy climbed every wall, tendrils stretching out like beckoning hands, brushing the shoulders of everyone who glided past. Everything was solid and real, she understood, deep down. Yet at this time and in this place, it was like watching beautiful, sinful creatures from another world, and she had no desire to break the spell. Had she been alone she would have cried at the majesty of it all.

Through the flames, Hunter's eye was immediately drawn to an ornate plinth at the centre of the courtyard. On the plinth stood a severe-looking man in a powdered wig, who used one hand to swing an incense holder on a chain and the other to grip a cat o' nine tails. He was dressed in a long scarlet robe that kissed the stone floor and wore an ornate crucifix which rested heavily on his chest. He was half confessor and half magistrate, a Spanish Inquisitor without a soul.

Despite his elevated position, the man did not speak. Instead, he chanted in a deep, sonorous baritone in accompaniment with some sombre orchestral music. Where the music was coming from was anyone's guess. But one thing *was* certain; his performance was a magical assault on the senses.

Hunter took her first tentative steps into the courtyard. It really *was* like going back in time. Everyone was dressed in different variations of the same eighteenth-century opulence. And everything they wore – the silk, the bone, the damask, the ebony canes, the powdered wigs – *everything* was original. Hunter never wanted to leave this place, especially if it meant submitting to the cat o' nine tails once more.

The entire scene pulsed to the ethereal tones of Purcell's 'What Power Art Thou', and she realised that was what the imposing man in the cape was singing. It was moments like this which had made her fall in love with Venice over the past twenty-four hours. The present hovered over the city's past like a translucent skin, with the past feeling far more real. Hunter considered the authentic Venice to be this long-lost dream, the Venice that was soul, not skin, deep. She felt as though she had crossed into the world beyond the looking glass and there was no going back. Part of her wished that to be true, the other part was terrified. She was no stranger to this world of sin; a world of vice, sacrifice, avarice, and depravity, but she was wary of it too.

Hunter was still lost in thought when Steward arrived to greet her with a click of his heels and a deep bow, kissing her hand as he did so. She curtseyed instinctively. He took her elbow without a word and led her towards the stone steps, the top of which were obscured by a large velvet curtain. Hunter could understand his silence; it was simply too beautiful for idle talk. She wanted to drink everything in. She wondered if this was what Shakespeare had really envisioned with his Midsummer Night's Dream.

When they reached the top of the stairs, they passed through the velvet curtain and into the old building that stood proudly to the north side of the courtyard. Ancient tapestries and deep velvet curtains had been intentionally hung to conceal every turn and doorway. As they made their way through the winding corridors, Hunter was struck by the most beautiful piano music she had ever heard. With a flourish, Steward stepped forward and swung one of the velvet curtains open to reveal a grand hall. Hunter continued on as if she was walking into a dream.

Four enormous crystal chandeliers holding real wax candles were suspended from the ornately corniced ceiling. Wood panelled walls held antique portraits of imperious and lavishly dressed long-dead Italian aristocrats. Although the atmosphere was such, that had they stepped from their frames to join the gathering Hunter would have accepted it as part of this new and ethereal world. The room was filled with a forest of elaborately dressed dining tables, and more candlesticks than Hunter had ever seen in one place.

As the curtain fell back into place behind them, it revealed the piano that had been playing for her since she entered the building. The piano was grand in every sense; huge and imposing, and elegantly embossed with golden roses. It was being played with evident aplomb by an older man in a knee length frock coat that was opened to the waist to reveal impressive breeches, knee-high silk stockings, waistcoat, and frilled cravat. However, Hunter was more startled by an exquisitely powdered but completely naked woman who was lying spread-eagled on top of the piano and being sensuously fucked by a dwarf with a ball-gag dildo in his mouth. Hunter's mouth dropped open. Much like the dwarf's.

'Exquisite, isn't it,' Steward asked rhetorically.

'I can't believe it. It's all so, beautiful, so wonderful. It's just...' Hunter didn't finish, unable to put into words the wonder, happiness, and gratitude she was feeling at that moment.

'Welcome into my world, Lady Diana.'

As Steward led her across the room, Hunter stared around unabashed. None of the guests were yet indulging in anything particularly debauched, but the room was dotted with entertainment which was clearly designed to arouse and captivate the guests. Hunter herself was already both turned on and enchanted, not only by the entertainment on show but also by the sheer spectacle of the room itself. She felt like she truly had gone back in time.

Hunter and Steward had reached their table. This, like all the other tables in the hall, was decorated with ornate bronze candelabra that bathed the celebrants in a sepia caress. Hunter was admiring the effect when, through the chess board of crystal glasses and the haze of candle smoke, she spied two guests sitting atop velvet stools on a raised dais in the centre of the room. When Steward noticed her staring in admiration, he smiled knowingly. 'I see you've found our Marie Antoinette and Casanova,' he said.

Hunter felt almost dizzy with happiness. Slowly, she sat down upon her seat, fanning her skirts carefully as she had been taught to do, the corset keeping her back ramrod straight. Never once did she take her eyes from the two guests of honour. They were dressed as convincingly as everyone else, if not even more so. The only difference was that they were also partially *un*dressed. The woman's corset was open to the waist, exposing her breasts, while the man wore no shirt under his beautifully embroidered gold jacket. His pantaloons were also open, though not indecently so; just enough for someone to reach into with an exploratory hand. Coincidentally (or perhaps not, given the occasion), this is precisely what Marie had chosen to do.

Further across the room, another couple, both men, were proving equally popular with the assembled guests. 'Who are they?' Hunter whispered. Steward looked to where Hunter was discreetly pointing. 'Ah yes, the absolutely divine Mozart and Salieri.'

'You're going to need to elaborate,' Hunter said. 'Are they even from the right century?'

Steward laughed. 'They are indeed. Although we don't get too hung up on that around here. I mean you, for example, are a fictitious Roman goddess tonight, are you not?' He smiled, as she nodded assent. 'Although everything from the cutlery to the embroidery is authentic eighteenth century, leeway is given to your avatar, as long as they fit in with the... the libertine spirit of decadence.'

Hunter nodded her understanding, then nodded towards Mozart and Salieri in the corner. 'I bet you'd love to join in with those two.'

'Sometimes. But in truth my eye is on someone else.'

Hunter raised a questioning eyebrow, but Steward just smiled.

*

They had had a truly spectacular dinner, with courses brought by servants who looked like they had stumbled straight out of the Palace of Versailles. In truth, Hunter was so enraptured by everything around her she barely registered what she was eating. She did, however, remark on how good the wine pairings were, causing Steward to respond that she would be the perfect addition to their little Italian Society.

Meanwhile Marie and Casanova had been undressing each other with soul-shattering slowness over the course of the evening. Pausing over every lick and caress, every tortured movement of reserved passion, it was as though they had been cast in slow moving resin, forced to release their majesty inch by agonizing inch. A hand sliding up a white stockinged ankle, a breath against a jewelled throat; it was unbearable to watch. Hunter did not know who these people were, but they were the most erotically charged individuals she had ever seen.

There was to be no fucking at dinner by the guests, and so the entire room acted with exquisite decorum. Hands were kissed and eyelashes batted, but beyond that there was nothing. Hunter understood the decision. It was heightening the arousal in the room to fever pitch. The audience were wolves, impatient to devour the erotic tableau, and each other.

To distract one another from their own sexual frenzies, Hunter and Steward had made as much small talk as they could bear. 'Oh my God who is that silken siren?' Hunter asked, looking around eagerly. 'I swear if you could fuck a voice, you would fuck his,' she finished.

'I couldn't agree more my dear. That is Louis VIV. The architect of the opulence you see before you.' Steward elaborated with a swish of his wrist showing the gentleman who had previously been at the piano who was now standing next to it with a brandy in one hand and fondling the breast of the woman who was still lying across the piano in the other, as he sang something uplifting in Italian.

'I would have thought he was a bit old for you surely. The powdered hair isn't a wig.' Hunter said in shock, 'he really looks like that!'
'Age doesn't matter,' Steward said with a sigh, 'it's the energy around him, his charisma or something. Don't you feel it?'
'God yes!' Hunter agreed, slightly breathless. 'But if you want him, then you definitely saw him first.' Hunter laughed, even though she was ever so slightly jealous.

'I do indeed, alas he is one of the more straight laced among us.' Steward said wearily.
Hunter nearly choked on her champagne. 'Oh please! You have got to be kidding me?! I thought you said that he, he created all of this.' Hunter said, incredulity writ large across her face.

'Yes. But he's also as traditionally hetero as anyone in this crowd can be. So not someone who is likely to give me the keys to paradise.' Steward finished sadly.

'Oh gosh I'm sorry. I was imagining some serious fun for you tonight!' Hunter said. 'Although I guess I'm surprised but also not surprised. The masculine energy he is exuding does have something viscerally straight about it... probably why I picked up on it, he reminds me of...' Hunter trailed off.

'Oh yes, and he's no spring chicken either now is he. Although I suspect a good twenty years his highnesses' junior.' Steward finished, motioning to the impressive man who was now wandering through the tables, briefly pausing to exchange greetings and pleasantries with everyone around him, before being swept on. Hunter watched him move, a clear predator among his prey.

This conversation continued until desserts, when an immaculately dressed servant arrived at Steward's elbow with an envelope on a silver tray.

Hunter's jaw dropped. 'Even here, at an eighteenth-century orgy, *in Italy*, you have staff? Good god, is there any limit to your power and connections?'

'Not exactly, my dear. Just an enquiry that I told my staff I needed the answer to as soon as humanly possible.'

Hunter shook her head, still trying to adjust to Steward's incredible status. Her affection for him grew as she realised that, while he could have legitimately lorded it over every single member of the would-be aristocracy at The Hall, he never had. What a true gentleman.

She had watched his expression as he had read the letter. He had been by turns disappointed, enraged, relieved, and then, finally, reassured. After settling on the final emotion, he turned to Hunter and offered a wide, encouraging smile.

'Good news?' Hunter asked.

'*You* tell me. It's about your man. The one you've been trying so hard not to get depressed about.' He held up a hand as she began to protest. 'Please, my dear, allow me to speak. I've known you since you were practically a girl, and I know how you've suffered these past months. There's no pride here, Hunter. I care only about your happiness. So. Do you want to hear what I know, or not?'

Hunter crossed her arms stubbornly. 'Not,' she said.

Steward had to laugh. 'Oh, for god's sake. Yes, you do! I know what happened, and for your sake, you must, too.'

Hunter was confused. 'You mean with the...? How do *you* know what happened?'

'I overheard something extremely unpalatable at the wedding, and it just got under my skin. I knew something wasn't right and I made it my business to find out. And I'm glad I did because it certainly cleared up a few things.'

Hunter felt like she couldn't breathe. The perfumed air had suddenly become choking and claustrophobic.

'Please, Hunter,' Steward continued. 'There are things you need to know. Please, let me tell you.'

The Revelation

Hunter stared hard at the stem of her wine glass. Then she took a deep breath and, raising her eyes, nodded her assent.

Steward inclined his head, took a long drink of whisky, and began his sordid little tale. 'First of all,' he said. 'The girl who died. It is *not* what you think. Not at all. I'm sure you're already painfully aware of what a heinous person Nick is, but I don't think even *I* knew how low he could stoop, and the things he is capable of, until I looked into what had happened.

'Nick has been with Stephanie for years, but that hasn't stopped him taking whatever woman he wants. Whether Stephanie consents to his practices, who can say, but that's a problem for another day. What I *do* know is that one of these women was Stephanie's best friend, someone she worked with in Las Vegas when she met Nick.'

Hunter winced despite herself. She instinctively knew that it was Stephanie's friend who had also been 'given' to Nick all those years ago. Though it would still be some time before she was inviting Stephanie out for drinks, Hunter's hatred of the woman ebbed away with every new thing she learned about Nick. In its place, her fury at Nick and his aggressive misogyny grew stronger.

Steward cleared his throat and continued. 'Apparently, Nick had been seeing her for months, calling on her whenever he wanted. One of those nights came when Stephanie was out with some of her other friends. This woman had... well, by all accounts, she had taken quite a lot of drugs before Nick had even sent his driver around to fetch her.'

Vice

'Well, wouldn't you?' Hunter asked rhetorically.

Steward smiled sadly. 'Quite. But unfortunately, he encouraged her to take more. He got very, very violent with her, and whether by accident or design, she... well, she went into cardiac arrest.'

Hunter was reeling. 'Wait. No. That... that can't be right. Stephanie said that her friend had belonged to Him, to Lord Byron. *My* Lord Byron, I mean. She was His previous submissive. And she died covered in cuts. That she bled to death.'

'And I've no doubt she was telling you the truth, as she understood it. Think about it, Hunter. She comes home and your gallant dominant is there, helping Nick get rid of the body.' Then, noticing the pain in Hunter's eyes; 'She was very dead by this point. I checked.'

'The... body...' Hunter croaked. 'But why?'

'Apparently, Nick had passed out shortly after she died. It was Natalie, by the way; her name was Natalie. When he came to, he was just sober enough to understand what had happened, and he panicked. Not, unfortunately, in the way any of the rest of us would, by calling an ambulance or administering mouth to mouth. He called the one person he felt that he could trust.'

'But why *Him*?' Hunter shouted. 'Why Him, of all people? Nick is just... awful! And He, He was dark and dangerous, but I always thought He was... good. I thought He was better than that.'

'He is darling. It turns out that about twenty years ago when all this public-school lot were in the military, Nick saved his life. Before you ask, I don't know where or how, but the fact that it happened is common knowledge, and apparently it was a big risk to even attempt to do so, if you get my meaning.'

She did.

'So, picture the scene. Your 'Lord Byron' gets a call from an old 'friend', one who perhaps he doesn't particularly like or respect anymore, but one who nonetheless saved his life at great personal risk and sacrifice many years earlier. Nick says he needs help – he offered no further explanation – so he goes. When he gets there, he finds a girl that is beyond all help and a panicking Nick.'

Hunter sighed. *That poor, poor girl.*

'Believe it or not this is where it gets a little bit worse.' Steward continued. 'Because this is when Stephanie arrives home. She sees your man holding her dead friend in his arms and justifiably panics. I know for certain that Nick sedated her, though whether it happened with or without her consent, who knows? Anyway, he did it, and fast. By the time she woke up, she could remember that her friend was gone, but she was very, very hazy on the details. She herself was drunk when she got home. So, imagine what Nick tells her...'

Hunter put both hands over her mouth. 'Oh my god.'

Steward nodded sadly. 'Blamed him entirely. Spun some complete fiction about how he'd used her as his submissive and she'd died when one of their little games got out of hand.'

'But why didn't He –'

'What? Set things straight?' Steward asked. He took a moment to consider. 'Do you know, I don't think he even knew what Nick had told Stephanie. He'd left with Natalie hours before Stephanie woke up. And since then, I suppose their paths haven't crossed that much. It's probably something he wanted to forget. It may be that he understood it as some sort of 'debt repaid.' I don't know. But what I *do* know, is that all of that changed when you were given the bastardised version of events by Stephanie.'

Steward was going to continue, but something made him stop. He shook his head slowly, a stunned expression on his face. The same shocking thought had just hit Hunter, too. 'She never believed Nick's story, did she? No matter what she said. Oh, maybe she did in those first hours, but afterwards, once she'd sobered up and time had passed, she would have known, deep down, that Nick was really to blame for her friend's death. She would have worked it all out. She knew.' Hunter shook her head, sadly. 'She wanted to cause me pain because at this point, I think pain is all she knows. I've never met anyone as broken as her.'

Hunter fell back heavily in her chair. She felt nothing but sorry for Stephanie now, and she understood that Astrid had intuited her pain immediately, in a way Hunter just hadn't seen. Stephanie's pain was an almost physical presence, it followed her like a malevolent shadow, tainting everything around her. Now at least, Hunter understood why.

'So, there you have it,' Steward said, his eyes glistening with sadness. 'The poor girl's death was nothing to do with your chap. He wasn't to blame for anything, really. Just a rather extreme case of being in the wrong place at the wrong time.'

Hunter's eyes were fixed intently on the candle in front of her. 'What happened to Natalie?' she asked, dully. For better or worse, she was determined to know even the most painful details.

Steward took a long drink of his whisky before answering. 'He dropped her off at a hospital, said he had found her unconscious in a doorway. The staff had no reason to disbelieve him. An upper-class man in a suit appears with a known sex worker who's chock-full of drugs and been dead for hours. She's battered and bruised, He's immaculate and stone cold sober. It would have looked exactly as he'd explained. I doubt if they even made him wait to give the police a statement.'

'I wish He'd told me.'

'Did you even give him the chance? Because if I know you...'

Hunter lowered her eyes and grimaced.

'Maybe he was frightened you'd hate him for it. And as I said, he didn't know that Nick had actually blamed *him* for what happened. I imagine he felt he owed it to Nick to keep the whole sordid thing secret.'

Hunter squeezed a hand against her temple. Her head was reeling. Unable to process what she had just heard, she took a deep, long draught of her Barolo, and then another, and then another. Steward waited, understanding that she needed time to think about his revelation.

Hunter was somewhat recovered by the time Marie Antoinette appeared at Steward's elbow and entreated him to follow her. He looked to Hunter who smiled back wearily. He was reassured. He had done the right thing by telling her. He stood and allowed himself to be steered towards the entrance to heaven. Now, perhaps more than ever before, he felt like he'd earned it.

The Revelation

The Submission

"But hurry, let's entwine ourselves as one, our mouth broken, our soul bitten by love, so time discovers us safely destroyed."

Federico Garcia Lorca

Hunter sat alone at the table, her eyes listlessly following the candlelight that flickered off the crystal glassware. She couldn't believe what she had heard. A part of her, she supposed, had always suspected that He was incapable of doing such harm to a woman, but to have the fact confirmed to her was a very different matter completely. She was relieved, of course, but she had spent so long swallowing back her desire for Him that she wasn't sure those feelings were still there. Maybe it was all too late?

Hunter was no closer to making sense of this internal chaos when Casanova crossed the room, only to stop by her shoulder. 'Heaven or Hell?' he asked. His voice was pure seduction. Hunter gave her answer without even thinking. 'Hell,' she said. In many ways, she felt like she was there already.

Casanova gently handed her a crystal ampoule of thick, sticky, red liquid. 'Drink,' he commanded.

She swallowed the liquid down, trying desperately to ignore the thought that it looked like arterial blood. It tasted sweet, and very alcoholic; it reminded her of the tea that He had given her the morning of the wedding. It brought a sad smile to her lips. She swallowed, and in that one action she knew that she had accepted everything that would befall her in Hell that night.

Casanova motioned to the waterfall of red velvet that concealed the descent into Hell. Hunter rose slowly, as if in a trance, and followed his languorous gesture. She passed through the curtain into a starkly lit stairway that descended so far into the darkness that its end was out of sight. Perhaps it wasn't precisely what Dante had had in mind, but it was intimidating, nonetheless.

Hunter filled her lungs with the smell and smoke of innumerable candles and took her first deliberate steps down into the inferno. She would go gladly into the smoky lustful hell if only to clear her mind of images of blood, death, betrayal and pain.

Marie Antoinette watched Hunter descend the stairs from her vantage point above the party. Casanova had returned to her and was already embedded between her thighs, the folds of her skirt spread wide to afford everyone an appropriate view. She sighed, partly in obvious pleasure and partly in a sort of ennui. She knew the woman who was descending to Hell; liked her even. She had noticed that she had seemed far from her usual self. Perhaps that was why she had failed to recognise *her*. But then, no-one *ever* recognised her, because no one ever really looked. She left as many clues as she considered decent, but they withered before blind eyes.

Not one of all the women who frequented The Hall had ever noticed that all the invitations that were sent out at the behest of Tiffany were almost *identical* to the ones that arrived from The Duchess. The only difference was the absence of antlers and the addition of a fleur-de-lys. *Well, if they were too slow to understand such simple clues, they didn't deserve to know anyway.*

Marissa smiled a slow, sardonic smile behind her mask, and wondered when their paths would cross again. No doubt at The Hall, she supposed. She smiled at the thought, until her mind was brought shudderingly back to the moment as Casanova's expert licking brought her to a thundering climax. The Duchess moaned appreciatively.

*

Hunter followed the dull, repetitive thump of the music down the endless stairway. Through the half-darkness, she could see that the walls were coated in hot, sticky wax which dripped from the antique candle sconces. The air was full of twisting smoke reminiscent of the decaying opium dens of days long past. When, finally, she reached the bottom step, she took a deep, shuddering breath. A breath that escaped her when a man appeared in front of her from nowhere.

He was enormous, and intentionally terrifying. His head was clothed in oil-black leather and topped with a silken black horse's tail that flowed from his crown. His mouth was invisible beneath the leather, but his eyes were mocking, and fixed firmly on her.

'You must be the Devil then?' Hunter said, her natural bravado returning like a reflex.

'You're the first,' he growled. God (or perhaps the Devil) only knew what he meant by that. 'Do everything I say, and do not move in the restraints. Whatever happens, do not move an inch.'

Hunter complied absolutely; she was well-practiced in obedience in the face of such clear masculine power. *He even sounded like Him* she thought, as desire for her Master overwhelmed her. The feelings she had suppressed for months heaved to the surface like drowning people gasping for air in a churning ocean.

She felt the coldness of iron chains against her skin, heard the tinkling of the bindings through the cacophony of moans and sighs. More patrons had descended and were being administered to in similar fashion. Hunter turned her head as she lay on her back on the leather clad stone plinth, another ritual sacrifice. The room was very dark, the candles throwing shadows like fairy tale monsters across the walls. People were entwined all round her, on the stone floor, against walls, over cushions and chaise longues. Many more were tied to St. Andrew's crosses and strapped to tables like hers. It appeared that there was more than one Devil in the room tonight.

Her tormentor had removed her dress before chaining her down, the careful removal of which was an impressive feat in itself. She tried to lose herself in the moment, submit to the thrill and the pain and the pleasure of it all. But it wasn't enough. It would never be enough. Steward was right; she was lost. The fact – the very *simple* fact – was that She belonged to Him. Nobody else would do. She could be with other men, she knew, but they would never fulfil her. She could try other relationships, but they would inevitably pale into insignificance when compared with that she had shared with Him. Or she could be with Him. Then, despite His darkness and His flaws, she would have the life she had always dreamed of.

The decision had already been made, of course. It had been made the moment Steward's story had ended. Her return to Him was inevitable. Yes, He was dark, and yes, He was tainted, but He was far from evil. Hunter could live with tainted; she could even enjoy it.

She was lying on the table, dressed in nothing but her white silken stockings. Her tormentor was tightening his chains around her. Normally, a situation like this would have both excited and calmed her. Normally, there was nothing she wanted more than another night among the cliterati. But as the final chain was locked into place and he raised his cat o' nine tails, as she braced herself for what was to come, she had a sudden thought - *She shouldn't be here!* It was as if someone had spoken it clearly into her ear.

The clarity of her situation bit her like the whip her erstwhile master was trying to use with effect. She barely felt the sting. Big and scary as he was acting, impressive as he was, he'd never measure up to Him. No one could. Even with his mane of black hair, his growls, and his leather flogger.

Her tormentor moved to bring the whip down once more, but he stopped when he noticed that his victim was grinning.

'I have to go,' she said, looking up at him through her mask.

313

'Now?'

Hunter nodded, tears prickling her eyes. 'I'm sorry, but I really must go.'

The man suddenly deflated; he was clearly put out at the sudden break in the erotic scenario. However, consent at these events was sacrosanct, so he had no choice but to comply with her wishes. He unlocked her chains and watched as she practically leapt from the table without so much as a thank you. Her discarded dress was on an ornate silk chair against the wall. She grabbed it and wriggled back into it as best as she could. It had taken her nearly two hours to carefully construct the dress around herself at the hotel earlier. Now she was trying to achieve the same effect in two minutes after at least a bottle of Barolo.

'Would you mind?' She asked a passer-by in nothing but a frock coat, motioning to the corset lacing at her back.

'But of course,' he replied smiling. Then, with a wry look around the room; 'Somewhere more appealing to be?'

'Actually, yes,' she said breathlessly, before thanking him with a kiss on the cheek and almost running back up the stairs. Her corset was haphazardly tied at best, and her skirts were all wrong but the dress was unlikely to fall off her so that was enough. She emerged into the cool night air that always tasted so deliciously of salt before pausing to catch her breath. Running up a flight of stairs in an authentic whalebone corset had caused spots to dance in front of her eyes, like tiny fireworks. *Calm down*, she told herself. *He is not going anywhere. He may be spectacular, but no man and no Master should ever be run for.*

Back inside the grand hall, Steward had been unsurprised when, from the gates of Heaven, he saw a dishevelled Hunter barrel out of Hell and run giggling into the night like a very, very, X-rated Cinderella. Sighing contentedly, he motioned to a servant and sent the message he had been hoping to send all night. Then, relieved of any more avuncular duties, he ascended to the delicious angels with whom he hoped to spend a satisfying evening.

Some minutes from the party, Hunter had suddenly realised that she was alone in Venice in the early hours of the morning. Walking home alone was not the most sensible choice she could make. Perhaps she had been a little hasty in leaving Steward; after all, the first flight back to Scotland wouldn't be leaving until after six in the morning. She leaned against a cold stone wall, damp with the rain that had thankfully stopped for now, and tried to work out what best to do. She needed to get back to the hotel, book a flight and get back to Scotland and then find Him. No doubt Tiffany could help track Him down.

Her head clearer, she walked carefully over the slick stones to a pontoon, where she was relieved to find another pair of partygoers already waiting. 'Done for the evening?' the woman enquired through her ebony mask. She was sensibly enveloped in a black velvet cloak, but Hunter could see the chain attached to the submissive at her feet dangling from one sleeve.

'Yes,' Hunter said, suddenly very aware of her dishevelled appearance. Her hair had come undone and was all over the place, catching the dew of the night-time air. She looked like a character from some bodice-ripping historical drama after the wrap party.

The woman nodded to her attachment. 'This one was naughty. So, it's home for punishment, I'm afraid.'

I wish I was going home for the same. Hunter thought, as the lights of the water taxi swirled into view through the mist.

The taxi slowed as it reached Hunter's hotel. She found balancing in the slight wave difficult in her dishevelled skirts, the weight of which pulled her with the sway of the boat. She managed to stay upright, however, and as she exited the boat with a breathless 'goodnight' to her companions, she knew she would owe the costumiers a serious apology in the morning. If she left Venice before she was able to return it, she'd write Steward a proper apology, as it would no doubt be he who had to face the wrath of the diminutive dominatrix.

Hunter entered through the glass doors of the hotel and received a pleasant greeting from the night manager, who asked if she needed anything sent up to her room. She did not. She was almost vibrating with a mixture of excitement and nervous anticipation. What she had felt on the way to the event had been nothing in comparison. She could feel her heart pounding in her chest all the way up in the lift, an old-fashioned affair with a gate that had to be pulled across before it would ascend.

She took her key from the inside of her left stocking and opened the door to her hotel room. Her suite had a small living room with an embroidered sofa and end table next to it. The lights had been set to low and a decanter of Amaretto had been left for her on the table. Hunter smiled; she could think of no better way to warm up after her night-time flit. She poured herself a glass, took a deep draught and set off for her bedroom to divest herself of her costume.

'Hello.'

The glass fell from her hand and smashed spectacularly all over the floor. Tiny shards cut into her ankles, yet she was unable to move, or breathe.

There He was, sitting on the chaise at the end of the bed as if it were His room she had just walked in to. She stood, eyes locked on His, the smell of almonds penetrating her senses. Tiny little pin pricks of blood were showing through the white of her stockings, but right then she wouldn't have cared if she were bleeding to death.

He reached into his breast pocket and pulled out a letter. 'It seems you have a fairy godfather.' Getting to his feet, He crossed the room towards her.

Hunter had begun to shake. All the fear and heartbreak and uncertainty of the past few months had evaporated like a warm breath of air on a cold winter's morning. She opened her mouth to speak, but still no words came. She couldn't believe He was here. Suddenly, her knees buckled. He caught her in His arms and kissed her ravenously. She wanted the kiss to last forever, wanted to be consumed by Him until she was nothing but His tongue inside of her and His body all over hers. Nothing but His, to do with as He pleased, to use her as He wished. She was utterly drunk on Him.

Vice

He pulled away and she looked up, smiling at the familiar stubble and delighting in the masculine scent that was all His.

'I came as soon as Steward explained what had happened,' He said. 'You don't need to worry. You never need to worry. You are mine. Always.'

She nodded her complete and utter assent, still unable to speak. He turned her around and tied her tightly to the bedpost with a thick length of silk rope that had been coiled next to Him on the chaise. He tied her wrists over her head, looping the silk rope over the thick carved wooden canopy to ensure she wouldn't slide down in her restraints. He was going to take His time with her tonight, and every night.
'I am going to fuck you, until even the Devil turns away.'

Her whole body and soul screamed 'yes.' This is what she had been longing for, the thing that would make her complete. She wanted to be stripped bare of all artifice and pretence, to feed her soul with the undeniable pressure of Him around her and the familiar force biting her wrists. This bondage filled her with fire and comfort. It electrified every nerve and licked at her wounds. She hung there, ready for Him.

Her hair had fallen around her bare shoulders, her breasts only just constrained by the corset that was already threatening to release them, her skirts pulled up around her waist. She was a fallen angel made flesh. He reached down to her ankle and took a drop of blood onto His finger, which he then touched to her lips. She moaned, her desire soaking her thighs and pulsing through every aching nerve in her body. She was His. At last, she was His.

The Submission

He removed his jacket, took off His shirt and took a knife, the knife that *she* had given Him all those months ago, from His back pocket.

'You kept it?' She breathed, her voice finally coming back to her.

'I did.'

'Use it.'

He did.

*If you enjoyed following Hunter
into her world of debauchery,
read on for a taste of the next
novel in the Sin Series –*

Sacrifice

The Party

'You do know,' Hunter complained, 'this would be a *lot* easier if we just pulled over to the side of the road for a minute or two.' She was in the front passenger seat of Darcey's car, balancing a false nail that had been filed into a deadly point in one hand and a tube of denture adhesive in the other.

Darcey turned towards her friend and threw her a quick death-stare, before returning her eyes to the road ahead of her. 'We're already going to arrive hours after the party has started. This is the sodding military, remember – they won't be impressed.'

Hunter sighed, exasperated. 'Tiffany, how long are you going to *be*?'

'I'm going as fast as I can,' Tiffany called, from the back seat of the car. 'But it's hard to dry your nails when you're balancing them on your knee in a moving car with Astrid's naked ass in your face.'

'It's not my fault,' Astrid said, as she attempted to slip a leg inside an orange fishnet stocking. 'I thought we would change on the base.'

'Well, too bad,' Darcey snapped. 'We're –'

'Yes, yes,' Astrid said, with a roll of her eyes. 'We're running late enough already. I just... oof! I hadn't banked on – ow! – getting dressed in this bloody car.'

Tiffany lifted one of the nails from her knee for a quick inspection, then laid it down again with an impatient huff. 'These bloody things just will. Not. Dry.'

'This one better be dry,' Hunter said. 'It's about to be glued onto my tooth. Darcey, for the next minute please, please, please keep the car steady. I don't particularly want to glue a blood-red nail to my eyeball.'

'It's denture adhesive,' Tiffany pointed out. 'It should only stick to teeth.'

'Why are we doing this again?' Astrid asked, as she settled back down in her seat. Despite having dressed in an ancient and knackered Ford KA speeding down the M8 on the way to Shropshire, her sunset-orange suspender belt, stockings, and nipple tassels were perfectly in place.

'The teeth or the party?' Darcey asked.

'The teeth!'

Darcey changed gear, provoking a groan from the car's ancient engine and a muttered expletive from Hunter. 'Those fake vampire teeth you buy in joke shops are just so tacky,' she said. 'These sharpened nails will look much more authentic, especially with the blood-red paint. More authentic, and *way* sexier.'

'Well, yes' Hunter admitted, as she pressed the nail against her canine. 'But can you imagine trying to fuck with these in?'

Darcey looked round to her friend with a grin. 'I've been imagining it all week, actually.'

Hunter laughed, then released the pressure on her tooth-nail. 'Bloody hell, Darcey,' she said, as she inspected her reflection in the mirror. 'You were right. Stuck solid and, my *god*, they look good. Wouldn't you agree?' Hunter turned in her seat and flashed Astrid and Tiffany a seductive vampiric smile.

Astrid clapped her hands excitedly. 'Ooh! Tiffany, they look fantastic! Do you have some ready for me?'

Smiling, Tiffany handed a couple of the nails to Astrid. 'There we go. Now, let me get my compact for you. I'm sure it's... somewhere.' She began to rummage through the bag at her feet, sending various bits of lingerie and make-up scattering.

'We are going to be the hottest women there,' Hunter said, as she struggled out of her bra and into a black leather corset, roughly elbowing the passenger side door in the process.

'Aren't we always?' Darcey asked rhetorically, keeping her eyes on the traffic in front of her.

'Damn right,' Tiffany replied. 'But... why "lesbian vampires"?'

Darcey laughed. 'Because it's Halloween. And because of that film that just came out. All the boys on the air force base are obsessed with it.'

Hunter rolled her eyes. 'Of course they are. Really, men have no imagination. I'd have expected more of our officers.'

Astrid grinned. 'Maybe. But at least they'll be standing to attention when we walk in tonight.'

'If we *ever* get there,' Darcey groaned, pressing her foot a little harder against the accelerator.

'God I can't wait,' Tiffany said, with a far-off look in her eyes. 'It's been ages since I've fucked someone hot.'

'Me too,' Hunter said, with a wistful sigh.

Tiffany looked to Hunter confused. 'I thought you hooked up with one of the pilots the last time you went to Darcey's squadron party.'

Hunter shook her head. 'They were all too young for me. I try to only sleep with the older, more experienced officers.'

'Why officers?' Tiffany asked. 'Why not the newer recruits? After all, they're young, dumb, and full of come.'

Darcey shuddered. 'God, I hate that expression. But you're not wrong, Tiffany. The stamina of those guys is incredible!'

'Their stamina may be good, but their seduction techniques are non-existent,' Hunter said. 'Plus, they're scared shitless of me. The older officers, on the other hand, really *do* know what they're doing. Firstly, they expect their orders to be obeyed immediately. And god, do they know how to discipline! So, yes – give me an officer any day. Just don't expect Darcey to follow suit.'

Darcey grinned. 'I can't help it if I like them young and… obedient. And their bodies are to die for. So many muscles, and so few hairs.'

'Ugh!' Hunter said. 'I like mine big and hairy. The more masculine the better.'

'I like refined,' Tiffany said, dreamily. 'I'd love to meet Prince William.'

'You know he's taken.'

'I do,' Tiffany said. 'But a girl can dream.'

'Well, I am certain there will be someone for everyone tonight,' Darcey said. 'The whole of 18 Squadron is there, plus some of 38 and even some visiting Canadian pilots or something.'

Hunter was now sticking nipple jewellery onto Darcey's naked breasts, much to the delight of the drivers in the cars she was overtaking. To a man, every person they'd passed had gaped, disbelieving, at the car full of half-naked vampires in lingerie. It's a miracle there hadn't been an accident. 'Yes, well, just remember to behave yourself tonight, won't you, Darcey?'

Darcey turned to Hunter with a mock-innocent flutter of her eyelashes. 'Don't I always?'

Hunter turned towards her friends in the back of the car. 'The last time Darcey invited me to one of her squadron guest nights, I may have struck out, but Darcey? Darcey hooked up alright… right on the Adj's desk!'

There were delighted gasps and giggles from Tiffany and Astrid.

'Who was he?' Tiffany asked.

'And what's an Adj?' said Astrid.

Hunter sat back in her chair and waved a hand to show Darcey that the floor was now hers. Darcey shook her head in mock outrage, but quickly caved. 'All right,' she said. 'The Adj is the Squadron Adjutant, basically the guy who's overall in charge. He's by far the scariest man in the entire Air Force. Wing Commander L.K.J. Talbot. Ex-paratrooper among other things. He runs the squadron.'

'And you fucked this guy on his own desk?' Tiffany asked.

Darcey barked a laugh. 'Not a chance! He's far too old for me. Too old even for Hunter.'

'That's true,' Hunter said, with a smile. 'Which is a shame because that man *really* knows how to take charge. But even if he was right for me, I doubt I'd stand a chance over Darcey – the Adj definitely has a soft spot for her. He always makes sure she's first on all the trips. Mind you, I'm not sure he'd like her as much if he knew what she'd done to his desk.'

'So, who was the guy?' Astrid asked.

Darcey smiled. 'He's called Sugar. And he was every bit as delicious as his name suggests.'

'Will he be there tonight?' asked Astrid.

'Indeed, he will,' Darcey said, with a smile.

'So…?' Tiffany said, leaning forward in her chair. 'Tell us what happened.'
Darcey gave a happy sigh. 'He didn't disappoint. He even took my thong as a souvenir, which was a nice little kink, I thought. But thank god the Adj doesn't know. I have never woken up with such regret in my life!' *Almost...* Darcey thought, as she had a sudden flashback to a French riverside.

'I'm so excited Sugar will be there tonight,' Hunter said. 'I can't wait to get another look at the man who made Darcey Bell throw caution to the wind and desecrate her commander's desk!'

'Ha bloody Ha. And don't you dare mention it to *anybody* tonight. I can still get kicked out you know. The military love their rules, and they don't make exceptions.'

'Suits you down to the ground then!' Hunter grinned. 'But you needn't worry; I'll be far too busy for conversation. While you're off dipping your fangs into something sweet, I'm going to find the biggest, most powerful man with a fetish and have him make me beg for mercy at least twice before the night is over.'

'Amen!' came the dual cry from the back seat as the car sped on to Royal Air Force Shawbury and the Halloween "wings" party.

Acknowledgments

My list of people to thank is a long one. Writing my first novel was a wonderful experience for so many reasons, but none more so than the help and support I received from almost everyone I know. My first thank you has to go to my gorgeous husband, for putting up with the endless commentary on my characters' lives, and for supporting me through the inevitable crises of confidence. You were always on hand with a glass of wine and a supportive word or two, I couldn't have done it without you.

Thanks also to my infinitely patient editor Andy, for immeasurably improving this book, somehow understanding what it was I was trying to say, and for stopping me from making absolutely everything *delicious*. To my first editor, my sister Debbie, who has possibly read this book even more than I have and has offered invaluable insight and criticism throughout - oh, and you were right about all the Latin! Thanks also to my mum for her help and support, for reading all my truly questionable attempts at writing from age four onwards, and for always believing I could do it. Thanks to Arthur for the never-ending support, critiques, and bottles of prosecco on the waterside. I can't wait to read your book when it comes out!

Thanks to Kieran for designing both the book cover and the podcast artwork, you are a true artist and a wonderful friend.

Thanks to Tiffany, Ashica and Chermaine for inspiring some of my characters and for being the best department a girl could have! A special shout-out to Caitlin for becoming my erstwhile business manager and actually getting my novel out of my office and into the world. Thanks to everyone who has encouraged, inspired, and helped on the book and the podcast over the (many!) years. Thanks to: Hope, Anna, Emma, Ellie, Anneka, Tash, Doddy, Rachael, Steph, Ali, Arthur, Jeremiah, Karín, Tara, Cassie and Sarah.

Finally, thank you to the original four, for everything. You know who you are.

About the Author

Terry Stewart is a Scottish novelist whose first novel Vice was released in 2023. Vice is the first in the four-part Sin Series that follows Hunter, Darcey, Tiffany, and Astrid as they navigate the debauched world of the sexual elite. The second book in the series, 'Sacrifice' will be released late in 2024. Terry has been to university and enjoyed it so much she keeps going back. When she's not writing she's usually cooking, or drinking wine in the bath. Terry lives in Scotland with her husband and cat. You can visit her online in the following locations:

terrystewartauthor.com

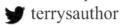 terrystewartauthor

 vicethepodcast

🐦 terrysauthor

Still to come in the Sin Series

Sacrifice
Avarice
Depravity

Printed in Great Britain
by Amazon